# HUSTLE HARD

## Also by Saundra

*Her Sweetest Revenge*

*Her Sweetest Revenge 2*

*Her Sweetest Revenge 3*

*If It Ain't About the Money*

*Hustle Hard*

*A Hustler's Queen*

## Anthologies
*Schemes* and *Dirty Tricks* (with Kiki Swinson)

Published by Kensington Publishing Corp.

# HUSTLE HARD

## SAUNDRA

KENSINGTON PUBLISHING CORP.
www.kensingtonbooks.com

DAFINA BOOKS are published by

Kensington Publishing Corp.
119 West 40th Street
New York, NY 10018

All Kensington titles, imprints, and distributed lines are available at special quantity discounts for bulk purchases for sales promotion, premiums, fund-raising, and educational or institutional use.

Special book excerpts or customized printings can also be created to fit specific needs. For details, write or phone the office of the Kensington Sales Manager: Kensington Publishing Corp., 119 West 40th Street, New York, NY 10018. Attn. Sales Department. Phone: 1-800-221-2647.

Dafina and the Dafina logo Reg. U.S. Pat. & TM Off.

ISBN-13: 978-1-4967-1199-1
ISBN-10: 1-4967-1199-8
First Kensington Trade Paperback Printing: July 2018
First Kensington Mass Market Printing: September 2019

ISBN-13: 978-1-4967-1200-4 (ebook)
ISBN-10: 1-4967-1200-5 (ebook)

10 9 8 7 6 5 4 3 2 1

Printed in the United States of America

# Chapter 1

# Secret

I loved life. There was simply no reason not to.

We'd fought to get out of the nightmare that our lives had become months ago when Penny was kidnapped and raped. I was with her while she fought to get back to some normalcy, not willing to give up, not willing to give in to the bullshit that tried to claim her sanity and mine. We had truly been tested. So I was ready for this good feeling, and I intended to enjoy every single moment of it, because I'd learned something important: We were not entitled to happiness.

No, in this life you had to go out and find it, fight for it even, shit, tooth and nail if you had to. Damn near kill for it. And I think we all knew that money was not given to us, we had to go out and get it. And *that* I understood well. It's a code I lived by: hustle hard.

After the hustle there was time to play, and I

didn't fuck around with that either. See, I loved the finer things in life. Some called it materialistic; I called it living life. Either way, I could give zero fucks about what other people thought. My sweat, my struggle, my tears, my life. Hands down, that's what mattered. That's precisely the reason why I was in this lot scoping the hottest, most expensive rides they had to offer.

"Jack, you know this is it. I knew you would get exactly what I wanted." I kissed my personal car salesman on the cheek. His name was Jack Ferguson, and he was down at Foreign Ecstasy. I had called him a week before and told him what I wanted, but I wasn't sure about the color. Jack had assured me he had my back and, true to his word, I had three of the same top-of-the line Ferraris sitting in front of me. All I had to do was choose the color.

"I will never disappoint you." I loved Jack's Jersey accent. Kirk, a childhood friend of mine, had given me his contact information, which, by the way, was not given out to just anybody. So I felt lucky.

"It's going to be this one." I gently rubbed the hood of the candy-apple-red Ferrari 488 GTB. "My baby right here." I had chills just thinking about climbing inside.

"Everything you need to drive away with is already inside. You are now the owner." Jack smiled at me. I knew he was just as happy as I was. He was in for a hefty treat from the sale of this vehicle. That was the case with any vehicle he sold, because they were all expensive.

"I guess that's it, then, the bag on your desk takes care of my end," I said, referring to the Gucci bag on his desk that contained three hundred and fifty thousand dollars. Yes, I had just spent that much on one car. Like I said, I worked hard and had no beef with playing harder. And I wasn't done yet.

"It was nice doing business with you." I slowly slid into the driver's seat of my new Ferrari and nearly stopped breathing. I had only dreamed about owning something as luxurious as this. I had to sit still for about two minutes to gather myself.

But soon I was in control of my emotions. I started up the car and floated out of the lot, then down the streets of Miami. I felt like Nino Brown in charge of the Carter. As soon as I merged onto the interstate, I let it rip. I nearly scared my damn self when I glanced at the speedometer and noticed I was going a hundred miles per hour. The ride was so smooth inside the car that it felt like I was only going forty. It was like driving a piece of heaven.

This was the life, and every day I had Kirk to thank for that. His bright ideas were still taking Isis and me to new heights. Thanks to him and his new newest scheme, we were pulling in top dollar as managers at his new car business called Custom Hot Rides. Custom Hot Rides was quickly becoming the spot in Miami and was bringing in mad money. We did some of the hottest custom jobs in the area. Vehicles were tricked out with the hottest features known to man, from top-notch paint to platinum and gold accessories, butterfly doors, and complete body overhauls. Whatever your wish was, it was Custom Hot Rides' command. And from ballers to celebrities, you name it, they were taking full advantage. We even sold vehicles.

Some of our cars came in special ordered with the intent to trick them out on delivery. Then there were the ones shipped in from other cities outside of the Miami, Florida, area at the owners' expense for our services. But that was all a cover-up for the kilos of cocaine that came tucked away in the engines or sometimes tires of the vehicles. And it was a gold mine. Because of it, I had more money than I even wanted to count. And it was easy. All Isis and I had to do was the paperwork on the shipments, which meant we had to receive the orders when they came in. And of course Kirk was our boss, and that meant we were in charge.

Pulling into Custom Hot Rides, I eased off the gas and coasted inside. Two black dudes were standing close to the entry door. I glanced at them briefly as they admired the Ferrari. I could only imagine how their conversation was going. Men loved to tear a car apart when they described the engine, down to the nuts and bolts of it. I climbed out slowly, still admiring it. I hit the alarm then looked up to see Courtney, the young receptionist, rushing toward me.

"Dang, Secret, that's you? That's yo' whip?" She did not hide her excitement as her hands went to her mouth. She looked as if she had just won the lottery.

"Hell, yeah. That's me all day. Hot, huh?" I gloated with no shame. I loved my ride, and I wanted everyone who came in contact with it to admire it for what it was: a hot piece of steel.

"Shit, all day, every day. You gotta let me borrow that."

"No doubt. Anytime you want to. While you're fast asleep in your dream." I laughed.

Courtney playfully nudged my shoulder. "Ha, ha. You are not funny." It was hot out, so we headed toward Hot Rides's entrance.

"Nice whip," one of the dudes standing by the entrance mouthed. "A 488, huh?" he asked. And just like I thought, they had the Ferrari birthright pegged from the time I hit the lot. It was a guy thing.

"Yep," I replied and stepped inside Hot Rides.

"Both of them are fine." Courtney referred to the guys once we were inside. She was a man-eater.

"They a'ight," I replied. "Where's Isis? I thought she was here."

"Nope, she left about an hour ago. Said she had to go do something about some ink. I think that printer trippin' again."

"I told her the other day to just buy another one. What about Kirk? He been in today?"

"You just missed him too."

"Damn, when I come in everybody ghost." I started toward the office that Isis and I shared. Kirk said he was going to remodel soon and build a new office for both of us, because with all the time we spent putting in work, it would not go to waste. No sooner had I put my right hand on the doorknob did Penny's name light up on my cell phone. "What's up, brat?" I teased Penny; she hated when I called her that.

"Whatever. You love me. Let's meet up for some smoothies at that new smoothie spot close to Spirals."

"You know I would much rather have some food than smoothies, but cool. I'm at the shop. I'll be there in drive time."

"Bet." Penny ended the call. I was sure if she in-

vited me out for a smoothie, it was because she
wanted one, and she wanted me to pay. The girl
was, and always would be, spoiled. But I didn't
care; it gave me a reason to jump back into the Ferrari, and I was loving it. I burned rubber out of
Hot Rides's parking lot just for the thrill of it.

Penny and I pulled up at the same time. Her
mouth flew wide open as I stepped out the driver's
seat.

"Hell, no. You didn't actually buy that thing."
She grinned. I had told her a few days earlier that
I was considering buying it.

"Sure did. You like?"

"No, I love." She walked around the entire car,
scoping it front to back, rim to roof. "I swear, Secret,
you about murder these hoes . . . I don't envy your
haters." She shook her head left to right, still grinning.

"I know, right. Bitches 'bout to be droppin' like
flies when I pull up and hop out," I boasted. I
could see the envy on the faces of the haters she
spoke of, and I laughed at it.

"And you better not trip 'bout me driving it either. Unless you want to put that insurance into im-
mediate effect," Penny threatened jokingly.

"Hey, you know I don't mind you driving it.
'Cause you know I'll bust ya ass about my whip."

"Yeah, you are a little crazy." We both laughed as
we made our way inside the smoothie spot. We each
ordered up a strawberry caramel split smoothie. It
was our favorite.

I watched Penny take the first sip of her smoothie;
I enjoyed watching the calm, peaceful look on her
face. For a long while I feared I would never see that
again. And I was glad I was wrong. She was back en-

joying her life and hanging out with her friends.
She hadn't gone back to school yet, but coming out
in the general population and mingling was a major
start.

"So I wanted to invite you out for smoothies just
to talk."

"Oh, so you invited me out. Well, I think there
was a misunderstanding, but we can clear that up
now. You go back up there, ask for a refund, and
you pay for the smoothies," I joked.

"Shut up." Penny laughed. "You the baller, remember, Ms. Ferrari? How much that thing set
you back anyway?"

"I won't tell you. It might make you nervous."

"I bet . . . But listen, I know things were rocky for
a while. You being patient with me as I got myself together . . . And I want you to know that I thank God
for you."

"Aww," I sighed playfully. But honestly, her
words nearly brought me to tears. I played it cool,
though.

"Really, you are the best sister a girl could ask
for, Secret . . ." She paused and took a swallow of
her smoothie, so I knew there was more.

"What now?" I said. I wanted her to get to the
point.

"It's time I take on some responsibility when it
comes to my life."

I breathed a sigh of relief. That was it. For a
minute I thought she might tell me she was preg-
nant, and I was not ready for that. But I was happy
to hear her say that; it showed her growth. My baby
sister was maturing into a grown woman.

"I want to move out on my own . . . get my own
place."

I glared at her hard, because I had not been expecting that. She had caught me off guard. I waited a few seconds to be sure that I chose my words correctly because I wanted to plainly say "hell no." "Penny, I get that you are trying to be more independent. I applaud that. But I don't think you ready for all that. I truly fear it's not for the best."

"Why not?" she questioned. I could hear the tone change in her voice. "It's time I got on with my life, Secret. I thought you could understand that."

"I do get it. Maybe you could wait just a little bit longer. Just to let things settle," I tried to reason. I didn't want to get detailed, I just wanted her to understand my reasoning. But the look on her face told me she was ready to challenge me.

"Well, I don't want to wait. I feel like the time is now or never. I have put it off long enough."

"What's the sudden rush?" I was becoming agitated. It was clear her mind was made up, but I was not one to give up easily.

"Ain't no rush. I'm just ready. And I'm moving out, with or without your help." She looked me straight in the eye and it said matter-of-factly.

I set the smoothie down on the table. It would have not been enough to just say I was pissed. I closed my eyes and counted to ten very slowly. I opened my eyes, and she was staring at me. She knew how I was: I could explode and probably shut the whole smoothie place down, but instead I held my breath then let it out slowly as I stood up.

"I have to go." With that, I snatched my smoothie off the table and left.

# Chapter 2

# Isis

The Custom Hot Rides parking lot was busy as usual. Cars were being picked up and dropped off or browsed by mesmerized admirers. People loved the work we did, and while we were not the only ones in Miami who specialized in custom work, we were definitely known as one of the best, especially since we had some celebrity customers. Throwing my truck in park, I jumped out, made my way inside, and headed straight for the office. Courtney was busy with customers, so I was able to slide by her.

Sitting down in the comfortable office chair, I was glad to be out of the Miami heat. I looked around the office and admired my position. Things were going well for us, and through the midst of the bullshit, I had found some sanity. And I was proud of my title at Custom Hot Rides. I had to admit that when Kirk first came to us with idea of running the business of the shop while being the front-runners for receiving kilos of cocaine, I thought he had lost his mind completely. But I was also at a point in my life where I needed something. Something less than normal to keep me busy and keep my mind focused. And this became the thing, because when you're dealing with cocaine, your head game has to be on, and I'm talking at all times. While we didn't personally handle the kilos—hell, we'd never actually even seen the cocaine—we were the front end for the receiving operation.

I wasn't proud of it, but I didn't have any regrets. The money was great, but that wasn't even my motivation, because I rarely spent it. Keeping myself busy and focused was my motivation. And to be sure, I did just that; I threw myself into my work. I spent most of my waking moments in the office at Custom Hot Rides. If someone was looking for me, I wouldn't be hard to find. And it had to be some of the easiest work I had ever done. No contact with the customers, which I loved, and even better, no going in-between with us and the customer. All of that was for Kirk to worry about, and thus far he had been handling it pretty well. So I couldn't complain.

"What's up, Secret?" I answered my cell phone when her name lit up.

"Bring yo' ass outside." I didn't even waste time questioning her. It would have been a waste of my time, because whenever she wanted you to do anything, she would worry you half to death. Dragging myself from my comfortable seat, I made my way down the hallway, through the lobby and outside.

"Wow, that's you?" My mouth dropped wide

open at the sight of the beautiful red Ferrari Secret was standing next to.

"All day." Secret rubbed it gently like she was rubbing her first real diamond. You could tell by the stroke of her hand she cherished the car.

"This baby is nice." I loved it. "When did you get it?"

"Earlier today."

"I can't deny it. It hot. I'm talkin' all that. How much you paid for it?" I braced myself for the digits I was sure she would be revealing.

"Three hundred fifty thousand."

"Fuckin' dollars." I almost screamed but was able to keep calm. "You spendin' crazy." I smiled. But I knew she had it to spend. Like I said, Kirk paid us well. I had more money than I wanted to count.

"Yep, I'm gone enjoy my coins, every goddamn penny. And you should too," she threw in with a smirk. And I knew she right. "You got to stop spending all your time at this damn shop. There is life after Custom Hot Rides. Make some time and experience it."

"I'm good." I wasn't sure if I was trying to convince her or myself. "But you need to be careful spending cash like that all at once."

"I know, but Jack down at Foreign Ecstasy takes care of that."

"Just be careful," I added.

"I feel you. But that's why we need to really focus on gettin' our own business going. Then we won't have to worry about reporting shit to the IRS as gifts."

I shook my head in agreement. "I'm with you on all of that, but we have to find the time. Right now we have to focus on this business; it's the money maker, and remember, Kirk say he gone help us when it's time," I reminded her. Just like Secret, I couldn't wait for us to go into business for ourselves. We both ran Custom Hot Rides and were really good at it. I knew we would be equally successful at managing our own empire. Minus the drug opportunity. But we had to be patient.

"True. I agree with you a hundred and ten percent. But I can't lie; I'm anxious. I'm really ready for us to have our own . . . but I'll chill." Secret gave her word. I hoped she meant it, but deep down I knew she would be saying the same thing in a few days. The girl had the patience of popcorn: she liked things quick. At a moment's thought, she wanted action, but I shrugged it off, knowing she would wait. "Check this out, though: Penny just invited me out for smoothies."

"Oh, so y'all didn't invite me? Did y'all go to that new one?"

"Yes, and I can't front, they bomb; we gone have to go. But she invited me out 'cause she wanted to talk. She kinda let me know that she ready to take on her own independence. And I'm proud of her about that."

"That's what's up. I knew it would just take some time."

"Check this out, though, then she drops the bomb on me that she ready to get her own place and move out." The sour look that Secret wore on her face and her tone of voice told me that she was not happy. But I was not shocked about that, either. "You already know I ain't wit' that." I was correct.

"Why not? If she say that she ready for independence, that's all a part of that. And you have to support that." I kept it real. When it came to Penny, Secret was like a mother bear with her cubs: she did not play.

"Aye, I know that. And I'm trying to support her, I just feel like she ain't ready to be on her own just yet. Eventually, yeah, just not now."

"But why? So that you can feel safe? She can't live her life like that."

"It's just that sometimes I worry that she still has nightmares about what happened to her."

"Secret, those are your fears, not Penny's," I pointed out to her. Penny staying with her was more about Secret feeling secure, not about Penny. "I don't think she would move out if she felt unsafe."

Secret just glared at me, then let her head drop low for a minute, then looked back at me. She laughed. "She even had the damn nerve to give me an ultimatum. Basically saying that she moving out whether I like it or not. Can you believe that bullshit?"

"No, I can't, because she normally does everything you want her to. So, do you blame her for the ultimatum? She had to come to you with her mind made up; it was the only way to stick to her decision."

"Aww, you exaggerating. I'm not that bad."

"Listen, I have told you before, Penny is not a baby any more. She is a young woman, and as much as you hate to accept it, it's true. Let her grow up."

"I know she's not a baby. And I treat her like an

adult. Let's be clear, I never said she couldn't move out. I just feel now isn't the time." She shrugged her shoulders.

"Have you considered that maybe this move is for the better? Maybe it's for her sanity? Maybe it will help her get over her fears, if she still harbors some. Or even help her feel stronger as a woman."

"Trust me, I hear everything you are saying. I just don't know if I accept it just yet. At least I don't today."

"News flash, you heard what Penny said. So you better take off them invisible ear plugs and all that stubborn and listen." I crossed my legs and leaned back in my chair.

"Whatever." She sighed. Secret was stubborn as a mule, and in most cases there was no changing her mind. "Listen, there ain't shit destroying my day today. I just drove off the lot in three-hundred-fifty-thousand-dollar Ferrari. Let's take a ride in my bitch."

That I didn't object to. I was ready to ride. "Can I drive?" I asked.

"Fuck yeah."

With that, we were out. The weather was perfect for a spin in Secret's new toy. And I was not playing. I took it straight to the interstate so I could lay it down.

# Chapter 3

# Secret

As always, Isis's words of keeping it all the way real lay heavy on me. And as much as I hated to admit it, there was some truth to what she had said. It was time that I let Penny grow up and be a woman. Not that I was trying to keep her from it, but the kidnapping had scarred me just as it had her. And even though the coward who had decided to cross me was six feet under, I still shuddered at the thought of Penny being out in the world alone. But Penny had made her stance on the matter clear, and she really hadn't left me a choice.

But I had other things on my mind, like protection. I told myself every day that I didn't regret any of the work I had done with Kirk. To be honest, I didn't know where Penny, Isis, or I would be if Kirk had not come back into our lives. But I had to be real: every job or scheme that Kirk had sent us on was a magnet for possible future problems. In some cases, deadly problems. And working at Custom Rides was just another chapter, because even though Isis and I wore the title "managers," we were in charge of the biggest part of the operation, which could make us targets. So I wanted to be proactive, and I had the perfect solution: a gun. Kirk had put me in contact with the best person for this situation: Mike P. Mike P was known in the streets to carry all the hot heat. He could get you anything you wanted, and however much of it you needed. And it would all be legal.

"Damn, Mike P, you ain't playin', you got everythang." I admired the machinery he had lying around. I was at one of his private locations, and I was impressed to say the least. I'm talking about machine guns, rifles, and shit I couldn't even describe. Simply put, if you were looking to start a war, Mike P was definitely your man.

"Sweetness, this is just the playground." I knew right away what that meant. He was trying to tell me I hadn't seen anything at all. And I believed him; his reputation preceded him in the streets. Not only was he the gun man, he was a trained killer. He was not to be fucked with or crossed. But what fool would be crazy enough to cross somebody with the guns and ambition he had? To even step to him, you would have to be connected to the US military, because he was locked and loaded.

"I know you got me then." I still was looking around, mesmerized at all the shiny.

He reached down and picked up two guns off one of the three glass tables covered with handguns. "Here is one of the two pieces you asked for." He gently laid a silver, heavy, metal piece in my waiting hands. Just the touch of it sent blood rushing through my veins.

"A nine-millimeter Glock, just as you requested. And this is her sister." He pointed toward the other nine-millimeter that lay on top the table

"What about the silencer?" I questioned. I had been adamant that I have a silencer for both guns. Who knew when something might pop off? I might not want everyone in my businesses to know if I had to make a rash decision that might lead to blood or loss of life.

"In the flesh." He pointed out the silencer on the gun. "You straight," he assured me.

"Thank you so much for getting me what I need and making the process easy for me. 'Cause I have no time for preliminaries."

"No doubt, that's what I do. And if you need anything else, you let me know, and I will make sure you have it."

After paying Mike P, I wrapped up our little gun meeting and hauled ass to Custom Hot Rides. It was a night for one of our midnight deliveries, and the last thing I needed to do was be late. Isis and I both always got there early so we could eat, meditate, or do whatever we needed to do to prepare. The nights were normally long and sometimes agonizing because we couldn't go to sleep. Tonight especially was big, because there were several kilos of cocaine coming in. Kirk was happy; the thought of money gave him chills.

"Secret, you have got to try to get here early sometimes. Pull up when you get ready."

"What you talkin' about? I ain't late. Just not on your time." Isis was so controlling; if I arrived ten minutes after her, she wanted to say I was late.

"Yeah, but we can get things set up without rushing."

"I'll remember that the next time I'm runnin' only five mintes behind." I said it sarcastically just to irritate her.

"Kirk called. He said he'll be runnin' late after the delivery. He rode out to Tampa for some last-minute business."

"Cool. That nigga always going somewhere." I shrugged it off. "Did Courtney pick up the tags for the locks?"

"Yep, she did that earlier. Where the food at?" Isis asked. I had forgotten all about stopping to pick up food.

"Shit, I forgot to pick something up. I had a stop to make."

"Order up some wings, then; I'm hungry. I been doing so much all day, I haven't even had time to have lunch."

"I done told your ass about that. Fuck around and pass out." I chuckled. Isis had a habit of letting work get the best of her. I told her time and time again it was not that deep, but she never listened.

By the time the wings arrived, we were chilling. I filled my plate with honey gold and hot flavor and popped open an icy cold can of Coke. Isis filled her plate with sweet teriyaki and honey gold.

"Do you think it's crazy how we sit here and eat like we ain't waitin' on shipments of cocaine?" Isis asked, then licked the sauce off her fingers. "If you think about it, we too calm. I mean, who does this? You know what? We need a man here to protect us. Real talk."

I couldn't help but laugh at her mention of a man. The way I saw it, we didn't need them for shit. If anything, they would make it worse. "For one, we don't need no nigga. Two, bitch, you clearly feel safe if you just sat there and gobbled down ten wings like somebody was gone snatch them off yo' plate. That seem pretty calm to me."

Isis couldn't help but laugh, knowing I was right. "I am not calm, but I have to eat to calm my nerves. You know what they say: food comforts you."

"I guess, but fuck being scared. Ain't no need for us to be scared of shit. Hell, Kirk would burn this city down if someone dared fuck with us . . . But in case he don't, you don't have to worry, because I got us." Isis looked at me, her expression confused, but she didn't have to wait long, because I was ready to lay it all out. "Yeah, that's right, I got heat for any nigga who want to fuck wit' us." I vowed that what happened to Penny would not happen to any of us ever again. To prove I was not playing, I pulled out my nine-millimeter. I smiled as I watched Isis's jaws drop and her eyes bulge at the site of the gun.

"Secret, what the hell are you doing wit' a gun?"

"What you mean? Shit, our lifestyle requires us to have heat more than ever now. We have to carry a gun for protection. Tell me you don't know that?" I glared at her, but she just stared at me without an answer. "Well, Kirk hooked me up with Mike P. I talked to him about it, and he agreed that a gun is not bad idea. He paid and everything. All I had to do was let Mike P know what I wanted. One of these is for you." The look on her face told me she was not having it.

"Most of what you said is true. This lifestyle we living is dangerous, I can't even deny that. But you

know I ain't comfortable with no gun, especially
one that I got to carry on me."

I was getting annoyed. Now was not the time for
fear or apprehension. "Fuck comfortable, Isis," I
spat. "I'm talkin' about safety at all times, never
being caught slippin'."

"I know that. But we cool around here wit' all this
security Kirk keep around. Look around you, it's
more than enough. I ain't carrying no damn gun."

I wanted to state my case further, but I didn't
want it to become a screaming match. Our heads
had to be clear for our deliveries. I would have to
wait to convince her at another time. So I chilled.
"Guess I'll be packin' double, then."

Isis looked at me and rolled her eyes. I had
pissed her off for a minute, but I knew she would
be over it soon. And at two hours she was. We sat
and laughed and talked until the delivery got
there. The delivery rolled in around midnight, but
we ended up staying two hours longer, waiting on
Kirk. Normally he arrived about twenty minutes
after the delivery. Really, he would be in close
proximity, watching just in case anything went
wrong. He always showed up with his team of guys,
which really was two of his close goons on his crew,
Sway and Busta. Sway use to be one of the dudes I
chilled with. But he wanted to be serious, so I had
to cut him loose, but we were still cool. Between
the three of them, they took the cocaine to another location where they were down and dis-
turbed. We didn't hang around for them to
remove the kilos from the engines, but we had to
stay until they arrived. It was a process, but Kirk
paid us well for our part. So I did my best never to
disappoint him.

# Chapter 4

# Secret

A few more weeks passed and I knew it was time, so I did what I hated to do the most. Reluctantly and stomping my foot all the way, I went out and found Penny an apartment. Talk about not easy; it was hard as hell. At one point I even shed a few tears. I simply was not ready, but every day I watched her watch me, and I knew it wouldn't be much longer before she tried to prove to me she was not playing. So I knew what I had to do. I wanted her to be somewhere where I knew she would be safe, which meant I had to pick it.

Finally, I chose a nice, quiet three-bedroom. I could rest well at night knowing she was in a safe, secure community. I wanted to surprise her, so I called her up and told her to meet me.

"Come on in." I met her at the door and invited her inside. "It took you long enough to get here. I thought you had got lost."

"Naw, I couldn't find my keys. I left them on the kitchen counter last night. I looked for them twenty minutes before even going in the kitchen to check." Penny chuckled.

"Why didn't you call me? I could have told you I saw them in the kitchen this morning."

"Didn't think of that." She sighed. "Oh, well, what's up? Who lives here?" She looked around at the bare living room area.

I smiled and handed her the keys. "It's for you," I announced.

She looked around the room and stared back at me, excitement lighting up her face. She jumped up and down, chanting, "Thank you, thank you."

It felt good seeing her excited. "Listen, the lease is only for one year, and you better not fuck it up."

"You know I won't."

"I had to put my name on the lease as head of household because of the credit. But I added you as another adult, so you need to go down to the leasing office tomorrow and sign your name."

"Cool, I got it." She could not stop smiling.

"If you fuck up, I ain't renewing the lease. And you know I will come all the way over here and bust your ass. You ain't too old."

"Secret, don't worry. I promise to be responsible. Plus, you know me, so you know you don't have anything to worry about. Have I ever given you a reason to believe I'm irresponsible?"

"No," I had to admit. For the most part Penny had been a good kid, always thinking things through and making good decisions. I was sure I didn't have anything to worry about.

"Plus, I have been thinking about getting a part-time job."

"I'd much rather you get back in school. You don't need a job. You know I got you when it comes to money and expenses."

"I know that. But it's not all about the money; it's just a part of my independence. And I plan on going back to school . . . just not right now."

I started to say more, but I really didn't want to push the issue, especially not at the moment. I wanted her to have a good feeling when she remembered being surprised with her first apartment. Plus, I knew why she responded the way she did when it came to school. Her kidnapping and rape had happened around school, so she associated the two.

"Let's explore the place." Penny led the way, ducking into each and every room, with a bigger smile on her face after leaving each one. "So what made you change your mind about me getting my own place? Because, honestly, I didn't see this coming."

"Isis, as usual. You know she sat me down and gave me the real. And you and I both know there ain't no ignoring her. She gone be heard."

"Isis what?" We looked up at Isis as she stepped into the room. She had come with me the day before to look at the place and help me decide that this was it.

"Don't be sneaking up on people like that. Fuck around and get dealt wit." I chuckled.

"I swear you always about the violence." Isis smiled.

"Thanks for always making Secret give me what I asked for." Penny gave Isis a hug.

"Don't be thanking her big-head ass. She ain't do nothin'."

Isis laughed. "Penny, don't listen to nothing she says. She will always be a hater."

"Real talk, though. I'm glad Isis helped me see that you are not a kid anymore. But I'm still gone bust your ass like one if you fuck up," I threatened for the hundredth time.

"I got this. So don't worry. Now, where my furniture at? Or do you expect me to sleep on the floor?"

"I swear, for this child nothing is never enough." I jokingly looked at Isis.

"I know, she just wants and wants and wants." Isis joined me in teasing Penny. Penny glared at the both of us and playfully rolled her eyes.

"All you have to do is go down to the furniture store that I use and get what you need. I already talk to them."

"Thank you so much, sissy."

"And don't go over twenty thousand, or I'm taking all the shit back."

"Thank you." Penny hugged me and kissed me on the cheek.

"And I put out ten thousand for you. Make it look nice up here," Isis added. Penny's jaw dropped again, and she hugged Isis for the second time.

"Y'all are so good to me." Tears formed in her eyes. "I'm going to pick up Erica right now. We got some shopping to do. Lock up when y'all leave." Without another word, she dashed past us, down the hall, and out the door.

Isis and I just looked at each other and smiled. "See, it was for the best. Look how excited she is," Isis said.

"She was too excited. I think she forgot me already." I was in my feelings. I would miss having her in the house, so close.

"Awww," Isis cooed. "Now stop being a baby and grow up."

"Whatever." I shooed her. "Since you want to talk about growing up and facing reality, did you think about the gun?"

"I know you ain't on that again, Ms. Trigger-Finger." She had the nerve to make up a name for me.

"Hell, yeah, I'm still on it, and you need to be. This shit is real out here. I want you to be safe, Isis." I didn't know what it would take to get it through her head.

"And I will be safe, so stop stressing about it. Now can we please go grab something to eat? I'm hungry."

"That and a drink. I'm too fuckin' sober." I released pure frustration. Talking about this gun with Isis was like talking to a brick wall. A drink would clear my thoughts, and the gun talk would slowly fade. Isis looked at me and laughed. We locked up Penny's new crib and were out.

# Chapter 5

## Isis

I woke up in a pool of sweat, my heart racing top speed, and a nervous, uncertain feeling in the pit of my stomach. I gripped my sheets and glanced around my room. I tried to find comfort in knowing that I had only been having another dream about Rico, my ex-boyfriend, who had left without warning. I lifted my head up for a brief second, then bopped it back down on my pillow. These dreams were coming more frequently and wearing me down. Each time, Rico disappeared in some form or fashion. Sometimes we would be happy, having a good time, and others we seemed to be in distress, as if we had been arguing or having a disagreement.

This time we seemed happy as we made our way through a crowd of people. It appeared we were sightseeing. Then, rapidly, the crowd seemed to thicken, and people were moving faster, and voices became elevated. I couldn't make out anybody's words, just the cackling of voices. All of a sudden, Rico disappeared, and I became frustrated as I desperately searched the crowd for him. Then I woke up drenched, and once again confused as to why these dreams were happening to me. I was over Rico and had written him off. Now I just needed the nightmares to stop.

Lying in bed, trying to gather my thoughts, I just stared up at the ceiling. The ringing of my cell phone annoyed me. I was certainly not ready to converse with anyone until I was calm and collected, so I let it ring until it stopped. I didn't even look at the screen; that way I didn't know who was on the other end. But no sooner than the ringing stopped did it start right back up again. "Uggh," I sighed out loud to the empty room. Why wouldn't people just leave me to my own peace?

Slowly I rolled over and reached for the phone, taking it off the nightstand. Kirk's name was on the screen, and I knew he was not going to ease up until I answered. I hit talk. "I'm still in the bed, Kirk. I will be in later," I announced right away. I hoped this would answer his question so that the call could end quickly. Kirk called me all the time to solve this or that. Somehow I had spoiled him, and I was living to regret it.

"See, why you got to act all mean, Isis? It ain't even like that."

"What, then?" I was not falling for that innocent act.

"I just called because I wanted to invite you and Secret to lunch at Nobu." That got my attention. Nobu was top-of-the-line, one of the most expensive restaurants in Miami. I wasn't bougie, but I loved expensive food and drink. But I was still nervous and tired and felt the need to get some rest. "I reserved a room already for us."

"You talkin' about lunch. What time is it?" Since I had opened my eyes, I hadn't even bothered to look at the time. And with the curtains pulled tight, I had no way of seeing the outside. I didn't know if it was night, morning, rain, sleet, or snow outside.

"It's ten o'clock now. So you have a couple of hours. I already called Secret."

Tiredness was really trying to call the shots for me. I yawned silently. "Cool." I gave in because he would probably just beg until I agreed to show up. "I'll be there, and you better not bring one of them whack chics you be foolin' wit'. 'Cause the last one wasted red wine on my all-way white bag."

"You still on that. I gave you like five thousand for that."

"True, but that ain't the point. I took time shopping for that. Minutes of my life I can't get back 'cause I stay too busy. So I would appreciate if your women had some type of class so they do not get drunk and destroy my things." I was still slick upset about my Gucci bag, not to mention that I hadn't been able to get another one because they all were sold out. I wanted to smack that girl. Thank God I'd never seen her again. Kirk had taken to bringing around his low-life, money-hungry slides, and they were all problem-causers. I was over it.

"Nah, but you ain't got to worry about that anyway; this for Secret and you. One hundred."

"Okay," I said with an apprehensive tone, then ended the call. Slowly, I climbed out of bed and made my way to the bathroom. As I turned on the shower I wondered what Kirk was up to. Sudden lunches at Nobu. My eyebrow was raised, but on the other hand I decided not to worry about it, because with Kirk it could be anything, good or bad.

I pulled up to Nobu's valet right behind Secret. We both climbed out of our cars at the same time.

"Hey, boo!" Secret gave me a huge grin.

"What's up? I see you brought the Ferrari out." I loved that car. I had contemplated getting one several times. Each time I thought about the price, I changed my mind. I wasn't as bold as Secret to drop that much cash on one vehicle. Not that I didn't have it, because I did.

"Of course. Why would I leave my bitch behind?" We laughed and headed inside the restaurant. The host greeted us and led us to the private area in back, which was VIP. This was the area the celebrities used when they wanted to eat in privacy. Kirk had it like that. To my surprise, Kirk was already inside.

"Damn, you beat us today." Secret did not hide the fact that she was shocked.

Kirk chuckled then gave us a shy look. "I'm a gentleman. I would never invite my ladies out and not be on time."

That was funny to me, because in the past, that was exactly what he had done. But it was all love. "Oh, yeah, let me backtrack, ummm . . ." I pretended to remember when.

"Okay, you got me. I turned over a new leaf." He laughed.

"Well, it's never too late," Secret said as she pulled out her chair and sat down. I followed suit.

"Yo, this place is nice. I heard about it a couple times, but I didn't know it was like this." Secret glanced around.

"I heard about it, too. I had thought about treating myself," I admitted. And I would have, if time permitted.

"I'm glad y'all like it, then. Nothin' but the best for my girls."

That got my attention. He was being way too over-the-top. "Oh, no, something is up."

Secret glanced at me then back at Kirk. "No doubt: VIP lunches, the extra added charisma. I agree with Isis, something is up. So what is it?" Secret folded her arms across her abdomen and we both glared at him with our undivided attention.

Kirk laughed again. He knew we were on to him. "Y'all know it ain't like that; we been rockin'." One of our waiters approached the table with a bottle of 1914 vintage Bordeaux

"Yep, the best." Secret observed the bottle and knew what I knew. That wine was expensive. It cost no less than five thousand dollars. The waiter looked at Secret and smiled before walking away. "Yep, Isis, this is huge, my nigga. Dude might need a kidney or something." Kirk and I both busted out laughing. There was no end to what Secret might say.

Kirk took a sip of his wine, and his facial expression took on a more somber look. Setting his glass on the table, he glared at us both. "Real talk, we are on top right now. We gettin' mad money. And I have to continue to let y'all know I appreciate you. Your loyalty is utmost. It's niggas in the streets that know the code, and they don't even have that. But you two, it ain't never a doubt in my mind."

"No doubt we could deliver nothin' else." Secret spoke up, and I shook my head in agreement. For the most part, I hated the schemes Kirk had put us on to, but not once had I ever considered crossing him or being disloyal.

"I want y'all to know that things can get deeper. We gone be monster big. I'm talkin' retirement. Y'all gone be able to live out the rest of your lives and do whatever."

That was music to my ears. That's all I ever wanted. "You know that's our plan. Be done and just walk away." I did a hand gesture like I was washing my hands of it.

"And you will," Kirk assured me. "But, listen, I'm going away for a few weeks. I got this thing I'm puttin' together. It's gone be major. All I need is for you two to step up at the shop while I'm gone. Just like you pretty much do now, the day-to-day. Deliveries will be the same. And you already know I got you protected, so ain't shit to be worried about."

"Listen, whatever you got going on is good. But right now everything at the shop is cool. That don't need to get messed up, Kirk, 'cause I ain't wit' the crazy stuff." I wanted to be clear. Kirk always had new ideas; he was constantly thinking about making more money and improving situations. That was cool. But sometimes it opened up new, unwanted issues, and I wanted to remain clear of that.

"Aye, no, it's all good. I ain't gone do shit to jeopardize what we got going. Trust everything I'm doing is just taking us up and beyond the top."

"I'm all for that," Secret chimed in.

"Good, then let's eat some of this expensive-ass food." Kirk picked up his fork and knife, ready to dig into the juicy filet mignon that had just been set down in front of him.

My mouth watered as I sized mine up. I was ready to eat, and I did just that. We all talked, laughed, got full, and left after Kirk paid the almost six-thousand-dollar bill. My assumption had been correct; that wine alone had cost him five thousand dollars and some change. Kirk didn't bat an eye at the bill. Afterward, we said our goodbyes, jumped in our vehicles, and were out. I felt good. Nothing felt out of the ordinary. I just didn't want any drama, and as long as we stayed cleared of that, I was cool. I had already told myself at the first sign of drama, I was out. I had zero tolerance for the bullshit. I just wanted to make money, start anew, and be happy.

# Chapter 6

# Secret

It had been a long day at Hot Rides, and I was glad to be home. As soon as I opened the door, I took in a deep breath then let out a sigh of relief. A shower and a glass of bubbly were calling my name; first things first, the bubbly. I headed to the kitchen and pulled out a bottle of champagne I had left chilling. Reaching the cabinet, I grabbed a glass, popped the cork on the bottle, poured, and watched as my glass filled to the rim. Taking in one sip, I let it slide down my throat and waited for the tingle in my toes. Once I felt that, I knew I was still alive and well.

Snatching up the bottle, I headed down the hall, and for the first time I realized how quiet the house was. No music playing, no television, nothing; just rooms filled with silence. A lonely feeling suddenly filled the pit of my stomach, and I felt ill. It had been weeks since Penny had moved out, and I missed her. I called her every day, but it still was not the same as having her there.

I went back into the kitchen, grabbed a few snacks, and headed toward the den. I knew exactly what to do to get me out of the funk. My favorite movie, *Something New* with Sanaa Lathan, would do the trick. However, twenty minutes into the movie I was lonelier than when I started. Plan B was my new hope. I picked up my cell phone and dialed Calvin. Calvin was a dude I kicked it with for company and my needs. To my surprise, his phone went straight to voice mail. Realizing quickly that I was out options, I contemplated calling Penny. But I dismissed that thought as soon as it entered my mind. The last thing I wanted to do was bore her with my complaints of missing her.

"What's up?" Isis chirped into the phone after the first ring.

"This house is so damn quiet. I could hear a pen if it dropped in the neighbor's house." I pouted. "And I'm tired of eating the loneliness away." I fake-cried with my eyes pulled tight as if Isis could see me through the phone.

Isis was silent for a brief second, then busted out laughing. "You're being a baby. Stop pouting . . . Why don't you get your things and come over here." Isis extended her hospitality, and I was not surprised.

Going over to Isis's house didn't sound like a bad idea. Nonetheless, I had a better idea. I always had the better idea. "Fuck that. It's a Saturday night and we sitting around the house like old Molly the maids. We need to hit up the club."

"I can't front; it has been a minute." Isis wasted no time agreeing with me.

"All we ever do is work. That shit gettin' old, and fast. I need fun in my life so I can blossom."

"I am so agreeing with you right now. But I'm tired." Isis let out a yawn.

"Fuck all that; we too young to be sittin' back 'bout to dry up. I ain't even tryin' to let that happen. Get you ol' lady ass dressed. I'm comin' through to pick you up. We hittin' the club tonight and that's that." I put my foot down. I was not about to give her a choice, because she was not ready to make the right one.

"Okay, I'll be ready." Isis sighed, but I did not care. She was going. I knew she would thank me later.

I wasted no time after ending the call. I raided my closet for an outfit, jumped in the shower, and sped over to Isis's crib. To my surprise I didn't have to blow my horn or get out of the car. As soon as I pulled up, she opened the door and stepped out. And as usual she was killing it.

"Damn, bitch, to say you wasn't ready to go nowhere, you sure put on quick," I commented. My girl was on point, rocking her white, pleated, high-rise shorts with a black Al cropped top, laced off with black patent-leather ankle-cuff Christian Louboutin heels. "That top is live. I need that."

"Cute all day. Ain't no sleep stopping that." She smiled. "I see you ain't disappoint."

"You already know how I do. Upstaging these hoes, even if it's simple," I bragged. I had decided to keep it simple and sweet, but I still was winning and ready to turn heads. And I was sure my Rag & Bone skinny blue jeans, simple tied off-the-shoulder white top, and red suede tilt-heel pumps would do just that. "We 'bout to be lit tonight." I was amped.

"Turn down for what?" Isis cosigned.

# Chapter 7

## Isis

I have to admit I was ready to snuggle up when Secret called me, talking about hitting up the club. Hell, I had worked all day, and the last thing I wanted to be around was a loud crowd of people and the endless thump of loud music. But Secret didn't leave me a choice when she all but demanded I get dressed, because she was picking me up. Not to mention she was talking that sad talk about feeling lonely. I had known Penny moving out would affect her, but she had seemed like she was coping with it well. Tonight, on the other hand, she really sounded like she needed me. So there was no way I would disappoint.

No sooner had we stepped off in the club, the DJ was on fire and that loud crowd that I had been reluctant to be around gave me energy. We grabbed a drink from the bar and stood close to the dance floor.

Future's "Magic" blasted out of the speakers, and Secret start dancing right away. "That used to be my shit," she yelled over the music.

"I know, right," I agreed. I bobbed my head and took a sip of my drink. Secret moved deeper into the floor, dancing. I continued to sip on my drink and rhyme the lyrics along with the song.

I wasn't sure at first, but this guy was coming toward me, and I was almost sure he would say something to me. I tried to look off in the opposite direction. It didn't help. "Hey, I'm Jackson." He was bold in his approach. I sipped my drink again, contemplating if I should even respond, but I didn't want to appear stuck-up or rude.

"Hi." I let the word slide off my lips.

"This may sound a bit corny, but you caught my eye from across the room. And I had to come over and tell you that you are beautiful." He was right. That was the corniest bullshit I had ever heard. But how could you say that to someone without hurting their feelings?

So instead I replied, "Thanks." Slowly, I took another sip of my drink. I wanted to shut my eyes with the hope that he would be gone when I opened them. Instead I tried to fix my eyes on Secret on the dance floor, but I no longer saw her. The crowd had swallowed her up.

"Would you like to dance?" he asked me. I guess he didn't see that I was trying not to pay him any real attention.

"Uh, no, actually I'm a bit tired." He looked at me like he wanted to protest.

"Well, if you change your mind, I'll be over there, across the room." He pointed back to the direction he had come from before walking away. I

couldn't lie: he was cute, fine even, but I was not in
the mood for no dude at the moment. And especially not him, because when he opened his mouth
it was clear to me that he had no game.

Secret suddenly appeared out of nowhere,
cradling her now empty glass. "Who was that cutie
over here talkin' to you?" I couldn't believe she
had seen that with all those people crowding her
view.

"Yeah, he might be cute but he super whack.
Talkin' 'bout I'm beautiful. Now what lame-ass
game is that? He might as well have wrote me a
note saying 'do you like me, yes or no?'" Secret
and I both laughed at the comment.

"Aye, aye." Courtney had come out of nowhere,
dancing.

"What's up, Courtney?" Secret spoke first.

"In this bitch about to shut it down. What y'all
doin' in here?"

"Secret got me here on empty, but I ain't trippin'." I grinned.

"Real talk. I had to get out. You know I can't do
all that work and no play." Secret turned to the bar
and ordered another drink. Lil Boosie and Web-
bie's old song "Wipe Me Down" came on, and we
all hit the dance floor. Future's "Percocet" came
on immediately after, and we had to jam to that.
Before long we had danced for several songs
straight. We were having so much fun; I didn't
want the night to the end. But finally it was coming
to an end.

We started for the exit, but the crowd was thick as
we tried to head outside. "This shit I hate, because if
one these bitches step on my eight-hundred-dollar

heels I'ma be ready to kill." Secret looked down at her feet as if trying to watch them.

"I told you we should have stayed at home." This was the first and only time of the night that I had regretted coming out. I wasn't shocked, though. This was usually the crowd, but normally we hung in VIP, so the crowd would be dispersed by the time we left.

"I guess I should have listened to you. Wait. Not." Secret laughed, and I did, too. We had enjoyed ourselves to the fullest.

A big, tall dude stepped in front of me, so I eased behind Secret and decided to follow her up but, somehow, in the blink of eye, she was nowhere in sight. Just like that we had been separated. I tried to sidestep some people looking for a clearing, but no matter which way I tried to turn, I just couldn't get through, and the crowd was moving slowly. I finally saw a clearing to the left of me and tried to break for it. I did a double take as I thought I saw a glimpse of my ex-boyfriend.

But suddenly, the crowd had thickened again, and the clearing was history. Not sure if I had seen what I thought I had, I paused for a brief second. With determination and ready to be rid of the crowd, I forcefully pushed my way through and saw Secret.

Secret looked relieved when she saw me, but I could tell she was agitated. "These motherfuckers reckless. I almost just smacked a bitch. Hoe gone step on my feet and instead of trying to say sorry, she had the nerve to jump bad. Before I knew it, I reached for that hoe's throat. Lucky for her, Walter grabbed me." Walter was one of the bouncers at the club; he knew us well because of Kirk. "I swear these hoes don't know." Secret's face was red, and I was getting red, too.

"Where she at?" I glanced around. I was ready to choke her myself. I hated getting upset, but I could not stand a disrespectful chick who wanted to try somebody in public. Stunting for the crowd. I would smack them myself. And after fighting my way through the vicious crowd, I could stand to hit somebody.

"That hoe gone. She got some since I skipped her TJMaxx–shopping ass right on up outta here."

"Good," I added. I also decided not to share with Secret the fact that I thought I had seen Bobbi. Secret hated him. She would probably search the club and crowd just to find him, and lord knows what ill will she might bring down on him.

At home, I climbed into bed and replayed the quick glance over and over in my head. Soon I knew the truth. I was tripping. There was no way in the world Bobbi had the nerve to come back to Miami. Besides, he had gotten what he wanted. I was sure he was somewhere off living the good life or planning to rob another poor chick blind. Either way, he was the last person I ever wanted to see. And I hoped to never lay eyes him on again.

# Chapter 8

## Isis

"Where you been at?" I questioned Secret. I was at Hot Rides as usual, doing some paperwork and spot-checking a few things. It was noon, and Secret casually strolled into the office. "I called you about three times last night, and you had your phone going straight to voice mail." I hated that she did that sometimes. I would worry. But I tried not to, knowing she went ghost sometimes when she was on one.

"Sorry 'bout that. I was at Calvin's house messing off. Then I left my phone charger at home. And Calvin was hiding his from me, talkin' 'bout he can't never spend no time with me when I come around 'cause people always callin' me. But you know I check his ass, right?"

"Well, you must didn't do a good job if he still didn't give you his charger," I added.

"I know he had the upper hand last night.

'Cause you know I didn't want to go home alone."
She pouted.

"Really, Secret, you still on that? I'ma need you
to get over it and now. Penny is gone for good.
Face the facts, she done had a piece of freedom.
She ain't movin' back in wit' you." I had to keep it
real.

"I know." She continued to pout. I couldn't help
but smile at her. You would think Penny was the
older sister and Secret the baby. She just couldn't
let go. "So why were you blowing up my phone, anyway?"

"Kirk was callin'. He wanted us to do a quick delivery around ten his morning to this church. He
donated twenty thousand dollars, and he wanted
us to deliver it. He said he'd been callin' you, of
course, too. So since you were nowhere to be
found, I had to do it by myself."

"My bad. Calvin kept me up and busy." Secret
giggled.

"I guess that's why you walkin' around in two-
thousand-dollar sunglasses and ain't no sun out. Because all I can see from my window is gray clouds
that's brewing a storm." I observed the weather.

"No doubt. But the sun is shining inside me."
We both laughed.

"You are so crazy."

"For real, though. What's up with the club?
When we gone hit it up again? It's been two weeks;
I ain't tryin' to let no long time pass again. That
night out did me all kinds of good."

"I know I enjoyed it. But I got to go shopping
first. Grab me some new fits."

"Maybe if you stayed away from this damn place
for two damn minutes, you could shop and some

more." Her statement hit home. She was right: I spent too much time up in Hot Rides, way more time than I needed.

"You right. I agree, but for right now, at this very moment, I would settle for some Starbucks. I didn't have none this morning because Kirk and his timing threw me off. He came by the house and dropped off the check, but I had to drive thirty minutes both ways to drop it off."

"Man, that's brutal. I know how you are about that coffee."

"You already know. So what I need for you to do is finish up this paperwork for me. I'm sleepy, so I'ma run and get me some Starbucks tea. I don't want to drink coffee this time of day; I'm already anxious enough. Then I'm going home. I'll be back tomorrow." I wasted no time removing myself from my chair.

"You do that. I got you." Secret pulled off her sunglasses and sat down in my spot.

I wasted no time getting up out of Hot Rides. I was craving Starbucks. I pulled into an empty parking spot and made my way inside. Thankfully, it was not packed. I jumped straight in line and placed my order. I was always all smiles when I thanked the cashier when she placed my passion fruit tea in my hand. I couldn't wait to sit down in my car and take my first sip. With my tea in my hand, I turned swiftly to make my exit. Stunned, I dropped my entire cup as I came face-to-face with my past: Bobbi. I had to be dreaming, but there was too much moving around me, and the cashier was calling me "ma'am" behind me. I glared at him, and the room seemed to spin. I tried to gather my composure, but I started to feel seasick.

For the first time, I realized that I had dropped my tea. I glared down at it, spilled out all over the floor in puddles. Then suddenly, I had the urge to get out of there. Sidestepping the puddle, I made a beeline for the door.

I could hear Bobbi yelling my name in an attempt to stop me, but that only made me increase my pace. Once inside my car, I could see him in my rearview mirror as I put my car in reverse. Burning rubber out of the parking lot, I sped off down the street at top speed. I was so nervous that my hands were shaking. I pulled over a few blocks later to try to calm my nerves. It took a few minutes, but I took a few deep breaths and continued to check my mirror to make sure he hadn't followed me. I was only able to calm down a little; I was still a bit shaky.

After pouring myself a glass of wine as soon as I got home, I sat down on my couch, undecided what I should do next. I thought about the club, when I thought I had caught a glimpse of him. I was right all along; it was definitely him. Was it coincidence that I had run into him twice? Either way, I needed to take action. Twice I picked up my cell phone to dial Secret, but each time, I laid it back down. One thing I knew for sure: Secret despised Bobbi. I worried about what she might do. The last thing I needed was her making a rash decision that might land her behind bars. Not that he didn't deserve it for what he had done to me; I still had a hard time accepting the fact that he could betray me like he had.

Bobbi and I had been close. We did everything together, and I was there for him when he didn't have anyone. I really believed we shared a bond. But it had all been a lie. Instead of him having my back, he was out making calculated and criminal moves against me. Just thinking about it made me angry and hurt all over again. But it also opened my eyes and made me understand Bobbi was not ever to be trusted. Never. I hadn't known what he was truly capable of, and he had proved that to me the best way a person could.

With all the thoughts and trips down memory lane, recalling what had happened, I soon felt drained and climbed into bed. I prayed sleep would find me, but my mind was too jumbled. I lay in the bed for hours, unable to sleep. Somewhere during the night sleep must have claimed me, though, because I woke up to my curtains still open and the sun shining bright. Sitting up in bed, I knew just what I had to do. I called up Mike P and drove out to see him. I did the unthinkable: I bought myself a gun. I had to be sure I was safe at all times.

# Chapter 9

# Secret

"Retail therapy, hunny, exactly what we needed. I can be in here all day." Isis and I were in Saks Fifth picking up a few things. And for one, I was happy. Shopping was what I did; I loved spending money. It released stress and gave me life.

"Secret, you shop every day, the last thing you need is retail therapy." Isis twisted up her lips at me. "Now me, on the other hand, it's been a while."

"That's because you stay tied up under the damn desk at Hot Rides like a slave."

"I do work too much, huh?" Isis asked.

"Way too much." I kept it real. We were looking at purses. Isis hadn't said much while we browsed, and I wondered if anything was up. "What's up with you, though? You have been kinda quiet lately."

"Oh, I'm cool, just maybe a little tired. After work I be staying up, catching up on my television shows since I don't have time to watch them when they come on."

"Well, you know how to solve that. Go home sometimes." I paused as I spotted the Burberry bag Penny had been asking about. "This the bag Penny been buggin' me about. I'm gone get it."

"It is a bad bag," Isis agreed, checking it out.

"Aye, I'm going to get this bag and fill it up full of money and take it over to surprise Penny." I had already given her like twenty-five hundred a month as spending money for whatever she needed. Not to mention I always took her shopping for whatever she wanted. So this money would be just like a bonus. I was just glad to see her happy with life.

"Now you know she gone like that. 'Cause you know she love money."

"I think she gets that from me." I laughed.

"So I been thinking about what you said about we need to get out more. You know work hard, play harder."

"Right, so what's up?" I was ready to hear what she had to say; anything that had to do with fun I was all in.

"Well, I was thinkin' instead of hittin' up the club, we do it bigger. Like take a trip to Las Vegas for a week or so. You know, sin city." Isis smiled, and I was actually surprised that she had come up with something so different. Because, lately, you had to damn near drag her out of the house or away from work with a bomb threat. I was down, but her timing was off.

"Bitch, go to Vegas while Kirk tryin' to be the kingpin. You know he ain't tryin' to have us leave the city, especially for no five days. That nigga would lose his mind."

Isis laughed at my dramatics, but I was keeping it real. "You right," she agreed. "But we got to make it happen. Maybe not right this second, but we have to."

"But what's really good, though? You must be holdin' somethin' out on me. 'Cause I can't believe you tryin' to go somewhere, Ms. Workaholic."

"Hey, I'm just ready to get out of Miami for a minute. We have been here our whole lives, born and raised. Don't get it twisted, this is my city and I love it. But it's time we explore beyond; let's do something different."

"I hear you, and I'm wit' it all the way. We just have to wait on the right timing wit' everything goin' on. So until then, we just gone have to chill."

"I agree." Isis was on the same page as I was.

After Isis chose some outfits, I paid for the Burberry bag and a few things for myself then headed out. I ran by the bank to withdraw some money for Penny's bag. I didn't feel like driving home to get into the safe for cash. I kept at least sixty thousand in cash in the safe at all times for just-in-case matters. But for the most part, all of my money was in safe deposit boxes in different banks. I placed the ten thousand dollars from the box inside the Burberry bag and headed over to Penny's crib. I couldn't wait to see the excitement on her face when she saw the bag and the money inside.

I was excited as I rang the doorbell to her apartment. I had a key, but I had promised to respect her privacy and only use the key if I had to. The front door swung open, and my smile faded, my blood pressure shot up, and I'm sure it showed on my bloodred face; my hands became so weak I al-

most dropped the Saks Fifth bag that carried that
Burberry bag filled with money. I was completely
speechless as I stared into my mother's white, familiar face. But I snapped back quickly as my
mother, Jackie, moved her lips to speak.

"What the fuck are you doing here, Jackie?" I
screamed so loudly my entire body seemed to
shake. "Answer me," I demanded, then pushed
past her.

"Penny invited me." Her tone was calm and
steady, and that infuriated me. I looked around
and didn't see any sign of Penny. I faced Jackie. I
needed her to see I meant what I said so that there
was no misunderstanding.

"Guess what . . . it don't matter how you ended
up here, you ain't welcome. That's coming straight
from me. So get out." I pointed toward the door
with my free hand.

"But . . ."

"Ain't no fuckin' buts, Jackie." I twisted my lips
at her. "I pay the bills, so what I say goes. Now
leave."

"Secret." I heard Penny call my name from behind me. I kept my eyes glued to Jackie for a
minute longer before half-turning to face Penny.
"Calm down."

"Girl, don't tell me to calm down. Jackie, get
your ass out of here now. I ain't playin'," I yelled
again, this time louder.

"I told her to come here. She didn't just do it
on her own," Penny tried to explain.

Jackie still stood, staring at me. "Is there something the matter wit' yo' feet or your hearing? I'm
being nice."

I placed my left hand on my hip; then Penny

grabbed it and started pulling me toward the back, to her room. I kept my eyes on Jackie until we turned the corner.

"What, Penny?" I yanked myself free of her grasp once in her bedroom. "Draggin' me an' shit." I straightened my composure.

"Would you just listen to me for one minute, please. Dang." Penny sighed as if she had the nerve to be annoyed.

"Make it quick, so I can get Jackie the fuck up outta here." My patience was on edge.

"Listen, she called me saying that she was hungry and didn't have money or food. And that she was homeless. Now, regardless how we feel about her, she is our mother. So I invited her over for a while."

"Are you done? Now first off, she ain't shit to me, or you, for that matter," I reminded her. I couldn't believe she had even said that to me.

"She is, Secret. You know it's true." Now I was pissed all over again.

"Don't say that shit to me no more. Now I don't give a fuck where she goes. But she gone get the fuck up outta here," I screamed. Upset, I tried to push past Penny as she blocked the door. "Move out of my way, Penny," I demanded.

With all of her weight, Penny dropped to the floor onto her knees in front of me. "Please, Secret, please don't make her leave." She looked up into my eyes and begged me. "Do it for me."

"Hell, no." I held strong.

Penny placed her arms around both my legs. "I need her right now, Secret." I looked down at her, and tears were streaming down her face. I was confused.

I asked, "Why?"

Loosening her grip on my legs, she shrugged her shoulders. But something in me shifted when, for the first time, I saw the sadness that had plagued Penny after the kidnapping. I felt so guilty. How had I missed it? I was so sure it was gone, but there it was.

Handing her the Saks Fifth bag that I still gripped in my hand, I gave up. "The Burberry purse you wanted is inside. It's filled with cash. Put it away in the safe I brought you." I felt as if all the fight had been knocked out of me, for the moment. I stepped around her, pulled on the bedroom doorknob, and exited. Back in the living room, I headed for the door without looking in Jackie's direction. With my back to her, Jackie tried to call my name, but I ignored her. Opening the front door, I stepped outside into the Miami heat and thanked God for the fresh air, then slammed the door so hard I think I felt the apartment shake.

# Chapter 10

## Isis

It had been the longest two weeks I could remember since I had laid eyes on Bobbi. I did everything in my power to rid my mind of him. But it was hard; I was literally fighting to keep the whole incident from replaying over in my head. And it was bothering me. No good could come of it. I wondered why he was here. How did he have the nerve to approach me? I had so many questions, but they were not for him. I didn't have anything to say to him; I never wanted to lay eyes on him again. The questions were the burning curiosity that I guessed anyone would have.

The confusion set off something in me that I could not calm. I wanted to speak to Secret about it so badly, but I couldn't bring myself to do it. During our early-morning shopping spree, I had really considered it. But I just couldn't.

It was time for me to see my mother, Felicia. It

had been a while since I had been down. I had just been too busy. We still spoke on the phone, and I sent her money monthly for her needs. I always made sure she had whatever she desired that was in prison's reach. So right after leaving Secret, I decided to make the drive down to the prison to make visiting hours.

"I'm glad you made it down." Felicia sat down in front of me with a grin. No matter how long it took me to come see her, she was always smiling and full of joy when I showed up.

"I know. I been wanting to come up for the past couple of weeks, but work has been keeping me busy."

"Are you eating? You look like you lost a couple of pounds."

I wasn't surprised she noticed I had lost weight; she always noticed everything about me. "Yeah, I lost about five pounds. I eat, but sometimes I get busy and don't eat as much as I should," I admitted. "But I'm trying to get better about that."

"Yes, don't neglect yourself. But you still have your shape I just don't want you looking skinny."

I chuckled. "I know. What have you been up to? Keeping busy in here?"

"Remember I told you that I wanted to get into those business classes they had that were overcrowded? Well, a few people dropped out, and I finally got in. I'm really enjoying them. It's an accredited college course, so if I complete it, I will get a certificate from the college."

I was glad to hear she was doing something constructive that she actually enjoyed doing. I couldn't imagine being locked away in the same place for years as she was, with nothing to do but wake up, eat, see the same people, and go back to bed with the same thing to look forward to the next day. But I guessed that's why they called it prison. Nothing but plain old misery.

"That's good. I hoped you got in."

"So how is Penny doing?" she asked. She was always concerned about Penny and Secret; they were almost like her daughters when she got locked up. And since Penny's rape, she had been extremely worried about her. Secret and Penny had come down a couple times to visit her, and she was always glad to see them.

"Good. She even moved out a while ago, into her own apartment."

"Say what?" She smiled. "What does Secret say about that?" It was a secret to no one how protective Secret was when it came to Penny.

I laughed. "You already know she tripped. It took a crane to pull the stubborn up outta her. But eventually she gave in, after I told her that she had to give Penny her independence."

"And it's a good thing that she even wanted to move out. That's a sign that she might be movin' on and getting over what happened to her."

"That's what I told her. Not only that, she had said that Penny basically gave her an ultimatum that she was going either way. Whether she supported her or not." I smiled again when I thought back to Secret saying that Penny had the nerve to give her an ultimatum.

"Right on, Penny." Felicia laughed. "She is growing up. It's amazing how all three of y'all grew up so fast."

"Happens quick, huh?" I looked off into the distance, but I could feel Felicia's eyes on me.

"What's going on with you?"

"Oh, me, same ol'." I tried to play it down.

"No, something is bothering you?" She could always tell when something was up with me. It amazed me every time that she could see it, because I always had a smile on my face when she saw me.

"I'm fine. You worry too much," I continued to deny.

"We have an hour left, so if you want to keep sitting here denying it, I'll wait." She looked into my eyes, and I could see all the love there that she held for me. A tear almost slid from my left eye socket, but I blinked it back. I was about to cry over some bullshit with Bobbi's punk ass. But I did need my mother's shoulder.

I looked away and around the room at all the strangers that I didn't know but saw from time to time when I visited. And every now and again there was a new face. That always made me sad, because I knew they would be here for a while. Then my heart would break when I saw their small children sitting across from them. Hopefully, they would be able to overcome their obstacles and still see their mother just as that. It had taken me a long time, but now I was able to appreciate mine. I looked at her.

"Bobbi is back. And I think he is following me," I released.

I don't know which part of my statement shocked her more, the part about him being back or the part about him following me, because her mouth dropped wide open and her eyes bulged at the mention of his name. But the way her entire face shifted, it was clear she was upset.

"What the fuck? Where did you see him?"

"Well, I thought I saw him one night while Secret and I were out at the club; I just wasn't sure. Then I was at Starbucks a few weeks back. I look up and he is standing directly behind me."

"That's some bullshit. You need to go to the cops and get a protective order. You don't know what to expect from his sneaky ass. Damn, I wish I was not in here. I would fuck him up myself."

"I don't know if I want to go to the cops. Besides, I haven't seen him since . . . And I went out and bought a gun just in case," I admitted in a whisper.

"I don't know, Isis. Who knows what he is capable of? And what I don't get is why he is making himself seen? What is he thinking? Dude got some fuckin' nerve."

"I know. But I don't think he'll try anything."

"What does Secret think? I know she hates him."

Again I looked around the room for a minute to avoid answering the question, but I had no choice. "I didn't tell Secret yet," I admitted, feeling a little ashamed of myself for not having done so.

"What do you mean you didn't tell her? Why not? I thought you said you saw him while you all were at the club?"

"She didn't see him at the club. I saw him, or at least I think I did. After the club was packed, Secret and I got separated for a minute, and I thought I saw him. The only reason I didn't tell her, and still have not, is for fear of what she might do. You know how impulsive Secret is, and I don't want her to do something crazy and get locked up."

Felicia softened a bit when I said that. "I guess you're right. She don't need to be in trouble. But you need to tell her, especially if you ain't gone put no protective order on him. I just don't think it's a good idea to keep it to yourself. I would feel a lot better knowing that Secret knows."

I knew she was right, and I didn't want her in her cell worrying about me and my safety. "I'll tell her," I agreed.

# Chapter 11

# Isis

After leaving the prison, I felt at ease on the drive home to the city. Telling Felicia about Bobbi had been a huge help. And I knew she was right about telling Secret about Bobbi. I should never have kept it from her in the first place. I still braced myself for when I laid the news on her. Soon as I got back to the city, I drove straight to Hot Rides.

I was tired from the drive, so I headed straight to the office and fell straight into my chair and sighed. I sat in a daze for a while as I replayed the conversation with Felicia. Suddenly I wasn't feeling as confident about telling Secret.

Secret stunned me and interrupted my thoughts as she busted into the office with force. One glance at the scowl on her face, and I knew she was pissed. The question was, what about. But I didn't have to wait long for the answer.

"I'm pissed to the fuckin' max," Secret announced.

"What up? What happened?" I threw at her. I had seen her hours earlier, and she had been in the best mood ever. I couldn't imagine what had made her so mad.

"So I told you earlier that I was going to take Penny the bag."

"Yes." I shook my head in agreement, ready for her to get to the point.

"Well, I get over there, and Jackie answers the fuckin' door." Now that was a total surprise, but it definitely explained Secret's anger. "So I immediately tell her she had to get the fuck out, of course. Then Penny explains to me that she asked her to stay for a while because she hungry, penniless, and homeless. As if I give two fucks," Secret barked.

"Wow," was all I managed to say.

"Like I'm shocked that her drunk ass is in this situation and ain't got shit. A pot or window."

"Where the hell did she come from? It's been a while since y'all even heard from her," I said, thinking out loud.

"That's what the fuck I want to know. Penny talkin' 'bout Jackie called her. Girl, you know I hit the fuckin' roof on both their asses. I told Jackie to get her ass out 'cause I pay the damn bill up there."

"This whole thing is crazy." I wasn't the least bit shocked about Secret's reaction to Jackie. "What about Penny?"

"Fell on her knees begging me to let Jackie stay." Secret shook her head, and I could see her eyes filling up with water, but she blinked it back.

"But, Isis, I can't allow that. That bitch gotta go . . . I want her ass out. I don't even trust her with Penny . . . Hell, she might ruin her," Secret said, full of anger and emotion. Water refilled her eyes. "And for the life of me, I just don't understand the hold Jackie has on Penny, and why Penny can't just forget about her. She knows what our life was like." Secret looked totally lost. I felt so bad for my friend.

"I can't, either." I paused for a minute, because what I had to say next was hard, but it needed to be said. I loved Secret and Penny, like I always said, they were my family, and I always had to be honest when it came to them. "But pushing Jackie away from Penny may set her back . . . Maybe . . . maybe Penny needs this."

I could see the hurt still building in Secret from the way her chest rose and fell. "She has me and—" She was cut off when we heard Kirk's voice booming through the building. Kirk was arguing with someone. Secret and I looked at each other and rushed out of the office toward the front where the voices were coming from. There we found a few of the dudes from Kirk's crew pushing some unknown muscular black dude with a flattop out the door. All the while, they were kicking and punching him, and blood was on his shirt.

Kirk looked up to see Secret and me watching the commotion. "Y'all get back in the office," he yelled at us. Before turning, I glanced at the front desk, but I didn't see Courtney. "Get in the office," Kirk yelled again. This time I made a beeline for the office, almost running into Secret.

"What the fuck!" Secret said as we eyed each other with confusion.

"Hey, I didn't see Courtney out there. Did you?"

I asked. Before Secret could respond, Kirk burst through the office door. "What's going on?" I wasted no time asking him. I had never seen this type of unexplainable drama at Custom Hot Rides during business hours. "And where is Courtney?"

"She straight. I sent her out to make a run for me just before that crazy-ass dude came in," Kirk answered, never addressing the incident.

"But what the fuck was that? Why he up in here trippin'?" Secret asked this time.

"Man, this dude came in claiming they damaged his car, so he was refusing to pay. I tried to explain to him that Custom Hot Rides stands one hundred and ten percent behind its product. And we ain't damaged shit on his whip. This weak-ass nigga done took a swing at me, so I had his ass escorted up outta here properly."

"What about his car?" I inquired.

"What you mean?" Kirk glared at me. "He will pay what his ass owe, or he won't ever see that piece of shit again," Kirk spat. And I knew he was serious.

Secret laughed out loud. "Kirk, you cold as hell. Calling that dude's whip a piece of shit."

"Fuck that punk-ass nigga. He betta' be glad he still breathin'. It was almost nighttime for his ass."

And I had to agree. I had heard stories of Kirk and what he was capable of doing or had done. Thankfully, we never saw that part of him, but I felt safe knowing that he was always on our side and had our back one hundred percent. As for that dude, he better count his blessings and remember not to pull that stunt ever again, because the next time he might come out on the other side. And ain't no coming back from death.

# Chapter 12

# Secret

That incident at Custom Hot Rides with Kirk a few days back had been dead-ass. Just another reminder that Kirk was not with the bullshit. And just another reason why he was my nigga, I fucked with him the long way. There was no questioning that. But since business had been booming, we didn't kick it as much as we used to. Sometimes I missed that. So when he called me up this morning saying he wanted me to swing by his crib, I was geeked. 'Cause the one thing I knew for sure, he was about to roll up. And everybody knew Kirk had that fire.

"What's up ghost-ass nigga?" I teased Kirk when he answered the door.

"You got jokes."

"Listen, I call it like I see it. You ain't never got time for us small people no more."

"Nah, you know it even like that. Bring yo' ass up in, and stop trippin' off yo' boy."

I followed him through his huge-ass mansion into his den. "Where that housekeeper lady at? She usually answer the door." I nosed around as usual whenever I did come over.

"Shi'd, I gave her the day off. Sometimes I feel like I see her too damn much. Hell, all they ask to be serious. You know I got a cook, too, now. I gave all they ass a few days off. I need to be alone sometimes when I'm in this bitch." He giggled. "A nigga want to walk around naked sometimes." He continued to smile.

"Whatever, I hope not." I laughed. Then I took a seat on the sectional. "But next time let the chef be here when I come over. You know a sister like to smash."

"Don't worry, I got you. One thing I know about you is how greedy you are. So I ordered Chinese takeout." I playfully looked at him and rolled my eyes at his "greedy" comment.

"That's what's up. But call me greedy again and I'ma smack yo' black ass." We continued to play around.

"Nah, you won't. 'Cause look what I got." He pulled out a fat rolled-up swisher full of that good weed.

I licked my lips at the sight of the blunt. "Yeah, you probably right. Now fire it up." I was ready. Kirk never disappointed. He lit up and passed it to me for the first hit. I was cool, calm, and collected. "So to what do I owe this honor of being invited out here?"

"Girl, don't do that. You know you always invited. Hell, I told you, you can have a key whenever you want it. All you gotta do is ask."

"So you say." I hit the blunt one more time then passed it to him.

"A'ight, but don't say I didn't offer." He hit the blunt and exhaled. "On some real shit, though. A nigga need you to come through."

And there it was: the reason I had been summoned out to his crib out of the clear blue. I hit the blunt and waited.

"I got some shit going down, and I need you to sit in to be sure it goes off smoothly."

"Listen, you gone beat the drum or spit it out." I was growing impatient.

Kirk sighed. "Got this hit I gotta make on this dealer. This weak-ass nigga tryin' to move in on my territory. He beat in the street, so his goons strong. So I gotta set him up. And if it all goes right, I can walk away with his full delivery of kilos and his breath." Kirk's last few words rang loud and clear. Dude had tried stepping on the wrong man's territory, he was for sure a dead man walking. "Only way I can see myself making this shit go off smooth is if you back me up."

With a job like he was contemplating, I could hardly see what I had to bring to the table. Surely he didn't need me as a trigger finger. "Why you need me?"

"I need you to do a private dance for the nigga."

"Private dance," I repeated. "How the fuck that's gone help?" I was confused.

"Shi'd, trust it's gone seal the deal. That nigga into that kinda shit. He lives in strip clubs."

"Kirk, what nigga don't. Shi'd, you strip club hoe, too," I reminded him.

Kirk smiled. "You right. But this nigga's addicted,

trust me. One peak at that red ass of yours, that nigga will be whipped and lose all brain thought. I can move in and make my move wit' no problem . . . All I need for you to say is that you in. And I will set it up."

Once again here he was asking me to do something risky. To private dance meant to be alone with a stranger—and in all cases a dangerous stranger. Why did Kirk's favors always have to be so risky? Yet, in any case, he was my nigga; if he needed me I was there. "I'm in," I said with a nod.

"No doubt. I knew you would have my back."

"Always," I assured him. "Now give me the black blunt back." I craved more puffs than ever now to calm my nerves.

"My bad." He passed it back. "Oh, and this stays between us. Isis can't know about it. But I guess I don't have to tell you that."

"Aye, I already know." I inhaled deeply. That he did not have to worry about, because if Isis found out I was private dancing for any reason, she would be pissed. I had to keep it under wraps for sure. But I had enough shit to worry about, so slipping up with the extra I had going on with Kirk was the least of my worries. Kirk's secret was safe from Isis unless I ended up shot or something if shit went bad. I exhaled the smoke and thought, *Fuck it.*

# Chapter 13

# Secret

It was a challenge, but I tried to chill and forget about Jackie for a minute, but only because I thought about what Isis had said. She had a point, and as hard as I knew it was for her to say it, I was glad she had. Maybe pushing Jackie away from Penny was not the best idea. The last thing I ever wanted to do was hurt Penny; that was never my intention. So as hard as it was for me, I tried to understand. Fuck that, there was no understanding her point of view. Tolerating would be the best I could try to do. Each morning I woke up, I fought back the urge to drive over to Penny's place, wake Jackie up, and toss her and her shit out in the middle of the street.

Each time I had to picture Penny's sad and broken face as she begged me not to make Jackie leave. And then Isis's words of truth, that maybe it was for the best. But tonight was going to be an even bigger challenge. Penny had invited Isis and me over to dinner at her place. The last thing I was in the mood for was an intervention with Jackie, because that simply would not happen. I had almost turned Penny down, but I did not want to disappoint her. And, of course, Isis had put in her words of encouragement, basically saying she did not want to be alone with Jackie, either.

So I agreed to go, but I invited Calvin along. I figured with him around I would keep my cool, since I considered him company. I tried to behave in front of company . . . most of the time. Penny also had shared that she had invited a new guy she had met, Patrick. With all the company that was now involved, I figured everything should go smoothly enough. Calvin and I arrived first, and thankfully Penny answered the door. I was glad because Jackie's face was not the first thing I wanted, nor needed, to see when I stepped inside.

"Hey," Penny said when she opened the door. She had a huge smile on her face. I wasn't surprised, though. She was still in denial that this was a combination for disaster. "What's up, Calvin?"

"Hey, Penny," Calvin said back. They hadn't seen each other since Penny had moved out of my place. Of course she liked him, but she knew I was not on any commitment-type thing, so she let it be.

Jackie wasted no time making an appearance, and I had to fight to keep from rolling my eyes. I silently counted to five. She smiled as she approached us; shockingly, she looked sober, or at least not sloppy drunk. I was not used to seeing her this way. "You made it." She looked directly at me; the eye contact was brutal in my mind. It took so much for me not to just look away.

"Jackie, this is Calvin, Secret's . . ."

I wasn't sure what Penny might introduce Calvin as, so I finished her sentence. "My friend." No sooner did I have the words out of my mouth, the doorbell rang.

"I'll get that." Penny smiled at me.

"Hey, Calvin," Jackie said.

"Hi." Calvin extended his hand. I contemplated smacking his hand out of Jackie's reach, but that would be petty.

"I'm Jackie. Penny's and Secret's mother." I nearly fainted when she let the bullshit seep from her lips. I was sure the scowl that suddenly appeared on my face burned a hole through Jackie as she looked away from my stare.

"Isis." She walked away quickly, acting as if she was surprised to see her.

I looked at Calvin briefly, then turned to see Isis's eyes glued to me. She knew something was up.

"How you been, Isis?" Jackie asked. The doorbell rang again. This time it was Patrick.

Suddenly we were all standing in the living room, and it was clear Penny was now nervous. She introduced Patrick to all of us. He was cute; he was about six foot one, thin build, with a flat fade, kind of a mocha chocolate skin tone, and a slight dimple on his left cheek. He spoke to all of us and stood back and waited. After we all said hi, silence overtook the room. There was definitely an elephant in the room. But I was a raging bull, and I wanted to attack Jackie. I just couldn't help myself.

Penny broke the silence. "I hope everybody brought their appetite, 'cause I cooked a lot."

"I'm ready to eat then," Isis said with a nervous laugh.

"Y'all head to the table then, and I'll bring it all out." Penny looked at me like she needed some type of confirmation.

Everybody followed her direction and went to the dining table. I went into the kitchen behind Penny. I figured the least I could do was help her grab a few things. You would think Jackie would have gone into the kitchen to help her, since she was living there. But Jackie was always just that, Jackie, selfish as hell. Everything was all about her. She took her butt to the table and sat down with the company.

"So what do you think about Patrick?" Penny asked me right away, as soon as we were safely away from everyone else in the confines of the kitchen.

"He's a cutie. What he do, though? He looks blue-collar."

"He's in school to be a psychologist. He's in love with the way the mind works." Penny smiled.

I was actually impressed to hear he was educated, because that's exactly the kind of man Penny deserved. Not that I wanted her in a relationship because, personally, I preferred she lived life and got herself together first, but if she had to be in love, a guy with a real future was the route I wanted her to take. "That's what up. Cute and he got brains." I opened the cabinet to fish out the hot sauce. It wasn't sitting out front, so I had to move some thing around. "What the fuck is this?" I snatched the bottle of vodka from the shelf.

I was immediately pissed and wanted answers. One of the conditions for Jackie being able to stay in the house was no drinking or being there when she drunk. "Why is it here, Penny?" I said through my clenched teeth. I tried to keep it down; I didn't want to scream and alarm the guests.

"Calm down, Secret." I was getting tired of Penny telling me to calm down. It was becoming a habit.

"Fuck me calming down. You better say something real fast."

"It's not what you think." she sighed. "Erica came over the other night, and we made frozen Jolly Rancher drinks. It's not Jackie's vodka, okay. She is tryin' to get clean."

That was a new batch of bullshit, and I was not trying to be in the mix of it or hear it. "Sure, she is," I said sarcastically.

"She is. Whether you wish to believe it or not." Penny wanted to convince me, but it was falling on deaf ears.

"Whatever. Just keep alcohol out of this place. Jackie is an alcoholic, a chronic one at that, so keep this shit from around her so that she won't be drunk in this house. 'Cause if she is tryin' to be clean as you say, it won't happen if you give her free access to it."

"You can be sarcastic if you want to, Secret, but I believe her. So I will take your advice and be more careful." Penny grabbed the platter of catfish and headed to the table. I rolled my eyes and followed with the pan full of homemade macaroni.

Once all the food was on the table, we all wasted no time digging in. Penny had fried catfish, macaroni and cheese, cabbage greens, corn on the cob, and homemade red beans and rice. In my opinion, little sister had shown out, and Patrick was enjoying all of it.

"So how is Felicia doing?" Jackie decided she wanted to start conversation. My skin started to crawl just hearing her voice. I hated when she pretended to care about something. We all knew she didn't give two fucks about Felicia. I remembered when she would get mad and curse Felicia out for buying us new clothes or feeding us. Jackie was full of shit.

"She's good. Taking some college courses and staying positive," Isis replied.

"That's good to hear." Jackie bit off a piece of fish.

"Yeah, she made a mistake but is on the right path to turn her life around." I looked at her and watched as she chewed her fish. She kept her eyes on her plate as she tried to ignore me. The room went silent again.

"This food is good," Calvin complimented, breaking the silence, which I was sure was awkward for him and Patrick.

Penny gave a nervous laugh. She knew what was happening, and she glanced at me. "Thank you. I cooked everything."

"Well, you are a good cook," Calvin said.

"Yep, she learned everything from me. You know how it is when you grow up and don't have parents. Some things you learn from your older siblings," I said as I stared at Jackie.

Jackie looked up from her plate but tried not to look in my direction. She grunted out loud to clear her throat. "So, Isis, you're not dating?"

"Yes, actually I am dating myself." Isis chuckled. I knew she was just trying to lighten the mood. "No, really, I'm focused on me right now. Relationships only complicate things."

Jackie's eyes left Isis and met Calvin's. I watched her like a hawk scoping its prey. "So, Calvin, are you Secret's boyfriend?" I could not believe the nerve of her. I had already answered that for her when I introduced them. But I was not surprised I had her bothered, even though she tried to pretend she was cool.

Calvin moved his lips to speak but I was not having it. "Like I said earlier, Jackie . . . Calvin is my friend. I don't have a boyfriend. I have fun." I gave her a fake smile.

"That's cool. Maybe I misunderstood." She tried to downplay her intentions. Thankfully for me, I was not stupid.

"I am young. I have a long time be in a serious relationship. I have to make sure I choose the right one. Or else I might become fucked up and weak." I glared at her so hard I could feel the steam rising off of myself.

For the first time since we sat at the table, her eyes met mine, and I knew I had sparked her fire. She dropped her fork. "A'ight, Secret, you got something to say to me, then spit that shit out."

Patrick looked at Penny, and she gave him a weak smile as her pleading eyes met mine, but it was too late. Clearly Jackie wanted to get a rise out of me, and unfortunately for her, I had risen. And I was just getting warmed up. "Damn right I got a lot to say. It was you who fucked us up. You were supposed to be the adult, the parent, but instead you was a fuckin' monster. Now you think you can come up in here like you deserve this mother-daughter shit from us." Spit flew out of my mouth; my emotions were all over the place.

"You think I owe you something, little girl?"
Jackie screamed.

And that was the Jackie I knew. I had wondered
when she would show up. "Damn right, you owe us
a fuckin' childhood, and I want it," I demanded as
I pounded the bare palm of my right hand on the
table.

"Me, me, me." Jackie beat at her chest with her
right hand. "It's always about you, Secret. You ain't
never been nothin' but selfish and demanding
from me. Always cryin' over your life like you're the
only one who has suffered. Fuck that, I don't owe
you shit. I gave you life and you alive and breathin'.
For that, you can thank me." Her words of bullshit
had, once again, cut me deep, and all I saw was red.

I was beyond hurt and in disbelief; I would
never have a mother. Before I could stop myself, I
jumped across the table. My destination was my
hands around Jackie's throat to choke her until she
stopped breathing. "Kiss my ass, bitch!" I screamed.
Calvin grabbed me just as my hands almost made
contact with her flesh.

Jackie stood back from her chair and stared at
everybody, then stormed out of the room. Penny
and Isis both stood frozen in their spots. Patrick
still sat in his seat with eyes bulging. I looked at
them and walked away, with not so much as a
goodbye. I grabbed my purse off the living room
couch and snatched opened the front door. Calvin
followed me outside yelling my name as I sped up
my pace. I just wanted to be away from there.

"Secret, just wait up." He was starting to annoy
me. I reached his Cadillac Escalade and stood
there.

"Unlock the door, Calvin," I ordered in an annoyed tone.

He hit the lock. "Wait, let me talk to you. Maybe you could go back and talk to your mom and work this out. It can't be that bad." I just stared at him for a minute. Maybe he was slow.

"Calvin, clearly you're deaf and dumb if you didn't hear what just happened in there."

"I did, but—"

I cut him off. "Listen, you don't know shit about my fucked-up life. So leave me the fuck alone and just take me home." I jumped into his truck, slammed the door, and sank down in my seat. As soon as he pulled up in front of my house, I jumped out and all but ran inside. He tried to jump out and come behind me, but I locked my door and ignored his knocks and the ringing of my doorbell. Eventually he got the message to leave me the fuck alone.

# Chapter 14

# Secret

Shit had been a bit fucked, and with all that was going on, I had kind of forgot all about what Kirk had asked me to do. But I had agreed, so there was no way I would back out. So here I was basically last minute trying to throw a banging outfit together so I could go shake my ass and bait some whack-ass dude.

While I tore my stripper wardrobe apart, I threw on some music and tried to practice my moves. But I was so pressed for time I gave up. Either he would like what I had to offer or he could kiss my ass. Jumping in my whip, I drove in the direction of the address Kirk had texted to me. According to Kirk, the dude thought some of the guys from his crew had hooked him up with a private dance for his birthday.

When I pulled up and stepped out of my ride, Kirk stepped from behind a bush and nearly gave me a heart attack. "Why would you sneak up on me like that? Is you crazy?" I scolded him.

"My bad." He laughed.

"That shit ain't funny. I should kick yo' ass." I pushed his right shoulder.

"Sorry. I didn't mean to do that. I was about to call you when you pulled up. Listen, everything straight. One of my niggas that work for him gone let you in. Just go in and do your thing. I'll be in when it's time. Don't worry. The kilos already inside."

"I ain't worried. 'Cause I trust you." I looked him in the eye.

"Good. Now go."

When I told Kirk I wasn't worried, I lied. I was shaky as hell. But I was no weak bitch, so I would do what I had to. The guy who led me to the room told me that Rock, which turned out to be the unknown dealer's name, would be right in. As soon as he shut the door, the lights went out and club lights came on. The room was small but looked like a VIP room with a comfy couch and glass table. Suddenly the door opened and this short, bald-headed, stout dude, with a lazy eye stepped inside. My first thought was that he did look like a rock. An ugly, beat-up rock. But my thoughts were interrupted by a familiar song that blasted out of the speakers: R. Kelly's "Honey Love."

I was disgusted. The last thing I wanted to do was dance for him. But I thought of Kirk and I fell into step. Rock smiled at me, and it sent chills down my spine. I ignored it and carried on twerking and gyrating my pelvis. I had his undivided attention; he used his middle finger and motioned me closer. When I got closer, he motioned for me to turn backward and dance on his lap. Against my better judgment, I complied, knowing Kirk would soon be coming in. I dipped my ass into his pelvis and froze as I felt something cold that resembled steel to the back of my head. Then his left hand came around my side, up my stomach, and stopped at my chest. Next I felt his vile breath as he stuck his head to the side of my face.

"I'm going to move this gun from the back of your head, and I want you to turn around and straddle me." He moved the gun, and I complied. No sooner had I straddled him facing forward did he put the gun to my forehead. "Don't let this gun scare you. I like thrills, and I want you to participate." I was so scared and in such shock. I instantly nodded my head in agreement.

I felt the coldness of the gun leave my forehead as he placed the gun beside him. I breathed a soft inward sigh of relief. But then I felt his short, stubby hands around my throat, at first lightly, but slowly he gripped tighter, then squeezed. I wanted to scream but couldn't. I could feel my face swelling and spit bubbling from my lips. I couldn't breathe. Suddenly he released me and I gasped for breath. And with one motion I jumped from his lap and grabbed his gun.

*Pop*. I squeezed off one round right between his eyes.

"Yo, what the fuck." Kirk burst into the room.

I watched the ugly-ass Grinch still sitting up with a hole between his eyes and blood gushing out of the back of his head. "It's done," I said without looking at Kirk.

"What happened?" Kirk asked.

I dropped the gun out of my hand and grabbed

at my neck, surprised that I was still breathing. "He was a sick fuck," I mouthed with disgust.

"You okay?" Kirk reached for me and tried to examine me.

"I'm good. Just take off this shit."

"I got this." Kirk bent down and picked up the gun.

"Don't leave not one kilo behind." I turned to leave without an ounce of regret.

# Chapter 15

## Isis

I had my own problems, but Secret's issues with Jackie trumped that. The dinner we had a few nights back had ended horribly. To hear the words that came out of Jackie's and Secret's mouths was just bothersome. Their relationship had always been beyond strained, for obvious reasons. But never had I experienced it to that degree and with such hateful passion from both of them. Felicia and I had had our problems with our mother-daughter relationship in the past, and it had not been easy getting to the place we were now, and still we were not perfect and needed work. But I honestly did not know if Jackie and Secret could ever even get close to having a civil word with each other, let alone have a relationship. I felt bad. For one, I always knew what to say to comfort Secret, or at least try to make some sense of things. But in this situation, I too was at a loss.

But what I wanted to do was get Secret and
Penny together so that they could talk. Secret said
that they had not spoken since the incident, and I
knew that was not normal or good. The last thing I
needed was them allowing Jackie to come in between them and rip them apart. So I decided to
get us all together for glam. I invited them out for
manis and pedis, because we all always enjoyed
pampering. What woman didn't?

"Hey, boo?" I said to Secret as she made her way
inside and took her seat next to me. I had reserved
our seats so we were good. The technician was already prepping Secret as soon as she sat down.

"I'm cool. Just done wit' the bullshit." Secret
pulled off her sunglasses. "I just cannot sit down
with Jackie and play the cool card. That shit is
dead to me." Secret jumped right to the situation
and kept it real. That was just her style.

"I feel you. I just don't think you should be getting this upset. And remember, everything affects
Penny. That's why I'm even more convinced that
the trip we talked about will be good. We need a
break from all of this. And we can take Penny; she
also needs a getaway."

"Aye, I agree. Shit, if anything, this will get her
away from Jackie's leeching ass."

"Good, we can tell her about it when she gets
here." The technicians in charge of doing our feet
instructed us to put our feet in the waiting water.
"Ahh, I needed this." I sighed as soon as my feet
touched the water. Penny walked in and sat next to
Secret. "Hey, Penny," I said.

"Hey, Isis," she replied. Her tone was not her
normal upbeat tone.

"You late," Secret said, just to torment Penny.

"Don't start." It was clear she was not in a good mood.

I signaled the technician over at the desk to start on Penny's feet. The technician wasted no time coming over. But Penny held up her right hand to stop her, then said, "No thanks, I'm good."

"What you mean, you good?" Secret asked. "Why you not gettin' yo' feet done? That's what we're here for."

"I'm cool, Secret. I got them done a few days ago."

"Whatever." Secret was getting upset. Things were already going left, and I had to do something to at least get a smile out of Penny. Then maybe Secret would come around.

"So what's up with Patrick? He is cute." I added his looks as a bonus to get her to smile, but she didn't.

"Well, actually I don't know how Patrick is, since he hasn't called since the disaster at my house. Secret and Jackie scared him off." I guess I had asked the wrong question.

"Gone wit' that weak shit. Ain't nobody scared him." Secret waved her off.

"Yeah, you did," Penny threw back. "All that jungle screamin'. I swear you was actin' like you ain't got no home trainin'."

"I don't. And his ass weak for that." I chuckled, but Penny didn't have laughing anywhere on her face.

"No, he not weak, Secret. But why you got to air our businesses out during what could have been a nice family dinner? That shit was not about Jackie, it was about all of us. But you have to give Jackie a coming-out VIP party." Penny was now sitting on the edge of the chair.

"Listen, I ain't do shit, so don't come up in here blamin' me. And furthermore, I can say whatever I want. I'm a grown-ass woman."

"But that wasn't the time, Secret. It could have waited. And yes, you are grown, and it wouldn't hurt for you to act like it. All the time, it ain't about you and your feelings."

"I know that, but I can't be fake, Penny. I told you I didn't want her ass around. The sight of her pisses me off."

"Again, you making it all about you." Penny shook her head with disappointment and stood up. "Have you ever thought about giving her a break? Allowed her to at least try?"

"Hell, no," Secret yelled and snatched her foot out of the technician's hand. "She had enough time to fuck us up. Or did you forget? 'Cause I didn't." Secret looked at the technician and gave her the okay to continue.

Penny stood for a brief moment glaring at Secret. "Well, that's sad, Secret. Because she is our mother, and maybe she deserves a try." Without another word, Penny walked away.

Secret watched as she walked out the door. She looked at me, then at the technician, and then rested her head on the chair. Then she looked back at me. "Did you hear that dumb shit Penny was ripping off to me? She act like she lived in a different house than me. See, that's why I want Jackie's ass out, she over there brainwashing poor Penny. Fucking bullshit." Secret pouted.

Again I was at a loss for words. I didn't know if Jackie was brainwashing Penny or not. But Penny and Secret were definitely on different pages when it came to Jackie. And that was not good at all.

# Chapter 16

# Secret

"So we got two big shipments coming in two days. Here are the pre-invoices I had put together. Isis, I need you to put the numbers in the system." Kirk handed her the papers he had cradled in his hand.

Kirk, Isis, and I were at Hot Rides in our office having a meeting on a couple of big shipments we had coming in a few days. Kirk always wanted to have a meeting right before, just to be sure we had everything together and we were always on the same page. Sometimes we did it the day before, though. We never wanted to get too comfortable or assume that things would just go right. We worked toward putting together a strategic plan that kept us on point.

"I got it." Isis studied the paper.

"Secret, I need you to call today to check the weight on the shipment to be sure that it matches up, as always."

"I'll call right after the meeting." Making sure the weight of shipment was spot on was always important. The weight being off could cause the haul to be pulled over, which could cause searches, and that was not okay. So we always checked several times, almost as if there was a trial drive, to be sure. So far we had been spot on with every shipment.

"I think we ready. Y'all be here on time ready to rock. And you know ya' boy got the rest."

"No doubt," I cosigned. "Stack up." I chuckled. Things with Penny and me were still in an uncomfortable position. But I smiled in spite of it. Penny was my baby sister, and I loved her with every ounce of myself, and no one or nothing was going to change or take that away from me. I believed that.

"Now in other news. I've been thinkin' about opening up another location out in LA."

"Another location? Like another Custom Hot Rides?" Isis questioned.

"Yep. I got a few connects out there, and the business is needed," he stated matter-of-factly. "I might need you two to go out there in a few months to help get it up and running."

Now that got my attention. Isis and I looked at each other. "Kirk, now you know I'm always down for the coin, but I got Penny, and right now I don't know if this is the time to be leaving her alone."

"Aye, you ain't got to leave her. She can go with you, and you know I'll foot whatever expenses y'all got. What about you, Isis?" He looked at her for an answer.

"I'll have to think about it," Isis said. But I'm sure he didn't expect any different from her. Isis never jumped right on board; she had to think things through first.

"A'ight. I just wanted to put it out there. It's just something to think about it. I don't have a definite yes just yet. I don't know if I'll even do it or not. But I like to keep y'all in the loop of all possibilities. I'll let y'all know."

A sudden knock on the office door stalled us. Courtney knew not come back or allow anyone back when we were having meetings. And she always called back first, so it was suspicious. Kirk reached for his hip where he kept it his gun locked and loaded at all times. Then the phone suddenly rang; the call was from Courtney's phone at the front desk.

I hit the speaker button. "It's Penny at the office door," Courtney announced. "I tried to tell her you all were in a meeting, but she wouldn't wait for me to call y'all."

I stood up to unlock the door; Penny knew the rules already, so I figured she was on one.

"What's up, Penny?" Kirk spoke first.

"We in a meeting." I stood in front of Penny.

"Hey, Kirk." She ignored me and bounced around, basically begging for attention. I wasn't sure what that was about, but I ignored it. I knew she was possibly still mad at me from the nail salon. Maybe she wanted to annoy me.

"Don't worry about the meeting, it's over. How you been, Penny?"

"Not up to shit. Just still tryin' to convince Secret to let me be a grown woman." She gazed at me. "But I guess you already know how that is."

"Life's a bitch." Kirk laughed and stood up. "I

got business. I'll catch up with y'all later. You take care of yourself, Penny." He bounced.

"Why you comin' up in here interrupting our meeting? Where the hell you been at? I been callin' you," I questioned her. "Talkin' 'bout being grown. Grown people answer they calls, they respond."

Instead of answering me, she laughed and sat down.

Courtney called from the desk again, this time asking Isis to come to the front desk to sign for a package.

"Secret, I seen your calls, and I know you think I was ignoring you. But I was not, and I'm not mad at you." I was glad to hear her speak some sense. "I just needed a few days alone. You know, time to think and clear my head."

"I understand," I agreed. I was glad she was talking to me. For a minute I thought I would have to curse her out just to get her to act right. But she was coming around on her own. "I'm sorry that I came off so strong the other day at the nail salon. I just was in my feelings. I really didn't mean to upset you."

"It's cool. I know you didn't. We just got a lot of pressure going on, but we gone be okay. Now can we please go grab some food? I'm hungry. I haven't eaten all day."

"No doubt. Let's grab Isis when she done."

Isis was game to go eat; we had been in a meeting with Kirk since we had come in and had not had breakfast. So we couldn't wait to eat. Courtney hadn't had lunch, so she wanted to roll. Shutting the office down, we headed out for Mexican, one of everyone's favorites.

# Chapter 17

# Secret

A few weeks had passed since the drama with Jackie, Penny, and me. But it still seemed like yesterday to me. I couldn't shake Jackie's hurtful words that she didn't owe me shit. But in spite of her bullshit, things were going well, at least with Penny and me. We were back on the same page, except where Jackie was concerned. I still wanted her out of Penny's house, but for now, I was biding my time, because one thing that I could count on was that Jackie would be Jackie and somehow she'd prove me right again. She was just a selfish drunk who had kids that she didn't give a fuck about.

But one thing Penny was right about: I had to try to get over it. I wasn't sure if I would ever be able to forgive Jackie, at least not anytime soon. The hate was rooted in me too deep. Something had to give, though, because my hate for her was weighing me down, and I no longer wanted that. Hanging on to it, in my opinion, made me no better than she was, and I longed to be nothing like Jackie.

The doorbell rang, bringing me out of my thoughts. "Coming," I yelled as I raced to get the door. I was sure it was only Isis, but she was clearly leaning on my doorbell.

"Would it be too much to ask to for you to hurry up when someone ringing your doorbell. It's hot out here," Isis complained.

"Would it be too much to ask impatient people to have patience?" I teased back. "Get yo' ass in here." I pulled her inside. I had invited Isis and Penny over for drinks and to hang out by my pool. It had been a minute since we chilled at the pool, so it was time. "I already got everything ready so we can go right outside."

"It's about time we chilled like this. I've been needing this." Isis sat down on the beach chair and scooted into a comfortable position.

"Me too. We use to do this almost every weekend. I'm tellin' you, we are turning into old-ass working ladies. And I tell you I ain't ready to get gray hair and start wearing no Depends just yet," I joked. I popped open a bottle of Cristal. Yes, me and my girl were about to sit outside in the bright sunny afternoon and sip Cristal. We had it like that.

"I swear, me either. No early menopause for me." We both laughed at our silly jokes. "Come on, hurry up and pour me a glass of that. I've been craving a glass of champagne since I woke up this morning."

"At your service." I filled a glass and passed it to her.

"Thanks." Isis sat up and reached for a chocolate-covered strawberry. "All this fruit looks delicious. But where is the food? I didn't eat breakfast this morning."

"I got you. I have some turkey and cream cheese roll-ups in the fridge. I'll go grab them." I hurried inside for the sandwiches and came straight back out. I didn't want to miss a second of the sun; it was soothing to my skin. "So I know Kirk hit us with the bullshit the other day about LA and all that. I ain't heard you say nothing yet. How you really feel about it?"

"Kirk, I swear, he never seems to amaze me. This guy just come out the ass with everything like it's nothing. LA. I could have never guessed it, but I guess I can't be shocked, this is Kirk we talkin' about. I can't lie, I wouldn't mind visiting the city, but workin' out there . . . That's a whole other situation . . . I'm just not sure," she said. I shrugged my shoulders.

"I can't front, it caught me off guard, too, especially when it comes down to me leaving Penny behind. But he cleared that right up, so I'm straight on that. I have to agree with you, though, LA a whole other situation. Yo, but remember when he took us out to eat and he was leavin' town saying he had other business that he was workin' on? Maybe the LA setup is what he was talkin' about all along," I replied.

"You know what, I never thought about that. But he also still sayin' it ain't definite yet. I'm just gone chill until he give us some facts."

"As long as I don't have to leave Penny behind with Jackie's unstable ass, we can talk." I was not playing about leaving my sister, and Kirk knew that.

"One other thing, I just worry if it's safe. This is LA we talkin' about. What about competition? That's a big-ass city, so I know they trickin' cars and all that. And the drugs, well, I guess we don't even need to talk about that. It ain't math." Isis was speaking some real shit. I had thought about that, too, but I didn't want to say it out loud just yet.

"Real talk. And we done received some of our shipment from out there, too," I reminded her.

"I know." Isis sighed, then took a sip of her drink. "Things could be different, I mean, I'm sure they will. And we don't know nothin' about LA. Miami is our home, it's easier to have things on lock."

"True that. But one thing is for sure, Kirk gone make sure we are safe. And that we can be sure of." Isis shook her head in agreement on that. "But hey, look on the bright side, maybe I could find me a man out there. 'Cause Miami ain't showing me no love. Hell, maybe LA got a man for you, too."

"Nah, I think I'm good. If I can't find a man out in Miami, maybe I should be alone."

"I feel you." I laughed. "Maybe it ain't the niggas, it's us."

"No, I ain't takin' no blame, it's definitely them." Isis reached for another strawberry and bit down hard. I laughed. "But what's up with Calvin? Why you trippin' off him?" Isis asked with her mouth still full of strawberry.

I gave her the driest look I could muster. "Look, don't start askin' me dumb shit. You know I ain't on that commitment shit. Calvin, he cool wit' that, but he really likes me. He be tryin' to spend nights and all that. You know I ain't into that, but I let him do it a few times. Well, he call himself tryin' to get mad when I told him a few weeks back I'm cuttin' that back. So I guess he want to be on some payback shit by ignoring my calls for a week. Hmmph, I guess didn't nobody warn him to be careful wit' that shit when it comes to me." I chuckled.

"What did you do?" Isis laughed. She knew me to all too well.

"Let's just say now it's been almost a month, and I'm still ignoring his ass. Who the fuck did he think he was dealing wit'?"

Isis continued to laugh. "Clearly he didn't know. Secret, you need to stop, though. Calvin's cool, a real good dude."

I knew what Isis was saying was true, but I never had any mercy for a man and his heart. Like them, I kept it straight gutter; that was the only language men seemed to understand anyway. First sign of weakness from a woman, and they take it and run with it. I was not having it. "Fuck that nigga. I will not get played. Ever." I felt bad as soon as that left my mouth. Isis and I both glared at each other, and things got quiet. I didn't mean to say that. The last thing I wanted to remind Isis of was Bobbi, and when he had run out on her. The worst part was him stealing from her. I hated his punk ass, but I felt like he had it coming soon in life anyway. Lucky for him, he had left Miami.

Again I saw this look on Isis's face that I had only caught a glimpse of briefly, but this was the second time I had caught it recently. And she hadn't been talking much lately; today was the first day that she seemed a bit more open. I had been so wrapped up in my own bullshit that I hadn't been paying much attention to my friend. "Aye, you cool? You been quiet lately."

"I'm good. You already know that. Like I said before, I'm just a bit overworked. I need to get that vacation in." Isis smiled for good measure, but I still wondered if she was holding something back. I didn't know what she would have to keep from me, but I still wondered.

"Heyyy." We turned to see Penny singing her introduction. "I had to use my key. You knew I was coming. You should have been waitin' for me. I even called when I was down the street."

"My bad. I left my phone in the house," I apologized.

"I see you came bikini ready," Isis said. "Normally you say you have to change when you get to the pool."

"Today I thought I'd be like you and Secret, ride the city with my bikini on."

"Aye, that's the best way to do it. I bet you felt free," I added.

"If you say so. I'm ready to take a dip, but first I need a drink. What you got here?" She picked up the wine bottle. "As usual, my sister got the good stuff, Cristal." Penny turned the bottle up and filled her glass. Isis and I watched as she drained the glass on sight.

"Thirsty, huh?" I asked.

"Yes." Penny smiled at me. "Miami is too damn hot today."

"Penny, where is Erica? It's been a minute since I seen her," Isis asked.

"I was wondering the same thing," I added. We

were used to seeing Erica whenever we saw Penny, but lately she was a ghost.

"Erica be busy all the time. I have to pencil my time in with her." Penny giggled. "Nah, for real she be busy. But I hung out wit' her earlier today for breakfast and drinks."

"Where the hell y'all have breakfast at that allowed you to have drinks? Ain't neither one of you twenty-one." I knew Penny drank sometimes; I even allowed her to drink around me. But now she was out ordering drinks at restaurants.

Penny giggled. "I knew that would catch you off guard. We had breakfast at Erica's crib. She cooked and made margaritas."

"Oh, I was about to say somebody 'bout to lose they liquor license." Isis chuckled.

"I know, right. But why the hell y'all drinking alcohol for breakfast anyway?" I threw in.

"We were celebrating Erica completing a paper she been workin' on for over a month. Now we can get back to kicking it."

"Well, y'all shouldn't make no habit of that," I continued to push the issue. Drinking alcohol in the morning sounded like some alcoholic shit to me. All I could see was Jackie up at the breakfast table, eight o'clock in the morning, with a six-pack, then another six-pack by lunchtime. "But you should bring Erica over sometimes."

"I will. Let's go for a swim." Before we could reply, Penny ran and jumped into the pool. Isis and I looked at each other and followed suit. We jumped around throwing water at each other and laughing.

I jumped up and down, splashing water; it went everywhere. "Stop, Secret, you gone mess up my hair." Penny faked like she was afraid of the water and swam to the edge, climbed out, and poured herself another glass of champagne.

"I miss having good old-fashioned fun with y'all." I couldn't stop smiling just thinking about all the fun we had shared, and some of the crazy things we had done just for a laugh.

"Me too," Isis agreed with a grin.

"Me three." Penny jumped backed in. I looked over and saw her pouring her third glass of champagne. I knew we were having fun, but she was putting the wine away.

"Dang, Penny, I know it's free, but slow down. You have to drive home, or did you forget?"

"Sure, Mom," Penny joked, then ran, jumped back into the pool, and splashed water in all directions. Isis and I ducked as if we could really avoid the splash.

We played around for a while until we were tired, then climbed out of the pool and ate the sandwiches, fruit, and, of course, finished off the Cristal—at least what Penny left for us, because, if I didn't know any better, I would have thought she was trying to finish off the entire bottle. We were having so much fun that before we knew it, the sun was setting, so we sat and watched it go down. Then Isis called it quits for the night. I refused to let Penny drive home after all the wine she'd had. So she stayed over. I had to admit, I was glad to have her back at the house. If it were up to me, she would live with me forever. But she was not having that, so I chilled.

# Chapter 18

## Secret

Kirk and I had not spoken about what had gone down with Rock nor did I even think about it. But I was on my way to meet up with him in some "undisclosed" location is what he told me over the phone. According to him, I was the only one he had shared the location with. I wondered what was up. With Kirk it could be anything.

I pulled up to this grassy area with nothing around but big trees and wind. It was beautiful. He let his window down. "Park and get in with ya' boy," he instructed. Shutting off my ignition, I climbed out of my car, hit the locks, and jumped in with Kirk.

"What's up?" I spoke.

"Shit," he answered. "Buckle up. You know we follow all safety guidelines when I'm in motion." He put the car in drive and drove off.

"Yeah, except you do a damn hundred," I joked.

"I be all the way up." He grinned. "Real talk. I

wanted to let you know that I appreciate you for
having my back a few weeks back. I know shit got a
little crazy, but you handled that shit like a pro."
He glanced at me, then back at the highway. We
were now on the interstate and out in the middle
of nowhere.

"Shit get crazy dealing wit' you." I smiled. We
veered off the interstate into another country area
and kept balling.

"I know. But here is a symbol of my appreciation." He handed me a brown envelope. From the
feel of it, I knew it was full of money.

"You know the way to a girl's heart." I opened
the envelope and glanced inside at nothing but
hundred-dollar bills.

"And that ain't all," he declared. The car slowed,
then came to a complete stop in front of an old
barn. We were at another undisclosed location.
And this time it was just that because I didn't have
any idea where we were.

"Where we at now? What's up?" I looked at the
other three cars parked with no one in them.

"I brought you out here because what you did,
Secret, can't go unnoticed. You got all it takes to
be on top. But I been knew that . . . Today I want
you to meet the connect."

"The what? I mean who?" My head shot in his
direction like a cannon. Now I was confused for
real. "Why would you do that, Kirk? I don't know
what you thinkin', but I ain't ready for that!"

Aye, yes you are. You may not know it. But you
ready. Trust me, it's a good move."

"But—" I started to speak, but he cut me off.

"Haven't I gotten you this far? Look at you now.
And this shit ain't even half over . . . Besides, one

day you might have to fill my shoes to keep you and Isis going."

"To keep Isis and I going," I repeated with a laugh. "Keep us going how?"

Kirk looked away, then back at me. "I don't know, sometimes I feel like my days are numbered, like someone is watching me." He then looked away again off into the distance. "I have done some foul shit, Secret. But I think you know that." He turned his attention back to me.

For a minute I thought he was serious, but clearly he was just fucking with me. I laughed. "Man, get the fuck outta here. You gone be straight."

"Probably." He smiled, and it seemed forced. I felt something in the pit of my stomach but forced it away quickly. "But shit always real, Secret. Remember that. Now come on, we got shit to do right now."

We walked inside. A few guys were standing around; they seemed more like guards than anything. One of them led Kirk to a tall, dark-skinned guy with a goatee. "What's good Kirk." He spoke first and reached out and shook Kirk's hand.

"Ain't shit. You got it," Kirk replied.

"And this must be the beautiful lady you been tellin' me 'bout."

"No doubt. Secret, this is Dough," Kirk introduced him.

"Hi," I spoke.

"So, Secret yo' real name?"

"That's what I was told." I smiled.

"Damn, well, it fits you. You are beautiful."

"I been told that, too."

"Aye, I told you she a trip." Kirk laughed.

"No doubt," he cosigned. "I like that shit." He looked me over. "So my man Kirk right here told

me a lot about you and your girl. What's her name
again?"

"Isis," Kirk chimed in. I could not believe he
had mentioned Isis to this dude. She would have
all kinds of fits.

"Damn, the names. But it's all good." Dough
continued to smile. "I like what I hear. It ain't too
many of y'all out there. And I want you to know
that I respect y'all to the full. You might not know,
but being here means a lot in the land of the living."

"Well, thank you. I'll remember that." I grinned.
I didn't need him to tell me that meeting the connect to any drug world was major and dangerous all
rolled into one. It was not game and to most it was
an honor.

"The shit you did a few weeks back is unforget-
table. So trust me, I won't. And I got something
for you." He signaled one of the assumed guards
over. "This is for you to do what you want." The
guy handed me two bricks of cocaine. "I want you
to know you are always welcome in my house and
my presence. Never forget that." I wasn't at all sure
what that meant, but I had an idea. I glanced at
Kirk, then back at Dough.

"I won't," I replied with my two full bricks in my
hand.

Kirk had one of the guards walk me back to the
car while he met with Dough. I didn't know what to
make of the meeting I had experienced, so I didn't
try. I went back home to life and tried to forget about
it. And I knew I could never mention it to Isis. But
there was still the question of what to do with the cocaine. I didn't have an answer for that, either, so I put
it up in my house. I had other shit to press about.

# Chapter 19

## Isis

I was in candle heaven up in Yankee Candle. Everyone who knew me knew how much I adored candles. Secret was a candle addict also, and normally we shopped for them together, but she was on something else today. So I was out in Yankee Candle alone, sniffing every candle I could get my hands on.

After placing the candle called Margarita Time down, I turned to grab the Lemonade Lavender from the shelf behind me; only I couldn't reach out for the Lemonade Lavender because Bobbi had me cornered. My eyes darted around in my head trying to find someone else close by, but there was no one. The store was empty except for the cashier and another black female with dreads at the front of the store.

"Isis, I just want to say that I'm sorry," Bobbi tried to apologize. I wouldn't look at him, but I felt his eyes all over me. I wanted to shut my eyes and just disappear. I continued to look around for an escape route, and Bobbi continued to talk. "If you would please let me explain, just hear me out." I'm not sure why, but I looked him in the eyes and, just like that, my emotions started.

Through clenched teeth I said, "Bobbi, you need to move out of my way. Now." I attempted to take a step to get around him. Bobbi did not budge.

"I'm sorry. Things are not what they seemed. I promise." His pupils seemed deep and distant.

I was beginning to feel disgusted with his presence, and his words made it worse. I had to be rid of him. "Listen, if you don't move out of my way, I will scream. And I will not stop screaming until they bring in the cops," I threatened, and I meant every word. He stood with a pleading look still in his eyes, but slowly he backed away.

I no longer wanted a candle, I just wanted to be away from my past. I walked as fast as I could through the growing crowds at the mall, trying to find an exit. I kept glancing behind me to be sure he was not following me out. But I couldn't be sure. Clearly he was still following me around town, but I was not catching him at it. I hit the locks to my Cadillac truck as soon as it was in view. Once inside, I locked my doors and dialed Secret's number. I was up to my neck with Bobbi's stalking bullshit; I could no longer keep it a secret. I had meant to tell Secret back when Felicia had encouraged me to. But so much had been going on, I just never found the time. That would end today.

"What's up, chic?" Secret sang into the phone.

"Are you out?" I asked. Not that it mattered, because either way, I needed her.

"Yep, just picked up some rib tips." I could tell she was in a good mood. I hated to be the one to ruin her day, because what I had to tell her would probably completely demolish her appetite.

"I need you to come by the house now." I tried to keep my voice calm. But I'm sure my words set off her suspicion.

"Why? What happened?" I knew she would throw questions at me, but I didn't want to talk about it over the phone.

"Just get to my house, Secret." I ended the call, jumped on the interstate, and headed toward the house. Now I was conscious about Bobbi following me. I could barely drive for viewing in the rearview mirror to make sure he wasn't behind me. I knew that wasn't safe, but I was paranoid he was on my trail, because it was clear that, at some point, he had been following me. Felicia had told me get a restraining order, but I didn't want to get the cops involved, but this shit was getting out of hand.

I pulled into my garage and waited until the garage door was down before climbing out of the truck. From what I could tell, he hadn't followed me home, but I wasn't sure if I could be certain of it. No sooner than I got inside, my doorbell was ringing. I rushed to the door, and just as I thought, it was Secret.

"What the hell's going on, Isis? You got me rushin' over here. I almost had two accidents."

"Girl, Bobbi has been following me," I released. I was so upset I could feel my blood pressure rising.

"Bobbi who?" Secret seemed genuinely confused.

"Bobbi, as in my ex-boyfriend Bobbi." I broke it

down to her. I wanted to get past this so we could figure something out.

"No, the fuck he didn't. Where the hell he at?"

As much as I hated to admit to the fact I had been keeping this from her, I let it spill off my tongue like lava from a volcano. And it felt good to let it go. Secret stood with her mouth wide open as I laid out how I thought I had seen Bobbi at the club, then how he had showed up at Starbucks, and his latest stalking addition, Yankee Candle. Honestly, as I revealed all he had done, I found it hard to believe myself.

"I don't know how, but he is back," I said.

"This conniving, thieving son of a bitch got balls the size of Godzilla. How dare he even think that he can come back and even approach you?" Secret's face was bloodshot red; she was pissed as she paced the floor.

"My thoughts exactly. I just couldn't believe it the first time I saw him at Starbucks. But to see him today was just way too fucking much." I rubbed my forehead, frustrated and creeped out at the same time.

Secret stopped pacing and faced me. "And how could you keep something like this from me? I should have known from day one, the first time you thought you saw him at the club. Fuck, Isis, you just can't keep shit like this to yourself."

I didn't even have a defense for myself. There was no excuse I could give that she would understand, but I tried anyway. "I know, and I wanted to tell you after Starbucks, I really wanted to. But I know you, Secret, and you blow your top off the bat. Half the time you have no chill, and I didn't want you to do nothin' crazy."

"Damn right. Shit crazy is all motherfuckers like Bobbi's scheming ass understand. And his ass is mine." Secret pulled out her iPhone. "I'm going to call Kirk right now; he gone take care of that ass. Nigga gone wish he never knew his way back to fuckin' Miami." Secret tossed out threats. And I knew they were not idle.

I dashed across the room at the mention of Kirk's name and snatched Secret's phone from her hand as she attempted to find Kirk's name in her call log. "No, Secret, I don't want to get Kirk involved in this. I need to handle this myself. I got it." I reached behind me and pulled out my gun to prove to her I was not playing. "And I have no problem using it." I wanted to be clear.

Secret's eyes bulged at the sight of my gun. It was probably the last thing she expected to see me unveil. "When the fuck did you buy a gun? Last you told me, you hated them with an extreme passion."

"And I did, but I had to do what I had to do. After the first run-in with Bobbi at Starbucks, I decided then and there it was for the best. I wanted to feel safe, and I thought this was the best form of protection."

"Who'd you cop it from?"

"Who else, Mike P," I shared. "He's the only one I trusted."

Secret stood back and glared at me. "Well, I'll be damned." She gave a hearty laugh. "You around cocaine being delivered, and you don't think you need a gun. But Bobbi's pussy ass comes to town, and you run out and buy piece. You're wild Isis, but okay." Secret shook her head like she approved. "The next time you see him, you better blow his fuckin' head off."

"Girl, I know this talkin' 'bout he sorry. I could have gutted him like a fish right in the middle of Yankee Candle if I had a knife." Just thinking about him standing in front of me blocking my way with his fake apology made me want to throw up.

"I don't think not doing anything right now is for the best. Because I really believe in my heart we should just call Kirk up and let him silence this nigga. He done proved he ain't to be trusted. But I want to respect how you want to handle it. So I'm gone chill, but if and when you need Kirk, just holla. 'Cause I promise he got this."

"Trust me, I will." And I meant it. All though what Bobbi had done to me was the lowest of the lows, I still didn't have a desire to see him dead. I honestly didn't believe it was worth all of that. But I didn't trust him, and if he crossed me or made me feel threatened in any way, I would pull the trigger on him myself. All I really wanted him to do was stay far, far away from me. What was done was done. I couldn't change it, I just wanted to be left alone so that I could move forward and shut out the past. Because as crazy as it sounded, when I thought of Bobbi it made me think of Rico. Even Rico had never stolen from me, but Rico had walked out on me, which was sort of the same thing Bobbi had done to me. And it hurt.

# Chapter 20

# Secret

Climbing out of the shower, I grabbed a towel and dried off, looking myself over in the mirror. I wondered if I would be this fine forever. I smiled at myself and mouthed, "Yep." Grabbing the French lavender lotion that I had picked up from Bath and Body Works, I treated my whole body to it. My phone started to ring. I glared over at it to see Erica's name on the screen. My hands were still slippery from the lotion, and I almost let the voice mail catch it, thinking I could just call her back. But the pit of my stomach tingled for some reason. It had been a while since Erica had called me. I worried something might be wrong. I caught it on the last ring. "What's up, Erica?"

"Secret, Penny over here laid out on the couch. I came over to check on her because she called me, and she sounded strange. When I first got here she was cool, but then she passed out."

I sat and listened to Erica, trying to process what she was saying before jumping to a conclusion. "What do you mean when you say she passed out? What's wrong with her?" I needed better clarification.

"I think she drunk," Erica said straight out. That caught me off guard. Why would she think that?

I had talked to Penny not even three hours ago, and she had sounded fine. So something was up, but talking over the phone was not going to get at it. I told Erica I would be right over. I threw on some clothes, jumped in my Mercedes, and skidded out at top speed. I had to find out what was up with my sister. Just as Erica had said, I found Penny on her living room couch passed out. And I knew right away what the cause was. There were empty bottles of liquor: bottles of Hennessy and Patrón scattered about the coffee table. Now I knew why Erica thought she was drunk.

"Penny." I started calling her name and shaking her lightly. A few times her eyes opened but closed right back up.

"This is what she's been doing with me when I try to wake her." Erica's voice was shaky; it was clear she was scared.

"Why didn't you call me when you got over here? Especially after you seen all this shit," I almost yelled. "Wait, I'm sorry. This is not your fault," I apologized.

"I started to, but I really didn't know she had actually drank all this herself." Erica started to cry.

"It's okay, stop crying." I turned to Erica. "She is gone be all right. Help me get her to the shower. Some cold water should do the trick."

Penny was a little thing; she didn't weigh more than a hundred twenty pounds, but she was heavy as a ton of bricks. Somehow we managed to get her in the shower. I let the water run down her face. I smacked her lightly; the last thing I wanted to do was bruise her high-yellow face. Eventually she started to come around.

"What are you doing, Secret!" she screamed. "Erica, what the hell is going on?" She continued to scream and tried to fight to get out of the water. "Get off me, this shit is freezing!" I grabbed her flapping hands and held her still.

"Stop flapping your damn arms around. This is what happens to people when they get drunk. Chill your ass out." It was my turn to get angry.

"I ain't drunk. Get off me." This time her words were sort of slurred.

"My ass, you ain't drunk. Erica, go put on some coffee." Erica raced out of the bathroom. I turned off the cold shower water.

"Put your arm around my shoulder." With Penny's help, I managed to get her to her room and changed into some dry pajamas. Then I helped her into the living room. Erica brought in the coffee, and I was able to get her to drink two cups. She was still drunk, but the coffee had worked miracles. Her words were now clear, and she was thinking clearly. But she was tired, so she went back to bed. Erica and I sat and watched her take a few breaths before heading back into the living room.

"At first I wasn't paying it much attention until about a week ago. Penny had been coming around all the time wanting to have drinks. Or she would invite me over and make us drinks—there was always a drink involved in whatever we were doing. And it didn't used to be like that, and I mean she was putting them away. I asked her about it last week, but she denied she was drinking any more than usual. And her behavior was a bit over the top for Penny. So when she called today, I could tell something was up. She was super happy, and her words were a bit slurred. So I came over."

Listening to Erica put a few things in perspective for me. Now that I thought about it, Penny's behavior had indeed been a little questionable the last few times I had seen her. And she was putting away the liquor at my house not that long ago. I guessed that would explain some of those vodka bottles in the cabinet. But I never put two and two together—not that I would have ever thought that my little sister was becoming an alcoholic.

And suddenly I knew the exact reason why. It was Jackie. I had known she would ruin Penny if I let her get close to her, and boy, was I on the money. That lady didn't care about anybody, not even her baby daughter, who had already been through a traumatic situation. I all but tripped over the living room couch as I raced to the guest room that served as Jackie's room. I rustled through every drawer, one by one, snatching all of her clothes out; next on my list was the closet. I threw everything she had back into the raggedy suitcases she had dragged them there in, and dragged them into the living room one by one. Just as I dragged the last one in, Jackie strolled through the door like everything was peachy keen. My eyes must have rolled into the back of my head.

"You got some fuckin' nerve!" I yelled out. "How you gone bring yo' fake alcohol-recovering ass up in here like you Queen B., knowing you turned your daughter into a mirror of you?" I was shouting so loud my head hurt.

"What are you talkin' about now? I ain't did nothin' but come home."

"Home? This ain't your fuckin' home. Get yo' shit and hit the bricks. You turned Penny into a funkin' drunk like you. Look." I picked up the Hennessy bottle and thrust it toward her. "She in here drinkin' bottles of this shit. This what you teach her while you claim to be getting clean," I accused, full of malice.

"Wait, this ain't my fault. I don't know nothin' about it." She cried innocence, but I knew she was lying. She would say anything to excuse herself and get out of whatever trouble she had caused. Never once in my life had I witnessed her taking the blame.

"Here you go with that shit. Lying again. Just admit it so we can get on wit' it." I clapped my hands together so hard they burned.

"Where Penny at? Get her out here. She'll tell you."

"I gettin' shit. What you can do is stay the hell away from Penny, so she can have a chance at life. Just stay the fuck away."

"You know what, how about you let Penny be a woman? Don't you think it's time you did that? Besides, you ain't Penny's mother, I am." She claimed the title as if she had earned it, and that burned my soul. What mother turned her own daughter into an alcoholic?

Once again, I lunged at her with all my might, but Erica all but sat on me with all her weight to hold me back. "Get the fuck up outta here before I end you!" I screamed with tears in my eyes. Jackie fixed her mouth to say something, but instead she turned and stomped out the door. "Get the fuck off of me," I yelled at Erica. I wasted no time racing to the front door. "And don't bring yo' ass back over here. Ever," I yelled out the door. "And take yo' shit." I ran back in the house and one by one tossed her suitcases out into the middle of the street. They were so old and fragile that each one flew open and all her things were dumped out as they landed on the ground. Jackie looked back up at me as if she was shocked at what I had done.

Slowly she bent down and attempted to pick up her things. I gave her one last smirk before slamming the door shut. When I shut the door, I realized Penny was now standing in the living room.

"Just don't say shit to me." I threw my hands up as if to stop whatever might come out of her mouth. But at this point it didn't matter. Jackie was not allowed back in the house, and that I meant. And no tears from Penny, no amount of falling on her knees begging to have her there because she needed her would work. She was out. "I don't want that woman back in this house under any circumstance. Ever!" I screamed.

I was exhausted and just over it. I snatched my keys off the end table. It was my turn to stomp out of the house as I slammed the door behind me with uncertainty. It just seemed no matter how hard I tried, shit just continued to flow downhill. There was just always something to fix, something to make better. One thing after the other. I was no weak bitch, I could handle a lot. Hell, I already had, but Jackie was a battle I wondered if I would ever win. Anything affecting Penny was my weakness. And now my girl Isis was going through it. I had to ask myself in all honesty and for sanity: what the fuck?

# Chapter 21

# Secret

I was beyond pissed and confused. When I got into my car, I had to just sit there for a minute and try to get my head together I racked my brain for some explanation of the craziness in our lives, but nothing made sense. The only thing I tried to do was calm down. I also realized that leaving was not the best decision. I needed to be with Penny. I went back inside and told Erica she should go home and get some rest. After she left, I sat in the quiet, deep in thought. I jumped when I heard the doorbell ring. I had told Isis to come over, so I was expecting her, but I guess my mind was so clouded I was in a trance.

"What's going on over here?" Isis asked, as soon as I opened the door. For moment I just shook my head. I had to fight to hold back the tears; I wasn't a crier, and I knew that tears didn't fix shit.

"It's Jackie. I told you she didn't need to be in

this house. Penny over here gettin' drunk, from the looks of it on the daily. Erica called me because she was over here passed out."

"What?" Isis's whole forehead crinkled. She was just as shocked as I was. "She okay?"

"Yeah, I had to put her in a cold shower and force coffee down her."

"Where she at now?"

"She in her room."

Isis stood up and without a word walked away. I watched as she disappeared toward Penny's room. I sat in silence and waited, my mind still full of all kinds of thoughts. I wasn't really sure how to fix this. But I had to come up with something, and fast. I had to make sure Penny got better. Alcoholism could ruin her life, for sure, and it didn't take much effort. Just a bottle and a dirty cup or glass.

"I couldn't get her to talk. She's just layin' there," Isis announced as she bounced down on the couch next to me. "Where is this coming from?" Isis glanced over at me. All I could do was shrug my shoulders.

"All I know is Jackie is responsible . . . I don't know what to do about this, Isis. It's a lot." I could feel a knot growing in my throat. I tried to fight the weakness of my emotions. I had to be strong. "This whole thing could ruin her life if it's not controlled, and quick."

"The only thing to do is get her some help. Because if it's anything like we think it is, we can't fix it on our own. She will need to be in one of those alcohol abuse classes."

"Shit sound crazy to even have to say, she too young for this shit." I held my head in my hands. "I should have never allowed Jackie in this house around her. Now look at the mess we have to clean up."

"Where Jackie now?"

"In hell, I hope. I threw her trifling ass out!"

"What did she have to say about all this?"

"What she known to say. She ain't have nothin' to do wit' it." I twisted my lips up. "Isis, you should have seen the empty Hennessy and Patrón bottles on the table."

"Hennessy?" Isis's eyebrows rose. "Damn, that probably explains why she was passed out."

"Tell me about it. But you know what, Isis, I should have known something was up. Remember that day she came by Hot Rides all extra hyped, or better yet, the way she finished off that bottle at my house when we were swimming just recently?"

Isis's eyes bulged. I knew she was remembering exactly what I was talking about. "Yes, she was puttin' that away. 'Cause you made her spend the night afterwards."

"Exactly. I can't believe I didn't notice then. Guess I just didn't see this comin'." I shook my head with disappointment. I had done a bang-up job protecting Penny, making sure she was good.

"Secret, don't beat yourself up. This ain't your fault. Now you just got to focus on helping her heal. And I got your back one hundred percent."

"I know you do . . . I'm gone get some of my things and come stay over here for a minute. I don't want her to be alone for a while."

"That sounds like a good idea."

Having Isis over was a big relief and helped me calm me down and focus on the problem at hand, and actually come up with sensible ideas instead of half-assed quick fixes that would work for a day and then dissolve with no real impact. I didn't want to leave Penny alone, so I gave Isis a list so she could run by my crib to grab a few things for me until I could go by the house the next day. After a long, hot shower, I lay down on the living room sofa and stared at the ceiling until sleep claimed me. I couldn't bring myself to go to one of the guest rooms. The couch did me just fine.

By morning I wasn't feeling any relief. I opened my eyes, and even though the drapes were closed, I could tell the sun was shining outside. Sitting up on the couch, I craved a fresh rolled blunt but, unfortunately, I had forgotten to tell Isis to grab my stash. After going to the bathroom, washing my face, and brushing my teeth, I went into the kitchen and decided to prepare breakfast. My appetite was nonexistent, but I hoped Penny would have one.

After throwing some bacon in the oven and putting on a pot of water for some grits, the aroma of breakfast filled the air. I was surprised to look up and see Penny standing in the doorway. She looked around, almost as if she didn't know why I was there.

I spoke first. "Good morning."

"Hey." She rubbed her eyes, then yawned. "What made you cook breakfast?" I hated when she questioned me about cooking. It seemed no matter how many times I did it, she always acted as if she was surprised that I did it.

"I figured you might want to eat since you went to bed with no dinner."

"Oh." She seemed confused about my answer. "Where Erica and Jackie at?" Stirring the grits, I looked up at her. I wasn't sure if she was being funny or trying to annoy me.

"Erica went home last night. And I put Jackie's ass out, remember?" I was not in the mood to toy around. Just because I was cooking breakfast didn't mean all was forgiven and, damn sure, not forgotten.

"Why you put Jackie out, Secret?" she asked me as if she didn't know.

"What you mean why? I told you last night."

"No, you didn't. At least I don't remember." She rubbed the left side of her face.

"Wow. Maybe you were still wasted. I put Jackie's ass out because she done turned you into an alcoholic. And don't bring her back to this house."

"She ain't done nothin', Secret. Don't start that."

"So you call you being passed out on the couch with all type of empty liquor bottles around you nothin'?"

Penny looked away and scratched her head like she was thinking of her next comeback. "Maybe I had a few drinks, but I was not drunk. And either way, Jackie ain't had nothin' to do wit' me drinkin'. She has never influenced me to drink. She has never offered me a drink or nothin' like that. She ain't never even been around me when I was having a drink. You got it wrong this time, Secret." Penny tried to convince me, but I was not in the mood.

I gave a fake laugh, because Penny would say anything to convince me Jackie was an angel. "So you expect me to believe that you became alcoholic overnight on your own? I'll wait," I taunted her. I stopped stirring the grits as they popped out of the pot, folded my arms, and tapped my right foot as if waiting for an answer.

Penny sighed. "You just refuse to listen to me when it comes to Jackie. She just has to be the villain in your book. All I have to say is the name 'Jackie' and you say guilty." I was getting tired of her dramatic thoughts and perceptions of how she thought I felt.

"Whatever, Penny. I'm not playin' these games wit' you anymore. This shit ends now. And it's not up for discussion. Don't bring Jackie's ass back over here. And no more drinking for you." I pointed my finger at her and raised my voice.

"Ughh . . . I'm not a drunk," Penny screamed, then stomped her right foot with her fist balled.

"Be pissed all you want, I'm gettin' you some help, and now. I'm not waiting until this whole thing is out of control."

"But I don't need any help, Secret. You can't just force things on me. I'm grown," she reminded me. And she was right, but that didn't mean spit to me.

"Say whatever you wish, Penny. Whatever makes you feel better but you gettin' some help, and you don't have any choice. It's not a negotiation, it's what I say it is." I laid out it and drew the line in the sand. There was no way I was going to give her a choice. I would drag her on the hot pavement to get treatment, kicking and screaming. "Now try me and see what happens to this apartment. I'll tell you what will happen, so you don't have to wonder . . . I will break the lease, and that will force you to have to move out."

"You wouldn't," Penny challenged me, but I was serious and not giving in.

"Try me and you'll get your answer." I smirked. I meant every word that fell from my lips. I would not have her fuck up her life while I was front and center.

Penny looked me up and down and rolled her eyes. "Ugh. I swear," she screamed and then went out the front door. I knew she was mad at me, but I couldn't be bothered with that. I had to do what I thought was best when it came to her. And she was always number one to me, so I had to make sound judgments.

# Chapter 22

## Secret

"Secret, where you been at? I was blowin' you up all day yesterday," Kirk all but yelled through the phone.

"Boy, you need to calm down and stop yellin' in my ear." I held the phone in midair.

"My bad. Aye, I need you and your girl Isis to hop a plane and come to California in the next two days."

"Damn, Kirk, just like that." I hunched my shoulders. "Just come to California in two days. Where the hell they do that shit at, dog? What you think, we ain't got no life here in Miami?"

"I feel you. But I need you here."

"What's so damn urgent that you can't wait at least two weeks?" I was sure the annoyance was in my tone. But I had my own shit to deal with.

"Moves being made out here. Major moves. I need you both for a couple days, or possibly a week at the latest. I already had Courtney book y'all flights, so basically just bounce."

"Kirk, I got shit going on here with Penny. I can't just leave."

"Aye, just bring Penny; you know that ain't a problem. But all I'm asking is for you to show up. I'll hit and have Courtney book her a flight."

I thought about it for a minute, but there was no way Penny was getting on a plane with me voluntarily. With the mood she was in, she would flat-out refuse. So that whole idea was dead. "Damn, Kirk, you a last-minute-ass nigga. And what 'bout Isis? You know she gone trip. Hell, she probably say no right off the bat."

"Then you got to convince her to come. Don't get on that plane wit'out her. A driver will be at the airport to pick you two up and will deliver you to me." With that he ended the call.

I stared at my cell phone for a minute and rolled my eyes. The nigga was bossin' up with his demands. I reminded myself to check him later. Now I had to muster up the energy to call Isis. I wasn't ready for that conversation, either.

"That nigga say what?" Isis screamed through the phone. "Girl, Kirk can kiss my ass." She continued without giving me the chance to answer her question. "Does he not realize we run a business here? Hell for him. We just can't up and leave."

"I know all that," I finally got out. "But he said set it up with Courtney. Either way he need us there." Between her and Kirk both yelling at me, I was becoming agitated. "Now pack yo' shit 'cause I ain't going alone. Plus, Kirk said bring yo' ass."

"I'm grown; he don't boss me around." Isis grunted. "What time the plane leave?" She gave in.

I filled her in on the itinerary and hung up. And just as Kirk had known she would, Isis handled everything with Custom Hot Rides before we boarded the plane. As the plane lifted off the ground, I breathed a sigh of relief.

The plane landed at LAX airport on time with no delays. We were both surprised to find Kirk at our gate waiting on us.

"I thought you were sending a car for us? 'Cause you too good to drive down here to pick us up."

"Fresh off the plane, and already you tryin' to start a beef with me." Kirk laughed.

"Shut up." I smiled.

"Kirk, I swear you got some damn nerve. You better be lucky I suddenly feel relieved to be in California," Isis said, looking around as we stood outside the airport.

"I know y'all pissed, but this gotta happen. Nobody else can help me wit' this. Ain't nobody else I trust. We gone handle this shit, and I promise y'all will be back in the air on the way back to Florida before you know it."

"Better be, 'cause I got shit to handle." I threw my hands on my hips and twisted my mouth.

"Well, let's do this." Kirk grabbed our bags and loaded them into the Cadillac truck he was driving. Once he was done, we all loaded up inside and were out. Kirk jumped on the interstate, and just like that we were in LA traffic. We rode the interstate for a while, then Kirk got off and we drove until we reached something like a ranch. We pulled in slowly. There was a house, a barn, and a stable. There was also a fence with two beautiful horses running around.

"Yo, Kirk where the fuck you got us at? *Little House on the Prairie.*" I laughed.

"For real," Isis added. "I can't front, though, it's beautiful."

"I know, right. It's peaceful. Clean wind, birds chirping, the whole nine." Kirk finally came to a stop, then shut off the engine. I almost broke my neck turning in Kirk's direction. Never had I heard him talk like that, describing things for their beauty and feeling. "Damn, nigga, is California making you soft?" I chuckled.

Kirk smiled at me. Then he looked over at the horses as they ran around the length of the circular fence. "Nah, never that. But sometimes you start to notice shit, you know."

"I can get wit' that," I agreed.

"Kirk, never mind her. You know she always a gangster," Isis chimed in, and we all laughed. Honestly, it felt good to be laughing and being around this beauty; for a brief moment I could forget about all the drama in my life.

"But this the spot, though, where y'all gone set up. I'm still trying to find an official spot. I looked at a couple places."

"But how you gone store shit at a barn?" I had to ask.

"See, things ain't always what they seem. Right there inside that barn is a makeshift warehouse. Trust it's all legit. Besides, out here shit gone be a lit' different."

"Different how?" Isis jumped right in.

"Now when I say this don't panic, Isis. It's safe, and I will have bodyguards here all day while y'all here. Trusted niggas y'all know from home."

"What's the scheme, Kirk?" Isis sighed. She was clearly impatient to hear.

"A'ight . . . So deliveries gone go down sometimes right here. I will need you two to take the delivery, weigh the product, make sure it's on point. And use the testers to make sure it's legit. I also need help counting the money . . . Well, at least running it through the machine."

"Wait, so you want us in the middle of the drug deal, basically?" Isis asked.

Kirk looked at me almost as if he needed help. "Yeah, sorta."

"What the fuck does 'sorta' mean?" Isis was becoming upset.

"What I'm trying to say is, you don't have to be in the room when the exchange is made. Y'all gone have the money ready and counted when they arrive. Once the product brought in, you will weigh and test. And vice versa: if they picking up product, then you will just count the money."

"You know this shit is risky, regardless of what you say. This ain't what I expected. You said you needed help with starting it up."

"I know, and eventually that's what it will be like here. I just got to get this shit going." Isis rubbed her forehead like she was in deep thought. "What's up, Secret? What you got to say?" Kirk asked me.

"Nigga, it's whatever. I just want to get this shit done and get home." I glared at Isis.

"Whatever, let's do this. But, Kirk, I swear you better get shot before I do." Isis sighed and sat back in her seat. I was shocked that she had agreed.

"Man, thank y'all. We gone do this."

Before we knew it, a whole week had passed, and Kirk had begged us to stay three more days.

And again to my surprise, Isis agreed. But actually, it hadn't been that bad: all the deliveries or exchanges were of course done at night. So during the day Isis and I would be out shopping and seeing the city. Kirk had booked us master suites at the Marriott, so we had no complaints. It was the day before we were leaving. Isis and I were out having lunch at this nice Mexican restaurant and having a drink.

"As much as I hate to admit it, I really have enjoyed myself out here. I'm kinda feeling California." Isis dipped a tortilla chip into her bowl of salsa.

"Me too. We gone have to come back out here whenever shit straight. Oh, hell, Kirk will be calling us back out here anyway."

"I know, right." Isis giggled. "But he better have his shit together. I ain't fuckin' wit' Kirk on this level no more. What we do at the shop back home is cool. But I don't like dealing with the coca this head-on. Touching that shit like that. Nah."

"I feel you. And he know that. He gone have it set up like home if he goes through wit' it."

"I get the feeling he ain't start that up. I think he like this quick way. Plus, the money seems to be greater. Do you realize he made almost a million in less than two weeks?"

"That's wild. I was checking that out."

"But the risk is much greater."

"Yep, that's a fact." I had to agree, but I knew Kirk wasn't worried about that.

"But Kirk is fidgety; something ain't right wit' him. And he gettin' high on that shit. The other night when we rolled up. Did you notice he stepped away? And when he returned, the cocaine was clearly on his nose. He ran those lines quick."

"He straight, though."

"Maybe, but you need to check up on your boy. Y'all been tight forever."

I shook my head in agreement. But I didn't want to dwell on the subject. Everything Isis was saying was true. Kirk was getting high on his own supply. And as for him being fidgety, I had also noticed, but I figured it was because of the deliveries; we all had reason to be fidgety. I was sure it was nothing.

# Chapter 23

## Isis

We had made it back from California, a few weeks had passed, and I still wasn't exactly sure if the storm that seemed to be brewing in all our lives was over. I hoped it was, but I was too scared to even think that, for fear that something else crazy would jump off. So instead, I just sat back and took each day as it came and thanked the heavens when nothing bad happened. I just wanted to get my head back in the game so I could focus on the business. Secret was wrapped up in Penny, and I had both their backs, but things just were complicated. On a good note, I hadn't heard from or seen Bobbi, so hopefully he had gotten the message to stay far away from me.

Today I was feeling good. I woke up feeling refreshed. I had taken off work the day before and pampered myself with a much-needed spa treatment. And I wasn't done. I took today off as well and went and got my hair done.

As soon as I got in the house, I went to the guest bathroom and played around, taking selfies of my new sew-in. I was looking too cute. Afterward, I went into the kitchen and pulled out the bottle of wine I had left to chill and poured a glass. It was time for me to sit back and unwind. I wanted to sip and think of nothing that was even close to serious. But no sooner had I sat down in the den and kicked up my feet, my mailbox popped into my head. I had been busy, so it had been a few days since I'd checked. And of course my fidgety mind wouldn't let me rest until I got the mail.

Setting my glass of wine down, I slipped outside to retrieve all my waiting mail from the box. Back in the house, I sat back down, picked up my wine, and sipped before I started sorting through the envelopes. Nothing important stood out; as usual it was just bills, the norm. Just as I was about to set the rest of the stack on the table, I noticed what one of the envelopes said. Check. I wasn't expecting any checks in the mail, so I wasted no time opening it. The last thing I was in need of was money, but money was one of those things that grabbed most people's attention, whether they needed it or not.

My jaws dropped as I read "twelve thousand dollars" spelled out perfectly across the light blue paper. As I separated the check from the envelope, a piece of paper fell out. Bending over to pick it up, I read the words over and over again. *I'm sorry.* Suddenly, without a doubt, I knew exactly where the check had come from. The only person who owed me twelve thousand and would apologize to me was Bobbi.

"Secret, where you at?" I wasted no time calling her up.

"I'm at the crib."

"Your house?" I asked to be sure. The last couple of weeks she had been at Penny's house.

"Yep."

"Stay put. I'm on the way." I ended the call right away; the last thing I wanted to do was discuss the check over the phone. No, that was some face-to-face action. I must have driven eighty all the way to Secret's house, because I arrived in fifteen minutes tops. She must have been sitting in the window, watching out for me, because before I could knock on the door, it swung open with Secret holding on to the doorknob. Before she could say one word, I placed the check and note in her free hand.

"What's all this?" she asked, still looking at me.

"Look at it," I instructed. I wanted her to see it for herself.

"That fuckin' Bobbi."

"Right? He so damn random," I commented. That was the only way I knew how to describe him and his actions. I couldn't explain him, because I didn't understand any of his moves.

Secret continued to observe the check, then she looked at me. "Well, I say definitely cash the motherfucker, 'cause he owe you that much. Actually, I'm pissed that he didn't think to add interest, for pain and suffering." Secret had a serious scowl on her face.

"Hmmph, I'm surprised he even sent that . . . I'm afraid to cash it, because knowing his snake ass, it's probably fake." I had to be honest. I mean, how could we trust him? He hadn't done nothing that made him trustworthy.

"You should cash it anyway. And if it's fake, we will hunt his ass down and kill him. And that's real."

"On some real stuff, forget the check. What I want to know is how he got my address. That is my biggest concern."

"That's a good question. Do you think he ever followed you home? 'Cause what about the other times he showed up in mysterious places you were visiting?"

"I know, I thought about that. But I honestly don't believe he ever followed me."

"But how could you be so sure?"

I sat in silence for a moment. I thought about how I had been concerned that he had been showing up in places I was. I just didn't believe he had followed me, but I couldn't be sure. "I can't be sure," I reluctantly admitted.

"Exactly. I think we should get Kirk involved. It's time. That nigga need somebody to kick some fear into his ass."

I was still apprehensive about that. Kirk didn't have talks, he caused funerals. "Listen, I'm not sure about involving Kirk just yet. And besides, I'm not worried. I keep my gun on me at all times."

"Ain't that just like a nigga, though? He think he can say sorry through the US postal mail, and the world will unfold for him."

"Yep, they think they are God's gift to women," I cosigned.

"Ha, never." Secret laughed.

"What's up with Penny, though?"

"She cool, still attending those AA meetings and seeing a therapist."

"How did you get her to agree to see a therapist?"

"For one, I told her she needed to speak to a professional about her feelings. And two, I told her if she didn't go, I would stop the lease on the apartment. And we both know that got her attention. She loves that apartment, and she will do almost anything not to come back to live with me."

"I guess you are right." I laughed. The thought of Penny refusing to stay with Secret made me laugh so hard. Penny was over Secret's momma ways. "Are you still staying nights over at her house?"

"Hell, no, three weeks was too long. I went home three nights ago. I didn't realize how much I was enjoying my freedom until I had to share space with Penny again. Now I don't see how I ever done it. We annoy each other."

"Poor Penny, I'm sure you are torturing her."

"Me, torture? I think you know better. I'm the best roommate ever," Secret gloated.

"I don't think so. Try the most annoyingly compulsive. All that snoring and all those damn sideways rules. I just don't have time."

"Whatever, listen. I'm gone stop by and see her this week. I got to let her see my face and see how she is doing." I had only been out to see Penny once since the incident. I wasn't really sure what to say to her. But I missed her smile, which always lit up the room.

# Chapter 24

# Isis

"When the next time we gone all hit the club like the last time? It was mad fun." Courtney chopped our ears off. Secret, Courtney, and I were all standing around Courtney's desk with nothing much to do.

"Soon. I promise." Secret gazed at me like she wanted an answer from me. "I need to party."

"Y'all just let me know. If I'm free I'll be there," I added.

"Your ass will be free; you ain't got no more to do than the rest of us. So get ready." Secret grinned.

"I went out over the weekend, and it was turned up. Mad niggas wall to wall; y'all should have been there. Because you both need a man, and I mean ASAP." Courtney laughed.

"Shut up." I playfully nudged Courtney's shoulder.

"Yo, I'm good," Secret declared. "These niggas ain't ready for me, anyways. I be giving it to them raw. They want somebody they can control they mouth and actions. I ain't wit' none of that. Plus, I ain't committing to no punk-ass niggas." Secret was cutthroat when it came to her views, and I couldn't help but laugh. My girl did not play about what she felt.

"Damn, Secret, you have no chill and no empathy for the male species." I grinned.

"Harsh, yes, but I agree with you, Secret. 'Cause for the most part these niggas is dogs. I'm talkin' straight pit bull. They don't mean, you know, good wit' they lies and deceit." Courtney rolled her eyes. I could tell by the hostile change in her tone that something was up.

"Let me tell y'all bout Rod's slick ass."

"Rod?" Secret had to think about who he was. "Wait, dude you been talkin' 'bout for the past six months?"

"He a cutie," I added. He was tall, dark, and wore a high-top fade like the Kid from the group Kid 'n Play.

"Yeah, cute, but the nigga ain't shit. Tell me why I just found out after six months that I'm his side chick." Secret's eyes and mine met; we were a little confused. We turned our attention back to Courtney.

"What you mean? Be a bit more specific," I said. I wasn't generally nosy, but I needed to know exactly what she was trying to say.

"Well, I just found out that he is married."

"What?" Secret stomped her right foot.

Courtney shook her head for assurance. I was stunned, I could not believe the guy had had us all confused. Never would I have even suspected he was married. "That's fucked. Nigga just raw." Secret groaned.

"Raw and out of pocket," I commented. I felt bad for Courtney. I knew better than most all about betrayal.

"I know! Here I am thinking I'm his woman, and all the time I'm side chick status like a motherfucker."

"What did you do?" I asked.

"It was hard, but I kicked his ass to the curb. I ain't got time for nobody's crazy-ass wife running my life. No, I'm good on that."

"I don't blame you. That could get really ugly," I added.

"Fuck that. You can't let him get away wit' that. You need to get his ass bad."

"By doing what?" Courtney asked.

"Bitch, it's a ton of things you can do to make him pay. First, what is that he driving? I know one of his whips is a sports Audi luxury edition." Courtney shook her head yes to confirm. "Fuck it up. I mean bad, sugar in the tank, the whole nine. Sneak in his house and bleach all of his clothes and only his clothes. How is he gone explain that to his wife? Exactly, he can't." Secret grinned.

I was all for revenge on a deadbeat, but this was going too far. And what would the risk be? Maybe something Courtney was not ready to face. I thought it best she just walk away. "Nah, Courtney, I think you should just dead that shit. It might not be worth the consequences." I hoped she listened to me and ignored Secret. "The best way to show him you good is to move on." I let the words trail off my lips. They parted as I watched Bobbi step through the doors.

Suddenly I realized he was everywhere, and Miami was not big enough. I was tired of being nice. There was not one excuse for him showing up everywhere I existed; he had to have been following me. I turned to face him head-on. "Are you stalking me?" I had to know. Because he had to know this was not normal.

Before Bobbi could utter one word, Secret leaped from beside me and was only inches from Bobbi's face. "Nigga, yo' hoe ass got some real motherfucking nerve to think it's okay to come around. Clearly, you don't value your life."

"Secret . . ." Bobbi attempted to speak.

"Bitch, don't say my name ever. Matter of fact, get the fuck up outta here. Now." Bobbi looked around Secret, at me. "Oh, you think this a game?" Secret turned around and speed-walked to the counter, bent down, and grabbed the bat that was kept there.

My hands grabbed for the bat, because I knew she would hit Bobbi with it if she had the chance. "Secret, let go. Calm down," I yelled, trying to grip the opposite end of the bat. A customer entered the shop. "Calm down, Secret. We have customers," I mouthed dryly in a low voice between my clenched teeth. The last thing the customers needed to see was Secret busting somebody's head to the white meat. Bobbi glanced at me once more, then walked out. I breathed a huge sigh of relief. "He's gone," I said to Secret, hoping that would calm her. She snatched the bat and walked behind the counter. "Just go to the office and relax," I demanded, knowing she probably wouldn't listen to me.

Putting one foot in front of the other, I made my way to the doors and tried to catch up to Bobbi. I wasn't sure what was moving me toward him, because it didn't feel like me. But I felt it was time for me to stop running from him, and I needed answers.

"Bobbi," I called out his name.

At the sound of me calling his name, he immediately stopped in his tracks. Slowly he turned to me. He approached my space. "I'm sorry, Isis," he let slip from his lips right away. "I didn't mean to hurt you. If you could just forgive me, I promise to make it right."

I'm sure his words were supposed to, in some way, move me, but instead all I felt was his betrayal, and it angered me deep down. I held up my right hand to stop him. I really wanted him to stop talking. "Listen, I know you might feel you mean what you say. But I personally don't give a fuck about words anymore. They no longer matter to me . . ." I had to pause to hold back my emotions. The last thing I wanted to do was cry, and I refused to do it in his presence. He didn't deserve my vulnerability, and I did not ever need him to sympathize with me.

The lump in my throat was growing by the second. I breathed in deep to fight it. "What I need to know is how do you know where I live and work?" I demanded.

Just as I thought he would, he stalled and stared at the ground before bringing his deceitful eyes back to meet mine. "Isis, that don't matter, none of it. Just know that I needed to see you." His words seemed scripted and almost laughable. And the fact that he thought simplicity would be enough infuriated me.

"Do you hear yourself?" I growled at him. "You

stand here in front of me and tell me it don't matter." I stepped closer to him, nearly closing the gap between us. "Bobbi, you were my man, we were in a committed relationship. We made plans to live together, or least I thought." I threw in my sarcasm. "Then I look up one day to find out you are gone, simply disappeared into thin air, and took my money with you. So unless I'm the invisible bitch, yes, it does matter," I barked. The look on his face spelled stupid to me. I couldn't handle looking at him any longer. I turned to walk away. He reached out and grabbed my left arm. I snatched it away from him so hard I heard my bone pop. I turned to face him.

"It was Melvin that told me. He told where you worked and how to find you."

"How the hell does Melvin know where I live? What, he's stalking me, too?"

"Nah, it ain't like that. He told me where you worked, and I followed you home."

"You know that's called stalking, and it is a crime." I rolled my eyes at him.

"I know. I just wanted to talk to you. I had to. I needed to make things right between us. Isis, I'm so sorry for what I did to you. Please forgive me?" His tone was pleading. "I have felt like shit since day one. I never wanted to do what I did, and I certainly didn't want to leave you. I simply had no choice . . ." He looked away. "I needed the money to pay off some debt, okay? I got in bad with the wrong people. And they threatened to kill me if I didn't pay, so I took the money and disappeared. My plan was to stay alive so that I could pay them back then come back to you. I always planned to pay you back one day. That's why I sent you the check, but I really just wanted to see you face-to-face so that I could apologize. That's why I kept showing up; it was important to me that you know I was sorry."

I believed him, because I did remember, in the weeks before he left, that he had been receiving these strange calls. But he kept saying it was nothing but salespeople or donation lines. So I ignored it. Now I understood what really had been going on. But I still didn't understand why he hadn't come to me. I loved him, and I had tried to make sure that he always knew that. So I could forgive him for taking the money, but I would never forget. "I accept the apology," were my only words before turning and walking away. He came for forgiveness, and I had given him that. I hoped that would be enough for him to get on with his life. He had his forgiveness, and I had my money back. We were square.

Walking back toward the Hot Rides entrance, I saw Secret was standing post, waiting on me. She had been standing there the whole time, so she'd heard everything. I wasn't shocked to see her standing there. I knew she wouldn't leave me alone with him.

"I heard him. But that shit still ain't cool. Do not trust him, Isis." She gazed over my shoulder at him, sighed, then turned and walked inside Hot Rides, and I followed.

# Chapter 25

## Secret

"What's going on with Penny?" Isis asked as we walked around the store.

"That's just it. Everything." I sighed. "She seems to be okay, getting better or whatnot. And as far as I know, she has not had a drink, so that's all good. She even seems to be upbeat again. But now she's saying the psychiatrist wants to talk to us both together. And I'm like, hell no. I ain't got time for that. Especially sitting down wit' no shrink. I mean, why the hell does she need to speak to me? Ain't she gettin' paid enough speaking wit' Penny?" I was being sarcastic just because I didn't understand.

"I don't know. I know talking to a shrink is scary in some ways. But look at Penny, she's doing it. Maybe it's not such a bad idea. Maybe the shrink got something she wants to share with you."

"What could she possibly have to say to me? I get the bill she sends paid on time. Either way, I'm not interested in talking to her." I meant that when Penny had mentioned it to me, I told her no flat-out. The last thing I needed was some mind person who thinks they're smart trying to get into my head and fuck with my feelings. I was fine, I didn't need the drama in my life. "This is cute also," I commented on Coach 1941 tote bag. "I might need to get this one, too."

"Maybe we both should. I got an outfit to match it." Isis eyeballed the bag with delight.

"I'm gone cop this one for you, then. We gone be twinzies." I smiled.

"Remember when Felicia use to boost us matching outfits?" Isis laughed.

"Man, she use to have us on point. I'm talkin' 'bout the shirt, pants, socks, headband, and shoes. We was shuttin' the school down." I giggled. "Yeah, that was the good ol' days. That's 'bout the only time me or Penny ever had somethin' new was when Felicia got it . . . Jackie used to be mad as shit when she seen how cute we looked, and she had nothin' to do wit it." The thought of Jackie ruined my mood. But I shook it off quickly. "I miss your mom."

"Me too." Isis sighed. "That's why I still take them long-ass rides." She referred to her visits down to the prison.

"Penny and I gone have to make a trip down there, it's been a minute."

"Y'all need to that. She'll be glad to see you. She asks about you and Penny every time I go."

"I know. I'ma make it happen." I looked off into the distance but not at anything in particular. Memories of the old days just always made me feel some type of way. My childhood was no walk in the park. It was complicated, and as much as I hated to admit it, I was scarred. Some would say I was damaged goods. I tried to rid my mind of it. But it was hard.

"I have been meaning to ask you. What's up with your boy Kirk? Remember I mentioned in California that he seemed fidgety?"

I gave Isis a confused look. I wasn't ready to revisit that conversation. Besides, that had been a minute ago, and Kirk seemed fine to me, at least when I was around him. "What you mean?"

Isis shrugged her shoulder like she had to think about it. "I don't know . . . just lately he seems a little distressed and uptight."

"That nigga cool, he said something to me about he's been having migraine headaches. Other than that, I ain't noticed no change in his behavior. California, that was just the risk of the scheme," I clarified, then briefly racked my brain to see if I could think of anything that might have been bothering Kirk.

"I'on' know, maybe we just need to watch him. Check this out, the other day he came in to look at the shipment me and you received the night before. And something just seemed too different . . . at least it did to me." Isis paused like she was trying to remember something. "I can't put my finger on it, or maybe it's just me . . . He just didn't talk that much. I know he not like a chatterbox or nothing, but Kirk usually talk about stuff, you know. Instead, though, he just kinda confirmed the order and was out. 'Bout an hour later I knocked on his office door because I needed him to sign a document. And I found him just kinda sittin' there staring into space like in a daze. It was weird."

"Damn, really?" I was surprised to hear that; that did sound like odd behavior for Kirk. "Maybe I need to check up on my nigga and make sure he's straight. To be honest, I haven't had much time to talk to him about anything but business. I been too busy dealing with Penny and this rehab shit.

"Maybe everything cool, then. I just wondered, 'cause his behavior was strange to me."

I silently made myself a mental note to get up with him. "Aye, what we all really need to do is get together and let's kick it VIP. Shit 'cause that's what we do."

"Hey, just tell me when and where, I'll be there. I'm tired of sittin' in front of the television snackin', because you know that's all I do."

# Chapter 26

## Isis

**W**ith Bobbi apologizing to me, I was starting to feel like I really had things in my life back into perspective. As for Rico, I tried not to think of him, and I prayed he would stop making appearances in my dreams. If that could happen, I would be closer to one hundred percent than I had been in a while. Either way, I felt good and welcomed all positive vibes, and today was no different. I allowed all of the sun that could enter my house from all angles in. I rejoiced in its beauty and warmth. Feeling energized, I dialed up Penny, since it had been a minute since we hung out, just two of us. In the past, we would take a day just for us. Secret would laugh, accusing us of plotting against her, but it was always just my day to spoil Penny all alone. I told her to meet me at her favorite store, Macy's, so that she could shop.

"I missed you, Isis." Penny came to me with her

arms wide open for a hug. She was standing over in the junior section, looking at some new Jessica Simpson jeans wear.

"Awww," I cooed and hugged her tight. "I swear I think you got taller," I teased.

"Nope, it's the wedges. I'm officially too old to grow any taller." She giggled. "What you think about these?" She stepped back and picked up a pair of blue Jessica Simpson jeans cut up about the thigh and knee area.

"Those are cute," I complimented.

"So what's been up wit' you? I know things been mad crazy." I kept it real.

"It has, I can't front . . ." She shook her head. "But since Secret and I got back on the same page, I feel better, a lot better."

"That's good. I was worried for a minute."

"Nah, it's all good . . ." She paused. "But I can't lie. I wish Jackie was still around. I know that Secret don't want to hear that, so I hate to bring it up, because it will make her upset. But Jackie and I were really building a relationship. And as crazy as it may sound, I had hoped that we could all eventually try to build a family." The look on Penny's face was hard to describe: it was sad, lonely, yet full of hope for something she knew was not possible. I found myself speechless. "I know it won't happen, though. Secret is too protective when it comes to me, and she will never forgive Jackie." She looked at me as if I held the hope but, unfortunately, that was a situation that even I could not repair. Secret was concrete in her decision. Jesus himself would be forced to battle for her change of heart. "Did you ever forgive Felicia?" That was a question that really caught me off guard. Never had Penny discussed Felicia besides asking if she was okay. She had never really gone into Felicia's and my relationship or the lack thereof. And as much as I would have loved to give her all positives, I had to be honest.

"Our relationship struggled for years. It got to the point where we barely talked. At times, I only visited her because I felt guilty for not doing it. And on most of those visits, I had nothing civil to say to her. The blame, the resentment, and all the negative things I felt for her were constantly written across my face, blaming her for all that she had put me through. I wanted her to suffer, knowing that I blamed her and would never forgive her. But deep down, I was suffering because I knew that I loved her. Eventually we talked, we shared, and started forgiving. It was hard, but I did it. . . ." Tears formed in my eyes just thinking about all the time I had missed with Felicia because I had allowed my pride to stand in the way. It made me sad just thinking about it. But I also knew that Secret, Penny, and I had different stories when it came to having a mother. I had to take that into consideration.

"But I have to say in all fairness our situations are a little different. See, I always knew, no matter the circumstance, that Felicia loved me. Yeah, I questioned that over the years when I blamed her for being selfish and chasing material things over me, which landed her in jail. I knew better, though. And never once had she abused me. Disciplined me, maybe, but abused me, no. I say that to say this . . . It's the abuse from Jackie toward you and Secret that triggers Secret's hate."

Tears started to run down Penny's face, and she

wiped them away. "I try to understand where Secret is coming from. And I know the pain is way
down deep in that place that no one can console."
Penny's face now held a distant look. "After the
rape I tried to begin a complete healing process of
myself for myself. I had to if I was gone have some
true sanity in my life . . ." The tears started to fall
down her cheeks again; she wiped at them. Sniffing, she went on. "Forgiving Jackie was of one of
them. I had to forgive her in order to move on wit'
my life. Or else I would still be standing still. Suffering even more."

I hadn't felt them, but my face was now wet
from tears. I wiped at them. I knew exactly where
Penny was coming from. I had forgiven Felicia and
now Bobbi, and the load on my shoulders was
lighter, the air I breathed was fresher, and the sun
had a brighter beam. And I could only pray that
Secret got there one day. "I understand, and
maybe one day Secret will come around. Because I
truly believe that masked under all of Secret's hate
for Jackie, Secret has love for her, and that's the
reason she's so emotional about everything that
concerns Jackie."

"Sometimes I believe that, too," Penny shared
with me, then shrugged her shoulders. "I got to
stop all this crying, though." Penny laughed and
sniffed back tears at the same time. "I can't have
my eyes all swollen and puffy when Patrick comes."

"Wait, Patrick coming by?" I was surprised to
hear that.

"Oh, yes, I forgot to tell you. He finally called."
Penny was all teeth and gums.

"Good, I'm glad he came around."

"I know, right. I guess he didn't want to miss out

on me. Actin' like he didn't know what he was giving up." Penny modeled in front of the mirror.

"I guess he figured it out," I cosigned. "Anyway, we got to get you the baddest outfit up in here, then," I boasted and I meant it. Penny needed to always be looking like a million bucks. Secret and I both spent the cash to make sure of that.

"You know it." Penny again held the overalls up to her body. "Let me try this on because we got a bunch more to grab before we leave."

"Get whatever you like," I sang in an attempt to mimic a T.I. song.

We tried to shut Macy's down, spending eight thousand effortlessly before bouncing. I had enjoyed the time I spent with Penny, as always. But I couldn't help but feel her pain; she was truly deeply affected by Jackie and her lifestyle. I made a mental note to speak with Secret about attending those psychology sessions. Somehow, I had to persuade her to attend at least one meeting with Penny. Penny needed it for her sanity, and it could possibly play a significant role in her healing.

# Chapter 27

# Secret

Watching rain pour like an overfilled coffee mug, and the gray sky that loomed over Custom Hot Rides, was doing a good job of making me feel sleepy. I had yawned at least a hundred times, and I blinked my fake lashes so hard, I feared a piece of them might fall into my eye. But it was the best I could do to stay awake. Custom Hot Rides was so quiet you could hear a pin drop on the floor. I was covering for Courtney; she had called in ill, and no else was around to cover her shift. I had been up most of the night waiting on a late shipment, so I was beat, but I didn't mind covering for Courtney; she was cool people, and she always did what she was supposed to do. And to be honest, good help these days was hard to find. So whenever she needed time off, besides the two days a week she already got, we all stepped up and stood in for her.

After my fiftieth yawn, I realized that staring

outside at the soothing rain was not going to help my sleep situation. So I decided to actually do some work, and that included my cell phone and Instagram. I figured catching up with social media could help me get my energy charged. For starters, I snapped a quick picture of myself. I knew my fans were always watching.

As soon as I snapped the picture, one of the double glass doors at Custom Hot Rides swung open. A smile went straight to the corners of my lips.

"What's up, bitch?" One of Isis's and my close friends, Trina, screamed and rushed over to me.

"Not shit," I replied and hugged her tight. I could not believe she was back. "It's about time you blew back through this bitch."

"Shit, I had to, I couldn't take the country no damn more. A bitch almost died in that damn heat with not enough wind blowing. And them big-ass horse flies, I just could not take it anymore."

"I told you when you ran your ass down there to plantationville," I joked.

"Girl, I know." Trina laughed. "So where my bitch Isis at?"

"She ain't here but should be any minute. She had some businesses to attend to this morning." I filled her in.

Trina observed the office. "I can't front: Kirk got this bitch on point. When I pulled up and seen all those tricked-out-ass cars, I got excited. Shit, Custom Hot Rides on point."

"It is Kirk doing his thing around here. But you already know how he do."

"What's up wit' Penny? She better?"

"Man, Trina, you wouldn't even understand.

Shit been wild around here. . . . I mean at first things were getting better. Penny was coming around to her old self—she even told me she wanted to move out. I think I told you about that over the phone once."

"Yeah, I remember that." Trina nodded her head in agreement.

"Girl, well, shit went totally left. Jackie done popped back in our lives; next thing I know Penny's an alcoholic and now in therapy."

"What the hell happened?" Trina twisted up the corner of her lips and waited.

I didn't feel like going into detail, so I kept it simple. "Listen, the shit was crazy, but I got it under control." I was relieved to see Kirk come in the office so we could change the subject.

"Awww, damn, trouble back in the city. Shit ain't gone be the same," Kirk joked.

"What's up, nigga?" Trina walked over and gave Kirk a hug.

"Not shit. And you?"

"A bitch just got off the plane from old hot-ass Alabama, but I'm good. Still thick." Trina smacked her big butt. Kirk licked his lips and grinned.

"That much I see." He and Trina loved to play around like that. "Tell that weak-ass nigga Terry I'm comin' over," Kirk teased about her boyfriend.

"Fuck him. I just threw his ass out." She waved the conversation of Terry off. "But what's up y'all know I'm ready to party."

"Me too," I chanted, excited.

"Kirk you gone hook us up, right?" Trina smiled at him.

"Man, y'all too much trouble in the club together . . . But you know I got y'all." That was music to our ears. Kirk was the man when it came to setting it out in the club for us. He made sure we were treated like royalty, and nothing was left to chance. In the words of T.I., we could have whatever we liked—he made sure of it. "Y'all just let me know what night. Shit go be ignorant off the hook."

"It's about to be super hype." I was excited. I could see the club lights now, music banging, constant flow of drinks. And me and my girls turned up to the max. My girl Trina was back. I couldn't wait for Isis to arrive.

# Chapter 28

# Isis

I was happy as shit when I found out Trina was back, because the girl was pure fun to be around. And I was not surprised that her first order of business was hitting up the club; she never wasted any time on that. Trina was a pure party type of chick. I truly believed the phrase "turn up" was invented to describe Trina. The only thing I sometimes wished is that she would slow down on the alcohol. The girl could drink. But she was never trying to hear that, so I chilled and left that to Secret. They were closer when it came to the friends arena. Secret had met Trina and introduced her to me, but either way we were all cool.

But tonight was the night, and it was going down. Secret, Trina, Courtney, and I were dressed to kill and ready to party.

"That is so cute," I complimented. We all gath-

ered around the cake that one of the waitresses
had brought in, loaded with fire sticks blazing.

"That's that cognac," Kirk announced; he was
standing behind the waitress. He had had the cake
made in honor of Trina coming back to town.

"Full of liquor, just the way I like it. Thanks,
Kirk." Trina kissed him on the cheek.

"Shit, cut me a piece of that," Secret said. "I'm
tryin' to be lit always."

"Don't worry, I got ya'." Trina reached for the
knife from the waitress and started cutting each of
us a piece of cake.

"Damn, I never had cake wit' alcohol this delicious." Courtney forked a mouthful.

"I know, right," I cosigned, savoring every bite
with the intention of getting a second slice soon
after.

"Yo, but next time bring a cake laced with the
chronic," Secret joked.

"Shit, please." Trina laughed.

"Damn, y'all's ass is wild." Kirk grinned. "Aye,
get me a couple shots of that Don Julio. We 'bout
to christen this bitch tonight," Kirk informed the
other waitress, who was approaching wit' a bottle
of Dom. She nodded her head in agreement and
turned on her heel.

"Yo, Kirk, this is nice. Thanks for setting it out for
us." Trina smiled. "And I'm so fuckin' glad to be
back." She stood up as the DJ dropped "Superfreak"
by Young Jeezy. "Once again, that's my shit. Come
on, y'all." Trina grabbed my arm first, since I was
closest to her. My plate barely made the table. We all
hit the dance floor, and we were twerking so hard,
Kirk stood up and started tossing money at us.

"You can't find his kind of action in no strip club in Florida," he yelled over the music. We all giggled at him. We were having a good time, I observed as some of Kirk's crew bounced into VIP. They stood back and watched the action. We danced to another song then made our way back over to the cake.

We were tossing back shots of Crown Royal when Duke, one of the guys from Kirk's crew, approached Trina. They started chatting while we stood back and caught up.

"Damn, I miss this so much. We don't do it enough." Secret referred to the club and fun.

"I know. You two stay acting like some old-ass ladies. But I be coming wit' my friends, though. 'Cause I can't be getting old before my time." Courtney threw in her two cents.

"Don't we know it." I laughed. "But real talk, I miss it, too. I just be tired. I'm get my stuff together, though, wait and see." I hoped to make a believer out of myself. Courtney and Secret both were right, we needed to enjoy ourselves. I spent too much time taking things too seriously and worrying about things that I could not change. I looked over at Trina, who was grinning while she talked to Duke. It was something about the girlish look and excitement that she had on her face that I missed. At least at that exact moment I felt like I did. Was I keeping myself from that feeling?

"Yo, I hope so. 'Cause if not, I'm dragging yo' ass up out the crib from now on. Real talk."

"And I'll help," Courtney threw in.

Trina approached us smiling, so we knew something was brewing. "Why you smilin'? What that nigga say to you?" Secret didn't waste any time getting to the point.

"Shit, really, but he got my attention for a minute."

"Ain't nothin' wrong wit' dat. He is a cutie." Courtney looked over Secret's shoulder to get a glance at Duke. He was about five nine, a bit shorter than I like them, but he was cute. He wore a regular flat-top, he was brown skinned and tatted all over his body, which was clear from his neck and arms.

"Yep, he not bad on the eyes," I agreed.

"Duke straight," Secret said. "But what you thinkin'? I know how you is."

Secret looked over at Duke like she was trying to size him up. She smiled. "I'ma see what's up with him. I got his number and, shit, you know me, I'm worse than a nigga. I gotta see how dat booty work first. 'Cause if that's whack, it's hard for me to fake it. After that we'll see . . . Shit, I could use a boo, job just getting started and pockets dry. And we all know that ain't enough cash for me anyway."

"Aye, I feel you. Cash coins, not that bullshit." Secret laughed, and we all joined in.

As much as I hated to admit it, she was right. Men could put you through so much. So it was sad that you had to keep money as the focus to even be entertained enough to stay in the conversation with them.

I excused myself to the bathroom, because all the excitement and drinks had my bladder on full. The crowd was thick on my way to the bathroom. That's what I loved about VIP: we had plenty of space to move around without bumping into people. That last thing I ever wanted was to be touching elbows with sweaty people who did way too much while on the dance floor. Just thinking about the crowd I had to fight just to get back to VIP made me wash my hands just a little longer to avoid it.

Back out in the crowd, I watched the two-thousand-dollar Gucci shoes that I had purchased like a hawk. I did not want them to be penetrated by another person's gym shoe or cheap high heel just because they were either too drunk to care or simply showing off and not paying attention. Just as my feet were about to be crushed, I looked up and almost walked smack into Bobbi.

"Hey," he yelled over the loud Gucci Mane song that was blasting out the speakers.

"Hi," I spoke back. His cousin Melvin was standing next to him looking surprised to see me.

"Hey, Isis," he said. I could see the guilty look on his face. I'm sure he knew that Bobbi had told me that he was the one giving up all my locations. But I didn't care about that anymore; I had moved on.

"Hey," I spoke back with a slight smile. I was still slick worried somebody might bump into me or step on the back of my shoe. And I was right: just as I was about to be trampled by a heavyweight chick in a skirt so tight she could barely move her legs, Bobbi snatched me out of the way.

"Thanks." I breathed a sigh of relief.

"I swear, she was about to knock the wind out of you. This crowd is beast." He laughed.

"Seriously." I grinned.

"You look nice," he commented. It felt awkward hearing him say that. Melvin had stepped over to the bar to order a drink.

"Thanks," I said. I felt a bit nervous as I kind of glanced around at the thick crowd. Knowing I had to eventually conquer it to get back to VIP annoyed me.

"So what's been up with you? I haven't seen you around town."

"Well, this is Florida. You don't just run into people unless you are looking for them," I said, glaring at him briefly. I knew that came out sarcastic, but it was not my intention. But I didn't feel I owed it to him to clear that up, so I didn't.

"True." He shook his head in agreement. "How are things at work?"

"Good," I replied. I wasn't really sure why he was asking me about work—he never had before when I worked at JCPenney—but I went along.

He was silent for a moment. "I know this is awkward, and I don't want it to be. I hope we can find some kind of common ground so that we can at least communicate."

I was glad he had said that, because I agreed. I had forgiven him; things had been laid out on the table. It was time to move forward, and talking never hurt anybody. After that was cleared up, we talked for a minute. Melvin came back over and we even talked, then Xscape's old song "Am I Dreaming" came on and Bobbi asked me to dance. I was surprised. I had to decline. There was just no way I could see myself standing that close him. People were on the dance floor, so walking space cleared up. I said bye to him and Melvin and headed for VIP without looking back.

I breathed a sigh of relief when I stepped back into VIP. The entire atmosphere was different. I made my way back over to Secret, who was standing alone. A glance to the other side of the room revealed Trina talking to Duke. Courtney, on the other hand, was nowhere in sight. I made it over to

Secret just as she tossed back a shot of something brown. She swallowed and glared at me.

"What the hell took you so long? I almost came looking for you."

I didn't realize how long I had been gone, but I knew it had been a minute, because I had heard at least eight songs since I left, possibly more. What I didn't think about was the fact that Secret would question where I had been. Even if she was having a good time, she would notice I was not there. I'd rather eat the words I was about to release to her, but I had no choice.

"I ran into Bobbi on the way back from the bathroom."

"So, and what?" Her attitude kicked right in.

I rolled my eyes, because she knew what I was about to say. "We talked for a minute, all right."

"That was no damn minute. You been gone a while," she pointed out.

"Well, maybe, but you wanted to know, so there." I signaled the waitress. "Get me a shot Don Julio." I needed something strong to drown Secret out in case she went berserk.

I could feel Secret's eyes on me. I didn't know what she would say next, but I was ready for her to just spit it out.

"What?" I looked at her. The waitress passed me my drink. I downed it right away as if it could ease the blow of the words she was sure to deliver. But to my surprise, her face softened.

"Listen, I ain't gone give you no speech. You're grown, and you already aware of how I feel. So I'ma just say be careful, and don't let him get his hooks in you. Because I know you might still be attracted to him."

That was a far cry from what I expected to hear from her, and I had to admit, I was shocked, because in the past she would have searched the club high and low until she found Bobbi and cursed him out. But she was right, being around him almost turned on something in me, but I pushed it back.

"I know, I thought about all that, and I wouldn't have talked to him, but he was looking good and smelling good." I smiled.

"Aye, aye, aye," Trina and Courtney both approached both singing along with Yo Gotti's song "Law" that the DJ was jamming. Secret and I jumped, singing as the waitress approached us with drinks. We all stood back and got to having so much fun that VIP was feeling up as a few of Kirk's other crew members stepped inside. It was all the way live. I was tipsy and feeling hella good.

"Which one of y'all is Courtney?" We all looked up at the same time and noticed this light-skinned, thick, like Remy Ma, chick questioning us. All of us looked at each other; it was clear none of us knew who she was. And apparently she didn't know who Courtney was, or she wouldn't be asking. Where we came from, when someone approached us like that, that's the treatment they got. Straight stranger to be watched.

Secret said, "Who wants to know?" The unknown chick had the nerve to roll her neck, but before she could respond, Courtney spoke up.

"That's me. What's up?"

The chick looked her up and down, then smirked. "So you the nasty bitch . . . that's been fuckin' my husband."

"Excuse me, what?" Secret started to step to the

unknown chick, but Courtney stepped in front of Secret.

"See, I think you got it all wrong. I don't sleep wit' married men. And as for your husband, I didn't know—" Courtney was trying to explain, but the chick swung on her, punching her right between the eyes. Then out of nowhere, another chick, the same as the unknown, appeared and jumped in. Secret jumped in and pulled her off Courtney and started punching her.

Kirk rushed over and started grabbing at Secret, trying to get her off the chick, but it was not working, so Duke and Trina chimed in. Then I started to pull Courtney off the other chick. She had managed to wrestle her to the floor and was on top of her, beating her blow by blow.

Just as I successfully pulled Courtney off the unknown chick, she swung and smacked me in the face. Pissed, I grabbed her by the neck, pushed her to the wall, and one-two punched her so hard I heard the dudes behind us sing, "Whew." Then Kirk pulled me back, because I had my fist up to go in for more.

"You ungrateful fat bitch!" I yelled. Here I was being a good Samaritan and pulling Courtney off her ass, and she gone hit me. Clearly she had me messed up.

"Fuck you, hoe!" she screamed back.

Security made it inside just as Kirk pulled me back. Duke was still holding Secret and guys from the crew had got hold of both the unknown chicks, who were not bloody.

"Get them two hood rats the fuck up outta here," Kirk ordered the security guards.

And just like that, the commotion was over. I

could not believe what had just gone down. Here we were, trying to have a good time, and these chicks come in here and ruin everything. Trying to fix ourselves back up, we looked at each other to be sure we were cool.

"Everybody cool." Kirk stepped in to check on us. "That was crazy."

"We good," Secret said. "These bitches got to learn a lesson in respect. It's levels, too, this shit."

"No doubt," I cosigned. I did not like fighting at all, but I would not sit back and be hit. Ever. I could go from zero to one hundred real quick.

"Yo, Isis. You one-two'd that big bitch real quick. It's gone be a minute before she forget that." Kirk laughed.

"She better remember. How she gone run up on me when I'm only trying to help?" I said.

"But who was them hoes?" Kirk asked.

"A dude I used to mess wit's wife . . . Yo, listen, I didn't know he was married. But when I found out, I cut him off. If she would have let me explain instead of tryin' to boss up, she coulda saved herself the ass whoopin'," Courtney mouthed.

"Next time she will." Trina laughed.

"I hope so. 'Cause I don't need nobody messin' up my hair and makeup. Now I'm mad," I complained.

"Don't worry, I'll buy you new hair and makeup." Kirk chuckled. "Now turn back up, the night still young."

"That's right. I'll never let a bitch ruin my good time." Secret was hype. "Aye, bartender, pour it up," she shouted. And just like that, we went back to our party, and the night was great. We didn't miss a drink or a beat.

# Chapter 29

# Secret

The altercation at the club with Courtney and her ex's wife turned out to be just a slight bump in the road. It didn't spoil our night one bit. We were still so turned up, we decided to hit the strip club for a while. Our mode was definitely *turn down for what*! I was in such a good mood, I decided it was time to call Calvin; maybe I could let him off punishment. It had been a minute, and he still was blowing me up trying to get my attention. And tonight I was ready, because I was sexually frustrated.

I rang his doorbell three times before he finally opened up. "Secret, what are you doing out here at three in the morning?" he asked me. I laughed at him because he looked so serious.

"What are you, my dad now?" I pushed past him. "Wait?" I turned to him. "Did you really want an answer to that?"

"I see somebody has been drinking," he pointed out.

This time I just looked at him. He was starting to annoy me quickly. "Listen, if you gone talk to me in the third person, I'm leaving." I started toward the door.

"No, Secret, wait." He blocked my exit. "Listen, babe, I just missed you, that's all." I knew he wouldn't let me leave. Plus, he was looking good, standing in front of me, so I let it slide.

"Well, if you missed me so much, then maybe you wouldn't play games." I turned on my heel and made my way into his den. He had a huge Italian leather sectional in there that I absolutely adored. I bounced right down and kicked off my Manolos, then leaned back and slid out of my one-piece, cropped, fitted body dress and laid back.

"What games?" He played dumb all the while lusting over my now naked body. Normally I would go off, but I was not in the mood. So he would get a friendly pass.

"The next time you decide to ignore one of my calls, just remember. I don't respond well to bullshit."

"Babe, so you ignored me for weeks because you assumed I ignored one of your calls? That's not fair," he all but whined.

"And what in life is fair?" I raised my right eyebrow at him. This told him that I was done with that conversation.

"Damn, woman, you have a heart that's cold like ice." He picked up both my feet and sucked the big toe on each. I moaned from pleasure. Calvin knew how to make me feel good. That's the only reason he had a second chance to be in my good graces. "Even still, I crave you." He smiled.

"I know you do . . . Now climb up here," I ordered, and I did not have to tell him twice.

Calvin lay on top of me, and we came face-to-face. He opened his mouth, and I slid my tongue inside. I sucked his tongue so good he froze still from pleasure. Bringing his tongue from inside my mouth, he let it trail down my chest, then it found each one of my nipples. He sucked them so gently yet with so much passion, I screamed. My middle thumped so hard it all but called Calvin's name. He lowered his head, and his strong tongue found my love and buried itself deep inside. My thighs wouldn't stop shaking and my walls begged him to fill me; he pulled down his silk pajama pants. I smiled as I watched his member standing at attention. I pulled him back down toward me, and he slowly guided himself inside. I moaned from deep within and rode him from below begging, encouraging him to go deeper and deeper until I exploded.

"After the long night we just had hanging out, why you up in here this early showing eighty-eight?" Isis referred to the smile on my face. And she was right, it was early, but I felt good after a night on the town with my friends. And four orgasms later, I was on cloud nine.

"Don't be a hater, okay? It ain't cute on you," I joked.

"I ain't no hater. But you actin' strange up in here. So what's up? Spit it out, 'cause you ain't never this happy in the a.m." One thing I knew for sure, there was no fooling Isis; she knew me like a book, and if need be could recite me by the page. There was no getting over on her.

"Girl, after I left y'all last night, I went over to Calvin's. And I already told you, homeboy got skills. And let me just say he relieved all my frustrations. I'm a happy bitch because of him."

"Wait, after the way you dogged that poor man, snatched out his bleeding heart, and stuck it in your toilet, shit on it, he let your ass back in his life, his house? He must be desperate or in love. Either way it's sad." Isis chuckled.

"Shut up." I laughed at her dramatic breakdown of Calvin and the wrong I allegedly had done him. "Ain't nobody dogged him or snatched out his pathetic heart. Hid ass know he ain't never got the upper hand. And if he remember that, he might stay around a little longer."

"I swear on all that's holy, you got game." Isis laughed. "You keep this up and you gone be pimp of the year."

"Whatever, I ain't interested in none of that. But you got to let these niggas know what's up. What you need to do is find a man so that you can relieve some that frustration that you got. Shit, Rico been gone, it's time to move on." After Rico had ghosted, Isis had all but shut down when it came to men. All work and no play was her new reality. I knew she was hurt about Rico leaving, but Bobbi had left, too, and she had eventually gotten over it. But things just weren't working out that way, now that Rico was gone. I had tried to set her up with all types of guys, but she refused, just saying she wasn't ready or didn't have the time. I hoped that she snapped out of that and soon, because at the end of the day she was a woman and she had needs. Needs that Custom Hot Rides, and all the money in the world, couldn't ease.

"See . . ." Isis started to respond but was cut off by a knock on the office door.

"Come in," we said in unison. Courtney opened the door and stepped inside.

"Hey, y'all, I hate to interrupt."

"Ahh, it's cool. What's up?" I said.

"I just wanted to say thanks again for having my back last night."

"No doubt," Isis and I said in unison, again.

"Besides, that bitch had it coming; she was all the way wrong. And I'll fuck up any bitch that ever tries to destroy my good time." I chuckled. "But real talk, you family; we always got you."

"And that's real," Isis agreed.

"But yo, for real. You still messin' wit' dat nigga?" I had to know. I know she hadn't told Kirk but we were women, it was hard to share our business with a man.

"Hell, yeah. I still got bills. But I'm 'bout to be done wit' his lyin' ass soon, though."

"I feel you." I laughed.

"I got to get back to the front, though. These niggas busy today droppin' off and pickin' up they whips. And they ain't playin'," Courtney said before shutting the door.

"Yo, that was crazy. That bitch had balls to come up in there like that."

"Yep, she did." Isis grinned. "I thought she was Duke's girlfriend or something first."

"I didn't know who she was, but I knew she was on some bullshit. Bitch wasn't about to sneak me." We both laughed. "That bitch did break code coming up

there while we having a good time. You don't fuck
wit' people's money. And how the hell she get up in
there anyway? I meant to ask Kirk."

"Hmmph, that's easy. Wit' that fat ass. You think
them horny security niggas gone stop her. I don't
think so," Isis said in a sarcastic tone.

"I guess you right. 'Cause they ass be thirsty."

The office phone rang, and Isis hit the speaker
button.

"Isis, Bobbi out here and wants to speak to you,"
Courtney said.

Isis looked directly at me. I held my tongue.
"Tell him to hold up," Isis instructed. Courtney
hung up.

"Here we go again wit' this thieving-ass hustler.
You just can't seem to get rid of him."

"Just chill." Isis glared at me with a grin. "I'll
take care of it and be right back." She stood up.

"If you say so." I sighed. Picking up my cell
phone, I dialed up Penny. "You up?" I asked. Penny
sounded like she was wide awake, which was a shock.
I expected her to sound groggy, like she was still in
bed.

"Yes, I'm up. Hung out with Patrick last night at
his house."

So that explained it. I didn't want to dwell on it,
so I didn't ask any questions. I got to the point of
me calling in the first place. "I called to remind
you that we are going out to dinner tonight. So
don't forget."

"Ahhh, that's tonight?"

"Yes, I see you forgot already."

"I know, and I'm sorry," she apologized, and
somehow I had a feeling she was not done. "Can I

please take a rain check, Secret? I got this date with Patrick tonight, and I can't cancel on him."

"Cool," I said reluctantly. I didn't much care for Patrick. I felt like he was too weak to date my sister, but I didn't want to upset her. "Call me later." I ended the call just as Isis stepped back into the room. Whatever Bobbi had wanted hadn't taken long, so I figured it was good news. "So what happened?"

"He asked me out to dinner." She released like it was no big deal. Her newfound calmness over Bobbi was a bit more than I cared for.

"I hope you let him down easy before you spit in his face." I was serious.

"Spit in his face. Now you know I would not do no disgusting crap like that." Isis chuckled. "I told him yes. I mean, why not? I don't see anything wrong wit' a free meal." I couldn't believe she was being serious. Maybe she was trying to get a rise out of me. But her facial expression led me to believe she was indeed serious.

"That's just it, it ain't free when it comes from a snake like him. I'm sure you know by now that his intentions are not always good. But okay . . ." I held up my right hand. "Just watch out for him. Who cares that he gave that money back? It don't change the fact that he is conniving. Maybe you have forgiven him, but I see right through him."

"I get it, Secret. Everything that you say about him, I agree wit' it. But I'm just going out to dinner wit' him, nothing more. And my position will be clear, and common sense should tell him that we will never be anything more than friends. Not even that too soon, but forgiving him does free a piece of me that I didn't want to keep hostage anymore."

"Just take your gun wit' you. Keep it close by, locked and loaded, at all times in case he tries to sneak you. And you already know to keep me on speed dial. Hell, matter of fact, just tell me where the dinner will be, and I'll wait outside in my car. That way if you need me, I'm not far."

"That's okay, I'm good. A Team," she joked, but I was serious.

I swear, I was beginning to think that Bobbi was to Isis like Jackie was Penny: baggage they could not seem to dump. No matter what these people did to them, they refused to just let them go. Why they couldn't see danger and just drop them by the wayside was a plain mystery to me. Nobody deserved to do so much harm to a person and be forgiven for it. In Jackie's case, she had done it to two people, damaged two people, yet she walked around with her heart in her hand, holding it out as if the ones she hurt should grab it. She convinced herself that we were selfish and ungrateful. Bobbi walked around with the feeling of entitlement. He felt that he was entitled to Isis's forgiveness because he had paid her back and said, "I'm sorry."

Neither Jackie nor Bobbi ever acknowledged the true pain they caused, because they were never truly sorry. See, sorry is a word that is used in everyday sentences, and hardly ever is it meant. For Jackie and Bobbi it was a word that could get them close to what they wanted: their prey.

# Chapter 30

# Isis

I know that Secret believed that I had forgiven Bobbi, and it was simple as that. But that simply was not true. Yes, I had forgiven him, but all was not forgotten. Going out to eat with him was a huge step. But something inside me urged me to take it, so I did, and I was not going to back out. Tonight was the night, and I was nervous; this would be the first time in a long time that we had actually sat down to a meal together and shared conversation. I didn't know what to expect, but I didn't expect too much.

The last thing I wanted to do was send him the wrong message. It taken me four hours to decide what to wear. I wanted everything to be right. I wanted to look my best, but I didn't want to wear something that said I'm available, looking, or hoping for something. But it would be hard. The old me that Bobbi knew had cheap knock-off clothes from the closest outlet mall to the neighborhood. Now everything I owned was designer, so my clothes fit me like they were custom made, but only because they were expensive. So anything I wore was bound to make me look good.

It was hard, but I figured out a way to tone it down. I threw on a pair of cut-up jeans, a cute designer blouse, and some red-bottoms. Even though I still had on over two thousand dollars' worth of stuff, with my bag included, it was the best I could do to tone it down; otherwise I would look like Beyoncé. I decided to drive my Mercedes. I guess it really didn't matter if I jumped in it, the Audi, or the Escalade; they all looked expensive. I put my music on, Xscape on Pandora; the last thing I wanted to do was listen to my Yo Gotti station. If I did, by the time I got to the restaurant, I might be shooting out his windows. Monica's "You Shoulda Known Betta" blasted out of the speakers as I drove over to the Benihana, the restaurant we had chosen.

After finding a parking space, I got out of the car and made my way inside. Secretly, I told myself that if he was not there, I would just leave. Unfortunately, he had already arrived. The hostess led me straight to the table. Bobbi stood up as I approached the table. He pulled out a chair for me. I was shocked. Never in the time had we been dating had he done that.

"So you pulling out chairs now?" I couldn't resist the sarcastic comment. But I was also being real. I wouldn't hold back anything that I wanted to say or do.

Bobbi gave a nervous chuckle. "You deserve that type of thing. But most of us men don't know shit when it comes to women."

"I might have to agree." I chuckled. Sitting down in the chair, I pulled it up to adjust to my liking.

"You look nice."

"I try," was my quick response. "I'm glad you like this place. I love it."

"Yeah, I ate here a few times. I forgot how soft your features were." He kept his eyes glued to me. "But you have always been beautiful." He was openly flirting with me.

"You can stop now." I looked up at him with a grin. The waitress came back, and we both ordered steak with shrimp.

"I know you don't want to hear what I have to say. But I have to be honest, I have missed you so much, Isis. It has been unbearable . . . You don't know how I wished I could have talked to you about was I was going through."

I wasn't sure how I was supposed to feel about him pouring out his heart. I had mixed feelings, but I had to be honest. "You know, Bobbi . . . you could have come to me, but you chose not to. I guess you didn't love me the way that you claimed." I looked him in his eyes. I couldn't take his cries; he was not the only one in pain. He had caused my pain. I couldn't help him through his.

"I did love you very much. I still do love you." I looked away, not wanting to see his eyes for fear of what I might find in them. "I wish I could have you back." He tried to touch my hand as those words left his mouth, but I quickly snatched my hand back. But my eyes met his at that same moment.

And I saw in them exactly what I wanted to avoid. Hope.

I cleared my throat. Clarification, at this point, was a must. There could be no misunderstanding of intentions. "The only reason I came to this dinner with you tonight is because I want to move forward . . . No, I need to move forward, not have anger anymore . . . Because when I accepted your apology I really meant it." A slight smile edged the corner of Bobbi's lips. "But that's it. Things can never be the way they used to be between us. We can never be together." That smile faded, but I could still see a hint of hope in his eyes. I was ready to handle his reluctance, but he surprised me.

He licked his lips and looked away for a brief second. "I got to say, those are not the words I wanted to hear . . . But I respect your wishes. I just really hoped they were different." I didn't have a response to that. I had said what I felt, and that was it. The back-and-forth of explanations or reasons were unnecessary and a waste of both of our time. The chef approached our table and began to set up.

Bobbi looked at me and smiled as the chef started up with his first set of tricks with the spatula and the breaking of the egg. "I swear I can do that," he bragged, as always.

"Boy, bye." I waved him away and laughed. "I swear, you always saying you can cook."

"You know I'm a chef, all those shrimp I steamed for you."

"You mean all those shrimp you boiled for me. Putting all that water in there." I continued to laugh. Bobbi always claimed he could cook but never did no more than fry chicken.

"It's cool. I know I got skills." He chuckled. It felt good to be laughing and be done with the serious talk. I started to relax, hoping to enjoy my meal. "So what have you been up to?" he asked.

"Nothing, just working. What about you? Where you been hiding at?" I hated that statement as soon as it came out. I didn't want to seem like I was trying to be funny.

"Well." He smiled and took in a deep breath. "I've been busy back in New Jersey where I've been. I opened a clothing store, and it's actually doing quite well." I was surprised to hear that.

"Wow. You mean you ain't fixing up old, dirty cars," I joked.

"Nope, I kinda let that go once I left here. I wanted to try something different. I met a few people, and the opportunity introduced itself."

"Real talk, I'm happy for you. Ain't nothing wrong wit' changing your dreams."

"Thank you. That means a lot to me coming from you." He looked at me and smiled. "Like I said, though, the store back in New Jersey is doing really good, so I'm in the process of trying to open one up here in Florida."

"Really? That's dope." I was really proud of him. Bobbi had always had business sense when it came to the cars. I never pictured him doing anything else, and this was really a good look for him.

"Enough about me, though. What's up with you at Custom Hot Rides? How long you been working up there?"

"For a while. We kind of new."

"Yeah, I don't remember that being around. But they got some hot whips up there, I can't front."

I smiled. "Yeah, they do." I used my chopsticks to pick up a piece of the steak the chef had just placed in front of me.

"So what you do up in there?" I figured that question would be next.

"Customer service." I wanted to be brief. Custom Hot Rides was not a job to be discussed. I wanted to tell him that and be done. But how would that look? I remained cool.

"Come on, you don't have to be modest. I know you important up in there." He used his fork and murdered two of his shrimp. I decided to fill my mouth with fried rice so there was less talking. But I knew he wasn't done. "No customer service person has their own office. You can be honest and admit you are the owner." He chuckled, but I was no longer in a laughing mood. I wished he would drop it.

I forced a smile and continued. "Nah, Secret and I are more like heads of Customer Service. We in charge of like all the paperwork." I hoped that put the issue to bed so he could shut up and move on, or I would have to open up a can of rude on him.

"Oh, so you good wit' paperwork. If that's the case, I could use someone like you over at the store. Maybe you can come through and help with the opening. I have good business sense, but when it comes to the paperwork, I struggle from complete boredom."

"But the paperwork is the most important part. In order for you to be successful, you gone have to get that together," I schooled him.

"See, that's why I'm trying to recruit you. With you on my team I'm sure to be one hundred." He tried to convince me, but there was no use. Secret would have my head and his. And Kirk would aid her in the crimes. There was no way Kirk was gone sit back and watch me go work for anyone else. He was like a spoiled kid when it came to my services.

"Nah, I can't do it. I'm booked far beyond what I can even imagine. But don't worry, you will be fine. If you running a successful one in New Jersey, I'm sure you don't need me. Besides, there are plenty qualified people right here in Florida who can't wait to work. Maybe you could take out an ad in the newspaper or something. Or you could call up one of these temp agencies." I was full of ideas that I was sure he could use, anything but me working for him. That was off the table.

He shook his head in disagreement. "I don't know about that. You can't trust people. And we both know Florida grimy as fuck." I glanced at him and almost cosigned, but I instantly thought about what he had done to me. Was that the grimy he was speaking of? I quickly brushed the thought out of my head.

"Listen, you have to trust somebody. Who helped you in New Jersey?"

"I do it myself. At least all the business and paperwork. I have two females who work for me, doing checkout and all that. But I do my own inventory and everything."

"I'm sure that's a lot."

"It is, but it works out."

"Yeah, you might need to come up wit' something different once you open a second store. 'Cause you will be busy times two." I kept it real.

"I know. I been thinking about it. I'm gone have Melvin help me out a lot here. I trust him, you know. And eventually I'll get some depend-

able people. I just believe in taking my time. You
know."

I nodded my head in agreement. "Like I said,
you will be fine. I can't come work for you, but you
can pick my brain for questions you might have. I
have a few successful pointers for you." I smiled.

"I'm sure you do. I appreciate that."

The rest our night turned out to be straight. We
enjoyed our food and had a few laughs. I had forgotten how much fun Bobbi could be. I really
missed the friendship we shared outside of the relationship we had had. But I didn't let that deter
me from my decision; neither of us did. We knew
better. That was clear now.

# Chapter 31

## Isis

Today was relaxation day, and I was all in. Secret had booked us a spa day, on her, and I was not in the mood to turn it down. Kirk was at Custom Hot Rides for the day holding the fort down so we could both be off. I was glad he had stepped up, because we both had made it clear we were taking the day, whether he approved or not. As usual, he called us bullies and fell in gear. The day was beautiful. I threw on a romper, some sandals, and sunglasses and raced out to the garage and jumped in the Audi.

I had a craving for my favorite Starbucks, but I had plans on drinking as much wine as the spa laid out for me. So I took a detour that wouldn't include Starbucks being in sight. A call from the prison came through on the phone. My heart instantly raced. I accepted the charges.

"Hey," Felicia's voice came though the phone. I

wasn't used to her calling me during the week. Matter of fact, she really didn't call much. That's why concern took over.

"Everything cool?" were the first words out of my mouth.

"Oh, I'm fine. I just decided to call. I hope I didn't worry you." The concern in my voice was apparent.

"Well, you don't call much. So I was alarmed."

"Maybe I should call more often, then." She chuckled. And I thought I heard something in it, almost as if it was forced. Something was up, but she was hiding it.

"Aye, don't get no ideas," I joked. "What's up in there?"

"Same ol', you know, it don't change much behind these walls. Just the shutting of doors and impatient bitches being impatient." She laughed. "Just been missing you, that's all."

"I know, been busy. But I'ma get down there soon . . . How are your classes going?"

"They good. I'm doing really well. Almost too well. Sometimes I forget how smart I really am."

"Hey, I had to get it from somewhere," I added.

"Sounds like you in a car. Where you headed?" I hated to share the fun things I was doing on the outside. I almost felt guilty. But I knew she wouldn't want me to lie to her, so I shared.

"On my way to meet Secret at the spa for a girls' day out. We both exhausted from all the work."

"That's not good, Isis. I mean working is good; being young and focused is especially good. But you need to enjoy life. It passes you by, and I mean fast."

"I'm trying to do better. And I promise I'm gone get down to see you soon."

"Don't worry so much about me. I'm fine, trust. I get plenty of rest and three meals a day." She chuckled. I didn't think that was funny at all, and I knew she didn't, either. That was her way of making light of the situation. The phone operator came on and made it clear the call was about to be wrapped. "A'ight. I'm gone let you go before this phone hangs up. Keep your head up, and have some fun sometime."

"I'll try," I managed before the phone went dead. It broke my heart to hear that. But it was our reality, no need to dwell on it. I pulled up to the spa, parked, and hopped out. The sun would heal me from the sadness that came over me.

"You gone beat me one of these times." Secret was at the counter checking in.

"Whatever. You so petty."

"Come on here. From the look of that face, you need some extra care today," Secret joked.

"Shut up." We fell in line behind the hostess as she took us back to get started. The first thing I reached for, as we made it back, was a glass of wine.

"Dang, Isis. You gone slow down on that." I downed the glass and reached for the second.

"Girl, I need this. I'm sad and thirsty." I sipped this time around.

"What's up?" Secret asked.

We sat down to have our feet done first.

"I just got a call from Felicia."

"Is everything okay?"

"Yes and no. I mean she fine, but, Secret, that time is coming down on her. I can hear it in her voice."

"Did y'all discuss it at all?"

"Nah, you know she ain't gone talk about it. But I can hear it so loud and clear. The shit breaks my heart." Tears threatened to fall, but I blinked them back. "She needs up outta there. Real talk." A knot was now in my throat.

"Man, I feel you. How much longer they gone make her serve? They really trying to make her do the full ten?"

"I don't know. I hope not. I was hoping she'd get out soon at least on good behavior. She don't never get into no trouble."

"Maybe you should try to get her a lawyer."

"That's what I tried to do last year. Every lawyer I spoke with said it would be a waste of money. The judge probably wouldn't reduce enough time before her actual time was served."

"Damn, that's fucked up. We just gotta pray they let her out soon."

"Trust me, I am . . . Anyway, thanks for the free spa day." I smiled.

"No doubt. But you gone tell me about this date you had with that bomb Bobbi or am I gone have to drag it outta you?"

"See, I shoulda known this free spa had strings attached."

"And you know this." Secret laughed. "Now spill the tea."

"It went all right, actually. Nothing bad like I'm sure you would like to hear."

"When it comes from a snake, it's always bad." Secret smirked.

"Would you stop calling that man names already."

"See, I knew he would brainwash you."

"He did not. The conversation was pleasant. And just like I told you I would, I made it clear to him that nothing was going to ever happen between us again. I forgave him, we can be cordial, that's it."

"Hmmph, you just better hope he heard you."

"And he did. I mean, he was honest and said that he had hoped for us to be back together. But he respected my wishes, and that was that."

"I guess time will tell."

"He actually left me impressed," I had to admit, and I knew she would trip.

"I can't imagine nothing he did would impress me. But I guess anything possible from a gutter rat." Secret would not let up. I laughed. The girl was hilarious.

"Well, he has his own clothing store in New Jersey and claims it's doing really good."

"Hmmph." Secret rolled her eyes. "So I guess he intended to impress you wit' his new business and you would fall in his arms."

"No." I chuckled. "He actually is opening up a location here in Florida. He did, however, ask me to help him with the paperwork."

"I hope you crushed his dreams, then. 'Cause you know Kirk ain't having that."

"I already told him no."

"Aye, but find out where his store is, though. So I can have somebody burn that bitch to the ground on Grand Opening night."

"I swear you evil." I sipped my wine.

"Fa' sho'." Secret gave me a snide grin.

"Check this out, though. I took Penny out and we talked about her therapy and all that."

"Yeah, she told me." Secret gave me a warning look. She knew what I was about to say.

"Well, she talking about the same thing you said about the therapist. I really think you should consider going. For her sake."

Secret looked at me and shook her head no, but I was not about to give up easily this time. Our feet were done. Another hostess approached and led us back for our massages next. I was glad to be on the table. I was full of tension.

"Listen, that look ain't getting nowhere wit' me today. You got to stop being so stubborn and really hear what's being asked of you."

"And maybe y'all need to understand what you're asking of me. I love Penny, and nobody knows that better than you, Isis. You been around us our whole life. It ain't nothin' I wouldn't do for her. Including die. But you know that already. So what you want from me?"

"It's not what I want, Secret. It's strictly what Penny needs from you. She is adamant about you speaking to that therapist . . . I don't know, maybe it's something we missed."

"I couldn't have missed much. I've been through her life with her. Nah, I'm sure I ain't missed shit. Her struggle been mine. I do all I can. Enough has to come sooner than later."

"Well, it ain't now. You got to see that. 'Cause all I know is Penny is crying out for something. And she needs us to be there for her. The drinking stopped. That was probably the easy part."

"I'm sure, 'cause that shit was Jackie's fucked-up ass."

"Maybe, but this can't be about Jackie, or least we can't assume. I'm sure it had a lot to do with the situation. But we know there might be other underlying things."

"Jackie is the underlying thing, and until you and Penny both realize that, the shit won't get no better. Jackie ruined Penny and me a long time ago, and she ain't done. But no one wants to see that. Penny can't stop fucking crying over her. And if she taking me to see that therapist to forgive Jackie or have some type of intervention, she can just fuckin' forget it. I don't want that woman nowhere close to me. Ever again, if I can help it." It hurt me so bad to see my friend in so much pain. I cried inside for her. I had to get through to her, though, if only for Penny's sake.

"That's another point you are missing. Penny didn't ask for you to see the therapist. The therapist requested that you come. There is a huge difference."

"Hmmph, well, it's still all bullshit."

"No, you mean and need to get out yo' feelings. Now what you need to do is get up off your ass, stop whining and bitching, and go sit on the woman's damn couch. Hell, you the one paying her ass."

"Damn, Isis, what could she possibly want with me? I have nothing to say. I ain't request her."

"If I knew what she wanted, this would be easy. I would tell you and be done. 'Cause you will straight run a bitch's blood pressure sky high." Secret held her head up, looked at me, and burst out laughing. I had to laugh, too. "I can't deal wit' yo' hard-headed self."

"Shit, I must be on your nerves. I got you heated up about this bitch. I'm sorry."

"Whatever. After this, I need you to take me out for a free meal, and I ain't talkin' tacos. When I get off this table, I'm making last-minute reservations and going home to get jazzy. You gone spend big tonight. Oh, and you leaving the tip."

"You call me mean, but you bossy as hell. Hopefully that restaurant got some men. 'Cause ass need to be smashed and quick, before you start picking up cars and smashing them to the ground." We laughed again. But I could hope that I had gotten through. Secret was like a brick wall. So only time would really tell.

# Chapter 32

## Secret

I would be the first to admit I was stubborn as hell to anybody who had ever said that, which was mostly Isis, who was kicking it to me straight up. But I truly believed that my stubbornness was fed by something else and that something else was a deep pain that even I could not describe. Not that I exactly had. And that was just another part of me trying to remain in control of myself. Isis, though, had put it all in perspective. The thought of me, facing me, was a lot to consider. I wondered and resented, even, the idea that that was the therapist's intention. I just wrapped my head around why she needed to speak with me. I think I could even have understood it better if she had wanted to speak with Jackie; after all, she was the one who had fucked us up. Either way, I had to dust myself off and go. A month had passed, but Isis had hit home with a lot of her tough love and getting straight to the point.

I slowly pulled into the parking lot that served the office Penny's therapist ran her business out of. It was midafternoon, and the lot was almost empty except for about six other vehicles. I didn't see Penny's car anywhere, so I assumed she was running behind. I had never been to see a therapist before, so I wasn't sure what to wear. I didn't want to dress up and look like I was coming to scope. And I didn't want to look too much like a carefree bomb. So I had decided to keep it neutral. I threw on a pair of jeans and a nice top with a pair of low pumps. To waste time, I pulled down my visor and gave my face one glance over, then fished out my Mac lip gloss and added an extra coat. I guess it was safe to say I was nervous.

Closing the visor, I looked up to see Penny pulling in beside me. Sticking a piece of spearmint gum into my mouth, I grabbed my Gucci bag, slid on my Gucci sunglasses, and exited the car. I wasn't sure how to judge Penny's facial expression when I got out of the car. She wasn't smiling but she didn't look mad.

"Hey," she spoke before I could say anything.

"What's good? You okay?" I asked.

"I'm fine. I just want you to know that I really appreciate you taking the step to come here today."

"No, it's fine." I wanted to reassure her. The last thing I wanted to do was make her think I was mad for coming.

"No, for real. Let me say this." She held up her hand to stop me. "I know this was hard for you to commit to. And not for nothin', I want you to know that I appreciate it."

"It's all good. Trust me, I wouldn't be here if it wasn't. Now let's go in here and get this over wit'."

Once inside, my nerves calmed a bit, as the office felt like home. The walls were decorated with fine African American art. I almost forgot where I was until Penny stepped up to the receptionist to check in. I took a seat on one of the plush chairs that were available. But no sooner had I sat down, a professional, petite black lady with her hair up in a bun stepped out and said Penny's name. She gave Penny a gentle smile and me a nod. Penny looked at me and gestured for me to follow.

Inside her office, I got the same feeling, as it was decorated just as nicely as the common area. African American paintings and art were placed throughout. She stopped at the door and allowed us to enter her office.

"You two can have a seat wherever you would like." I could tell right away she was soft-spoken. I took a seat on the love seat and Penny sat right next to me. "And who do I have the pleasure of meeting?" She smiled at me.

"Hi, I'm Secret, Penny's older sister."

"I guess I would be blind if I couldn't see that." She grinned. "Hi, I'm Dr. Cesaley Wright." She extended her hand to me. I wanted to say, 'I'm well aware of who you are; I'm the one who pays that expensive-ass bill you send every month.' But even though Jackie didn't raise me right, I knew how to act in public, so I chilled.

"Nice meeting you." I reached out and shook her hand. She walked over to her desk, grabbed a notepad, and sat down on a couch that was across from us. The room was silent a minute too long for me. I didn't come there to hang, so I cut to the chase. "So Penny has been telling me that you wanted to see me?"

"Yes and no." She slid a pair of glasses on. Now I was confused, because I was deaf or crazy. My eyes went to Penny, who glared at the doctor.

"Could you be more specific about that?" I swallowed hard. I had to check my mood and quickly. Penny seemed nervous. "What's up, Penny?" My eyeballs burned a hole in the side of her face. "Penny, speak up!"

"Secret, what I meant by yes and no was . . ."

"Yeah, hurry up and spit that shit out. I don't have all day." I was losing my control.

"Secret, don't do that." Penny turned to me. I was embarrassing her.

"Like I was saying . . ." Cesaley jumped back in. "I requested that you to come in here because Penny has some things that she needs to say to you. And as her therapist, my goal is to help her make comfortable transitions. In other words, her feelings, thoughts, emotions, anything that's inside, need to come out so that she can heal properly. Otherwise, nothing I do or say will be effective. She will crawl back into the hole, however small it might be, once these sessions are over, and regardless of the time spent here with me. But deeper into the abyss of her depression. The choice is yours."

Why Cesaley thought it necessary to be so dramatic was a mystery to me. But I had heard her, and now I needed to hear from Penny, because anything she had to say to me, she could have said to me away from this office. I turned my attention back to Penny.

"Penny, you do know that you can talk to me about anything, right?" I needed to clear that up right away.

"Yeah, but this is different."

"How?" My tone was demanding as I scooted to the edge of the couch.

Again Penny went quiet. I looked at Cesaley, writing on her pad. She looked up at Penny. "You have to start somewhere. There is no right or wrong. You can do it."

Penny looked at me. Something in her eyes was different, something I couldn't quite put my finger on whether I had ever seen it. My heart sped up; I took in a deep breath without opening my mouth or even meaning to breathing in. "Secret, we have always shared a tight bond. No matter how bad or good things were, I had you there. I could count on that, and I did . . ." She paused. "I came to you and told you I needed to be independent, and I felt that. Needed, even. I could no longer be your burden."

It broke my heart into a million pieces to hear her say that she thought she was a burden to me. "Penny, don't say that. You could never be a burden to me. You are my baby sister, I love you."

"I know that. But you needed to live on your own to be a person. All your life has been spent protecting and loving me. I had to think of you . . . Me moving out killed two birds wit' one stone: me gaining independence and you freedom. Only it wasn't that easy. Those sleepless nights since the rape wouldn't let me rest. No matter how hard I prayed, no matter what. They kept comin' and comin' like a thief in the night to claim me as bait . . ." I couldn't believe what was coming out of her mouth. I had had no idea.

"So I thought moving Jackie in and having someone else in the house would help. I was wrong . . . so very wrong. It only got worse. But I noticed that when I drank, my mind found silence, and I found sleep. And the more I realized the alcohol was helping, I found hope in believing it was my cure. So, see, I was never hooked, I was relieved." Tears rushed down Penny's face.

I stood up. I had to think there was no way what she was saying was true. There is no way she had done that to herself. I wouldn't believe it. I paced. I could feel Dr. Wright's and Penny's eyes all over me. I didn't care. I had to rationalize why she would lie to me. It came to me. "No, you just saying this because you don't want me to blame Jackie. But I do know she did that to you. And she still have you protecting her with these horrible lies that you turned yourself into an alcoholic."

"Stop with that, Secret," Penny screamed, and she balled her hands in her lap. I stopped pacing. "Just please stop fuckin' saying that to me. Didn't you just hear anything I just said? I sat here and poured out my truths, and all you think of is Jackie. Always Jackie. As much as you hate her, it will not change the fact that she did not start me to drinking. She never gave me one drink; she never even knew I was drinking. And I'm tired of repeating this to you. Just shut the fuck up wit' that already."

Dr. Wright stood up and walked over to Penny and rubbed her back, clearly to calm her down. "Penny, take a few breaths and relax. It's okay for Secret to question, she needs to rationalize."

I looked at Penny, and for the first time, I heard her and knew that she was telling the truth. She still suffered from the rape. And I had never paid enough attention to even see what was clearly there. I was in such a hurry to heal her so that she could be normal again and get on with her life. I never truly gave her time to heal her wounds, so she covered them up and hid behind a mask to please not only the world but me. Not only was I stubborn, I was selfish as hell, and to mask my bullshit, I blamed her drinking on Jackie. This way I didn't have to face the truth. I had caused my sister's rape and then her mental breakdown that led her straight to the bottle. Suddenly, I had no more strength, and my legs gave way. I dropped to the floor.

Penny rushed over to me. "Secret, are you okay?" She cried over me.

"I am so sorry for what I have done to you, Penny. It's all my fault. Everything that happened. The rape, your drinking. All me," I sobbed.

"That's not true. So don't say it." She lifted me up.

"Yes, it is, and I apologize. I'm so sorry."

"That's not what I want, because I don't blame you. I blame the person who raped me. We have had so many challenges growing up. And I know Jackie is the underlying reason for your hurt, your pain. She's mine, too. But I have tried to work toward forgiving her so that I can move on. I know you may never forgive her, but I want you to learn to deal wit' it. Because you can't go through life like this. We can't go through life like this."

I nodded my head in agreement. My heart was in so much pain, there were just no words that I could deliver. I needed peace and I needed it soon. Life was holding me in its fist so tight. I was sure to suffocate if I didn't come up for air. But there was no hole where that air could seep in.

# Chapter 33

## Isis

Bobbi had been calling up a lot with questions about this or that while he was preparing to open his new clothing store. I know I had extended the offer, but I hadn't really believed he would take me up on it. Or would have to. He told me had a successful business in New Jersey already. But he claimed he was sure there were things he could have been doing to work smarter, not harder. However, I was starting to believe he was using the opening of the store as an excuse to call me. I didn't mind, though; I actually enjoyed hearing him get excited over some of my techniques.

All that was finally over, though; Bobbi's new clothing store was all done. He had had a grand opening a few days before, but I couldn't attend. We had a huge shipment of cocaine being delivered, and there was no way of getting out of that. But Bobbi had been bugging me nonstop to come by and check out the store. So since today was my day off, I decided to take him up on that. Typing the address into my GPS, I balled out.

"I thought you had changed your mind." Bobbi grinned as soon as he had me in sight. I had to admit the store was nice. Kinda put me in mind of Buckle in the mall. I had to admit it looked all together.

"I think you know I'm a woman of my word." I took in the whole store. A dark chocolate, tall, skinny girl stood by behind the counter.

"Hi," she said when I glanced in her direction.

"That's Lesley, my new employee." He turned to face her. "Lesley, this is my close friend Isis. Whenever she in here, always give her the VIP treatment, discounts, the whole nine."

"Not a problem." She smiled.

"Trust, I will be looking for the hookup. Nice meeting you, Lesley." I smiled, too. "She looks young," I pried.

"She is nineteen. College and all that, her schedule works wit' what I need. Part-time and all."

"Oh, okay. That's cool."

"Yeah, I hired two other full-timers, and Melvin gone take care of the rest. I'll be back and forth from here to Jersey." It sounded like he had it all figured out.

"You got it all together; I must say I'm impressed. I see you got that True Religion up in here." I used my eyes to continue to browse.

"No doubt. Let me show you around." He took the lead, and I followed. I was glad to see he even had some red-bottoms for the ladies. "You got some stuff. How was the grand opening?"

"Packed. Sales were through the roof. I didn't

know Florida was still showing ya' boy love like that."

"Hey, don't doubt us. One thing for sure, we got money to spend out here." I giggled. "And I'm sure every drug dealer that was close showed up."

"Listen, I am not the IRS, I don't ask any questions about the coin. All money is accepted."

"I feel you." I laughed. "I'm for you, though."

"That means a lot, coming from you." He reached out and gently touched my cheek. I played it cool, but I was stunned, not because I couldn't believe he had done it, but because I didn't know how I felt about it.

"Soo . . ." I stalled. "Ummm, I kinda got a few things planned since it's my day. You know I spend so much time working. I'm going to spend the rest of my day knocking things off my to-do list. So I'ma get outta here."

He stared at me for a moment. "You're not upset wit' me, are you?" He looked me directly in the eyes.

"I'm cool. I told you I would stop by, and I did."

"A'ight. I won't hold you up. Thanks for coming through."

With that I was out. And it's not like I had lied; I did have plans, to do whatever I felt like doing. And today I felt like checking out some whips. A Porsche, to be exact. I pulled onto the lot and was in Porsche heaven. I couldn't wait to at least sit in one.

"I'm Jeff, and you are?" This short, middle-aged white guy with red hair approached. He wasn't attractive, but he smelled hella good. And oddly, he had a slick pimp to his walk.

"Just looking." I smiled. "Just kidding; my name is Isis." I reached out to shake his extended hand.

"Which one would like to drive off in today? Or are we going custom?" Dude didn't waste any time.

"Jeff, how do you know I got it like that? Maybe I'm just a dreamer who spends endless hours window shopping."

He looked me over and smiled. "There is nothing about you that says dreamer. There is nothing on this lot that you can't have." I was feeling Jeff's style; he was a charmer, which could in some cases make up for his not-so-good looks. He had my vote.

"Really." I grinned. "Yep, you good at what you do. Now show me around."

Jeff must have showed me every Porsche on the lot from the 911 to the 718 Cayman, and I loved each and every one. Now I saw how Secret had ended up with the Ferrari. The car lot was a complete addiction. I was craving a Porsche, now that I was on the lot. That craving reached an all-time high by the time Jeff walked me onto the showroom floor. I nearly crashed and burned when I got a glance of the all-black Panamera model with Bordeaux red leather interior and twenty-inch turbo wheels. I was in complete love with it. I told Jeff to have the paperwork started. I made a quick dash to the bank and visited my safe deposit box.

See, Jeff was like Jack, who had sold Secret the Ferrari. It wasn't a coincidence that I went to that specific Porsche lot. Jeff had come highly recommended by Kirk, and when I had called Kirk up the day before and told him I would be out looking, he had given Jeff a call, so even though we had never met or seen each other, we played the game well. All we knew about each other before today were our names.

Back at the lot I handed Jeff a hundred twenty stacks and he gave me legit paperwork and the promise that my Audi that I had driven to the lot would be delivered later that day to my house. With a huge smile I thanked him, jumped in my beautiful Porsche, and set out to give the streets a piece of my new blessing.

I pulled up to a red light and leaned my head back onto the headrest. It was so comfortable, I could just about close my eyes and go to sleep. A quick glance to my right told me my Porsche was pulling status already. A fine redbone dude was admiring the car. He looked at me and winked before speeding off in his brand-new Camaro. I almost forgot where I was until cars behind me started to blow. To show them I was a boss, I burned rubber, leaving my skid marks as memories.

I found the closet route to the interstate and got on it. I needed to put the Porsche to the test. And trust, it lived up to my expectations. I laid it down and the gas pedal felt like butter. I was riding high and on one. But the flashing of red and blue lights through the rearview mirror put things in perspective. Slowing down, I pulled off the highway.

"Would there be any particular reason you in a hurry, young lady?" the old black cop with a gray-and-white beard asked. The glass part of his eyeglasses was dark like shades, so I couldn't see his eyes.

"Not really . . ." I decided to just keep it real. "Listen, I literally just drove this car off the showroom floor. I had to try it out. But I promise I don't normally drive like this." I hoped he believed me.

He observed the car. I could tell he was holding back a grin. "This is a fine automobile."

"Thank you." I wasn't sure if I should smile or not. The last thing I wanted was a ticket.

"In honor of your new car, I'm just gone warn you. Slow this thing down, young lady. And you have a good night." He grinned.

"I will." He nodded and turned and walked away. I breathed a sigh of relief. Readjusting my thoughts, I pulled back into oncoming traffic, but I still did a cool seventy; hell, I was driving a new Porsche. I was sure it was a rule not to the do the speed limit. I couldn't disappoint.

Driving along, I began to think about Bobbi's store, and it got me to thinking about Secret and how we dreamed of opening up a business. To see Bobbi do it so effortlessly had me motivated. My thoughts were really about a shoe store, since we both were shoe fanatics. Obviously, we would excel at it. Actually, I believed we could excel at anything we decided to do. Secret and I were both smart; our ideas would only multiply. Our only hold-back at this point was Kirk; we did a lot for him, and he really needed us. But I knew eventually in order for us to get our own start, we would have to step out and just do it. Maybe we could start without leaving Kirk all at once. I was sure there was something we could come up with that could make it happen. We just had to put our heads together.

One thing I was sure of: I was ready to do something. There was no time like the present. I was feeling good about everything. But I needed to make sure Secret was still all in. She had her hands full with work and family and decisions. I didn't want to jump into anything that could be overwhelming for her at this time, because whatever we did, like always, we would do together and be on the same page. And I believed a shoe store could be perfect. Veering off the interstate, I decided to give Secret a call. I had to share the idea with her while it was fresh. Our biggest challenge was finding the right spot. The right location was the key to being successful because, in my opinion, you could have all the nice things you wanted, but if you were located in the wrong spot, it was for sure that you might never make a dime. I wasn't about to make that mistake.

"Call Secret," I said into my phone receiver. I couldn't stop smiling, I was so excited to introduce my idea. But her cell phone rang until it went to voice mail. I tried a second time but got the same result. I hated when she didn't answer and I had something I needed to get out. Annoying.

# Chapter 34

# Secret

It had been just one day since the meeting with Dr. Cesaley Wright and Penny, and I was still in awe. I was still lost. I had been up all night; I couldn't close my eyes to go to sleep. I just sat on my couch in a fog. The only place I had forced myself to was the toilet and hot shower. My life at the moment was a bad dream. Who was I really? I would never understand how I had missed so much when I thought I knew it all. Was it the material things? Had I been so caught up in a Ferrari that I failed to see what was in front of me? Penny's pain. Had I chosen the good life over her?

If I cried hard, and I shut my eyes tight, a resolution was bound to pop out at me. Nothing came, though, just the bottomless pit of my gut that wanted to release any fluids that might be available. 'Cause I had nothing else left inside me. I was empty and feeling all alone. I couldn't think of anyone. Every time I imagined Penny's face, tears flowed down my cheeks. My chest rose and fell.

I was in the mood to say a word, but I wasn't even sure that if I opened my mouth anything would come out. The ringing of my cell phone only annoyed me. I considered making a move toward it, but my legs felt like bricks. I couldn't move them, so I stayed still. I was in a fog that I wasn't sure would ever end.

The pounding on my door pulled me away from the silence that my ears had adjusted to. Then the constant ringing of the doorbell started. Slowly, I stood up and walked to the door.

"I know you seen my call. Why you playing around?" Isis accused as she barged in past me. "You have ten fits when I don't answer your calls." I followed her but said nothing. "Who you got up in here?" She glanced around the den as if she expected to see someone in there.

"I'm here alone," I managed. I didn't realize how dry my mouth was until that moment. My tongue felt like it got stuck on the roof of my mouth.

"And what's wrong wit' you?" Isis looked at me for the first time. When I had answered the door, she had barged in past me so fast that she never made eye contact.

"Just in here trying to clear my head."

"What's up, Secret? You look funny and sound funny. Something ain't right. Spit it out."

"Yesterday I went and met wit' Penny and her therapist, Dr. Cesaley Wright."

"Oh, snap, how'd it go? Wait, what happened?"

"Nothing happened, but I found out a lot. And I've been stupid, Isis."

"How? What do you mean?" Isis shrugged her shoulders.

"Penny, she blames me for what happened to her. The rape, all that. She blames me." My stomach again twisted up in knots. I had to fight to keep from throwing up. I had done that most of the night. That was the reason I had nothing else left in me but fluids. And I was sure I didn't have much of that anymore.

"Nah, I don't believe that." I was in denial, but that didn't surprise me. "Did she say that to you?"

"No, she says she blames the rapist, and I believe that. But she blames me, too. I just know she does . . . I could hear it in her tone. The things she said." I bit my bottom lip trying to hold back tears, to hide the choking noise in my voice.

"Well, what did that therapist say? She wanted to see you and all that."

"Yeah." I gave a sarcastic laugh. "That turned out to be sketchy." Isis's forehead twisted up with confusion. "Dr. Wright just wanted me to come in so she could be with Penny while she transitions. Meaning get shit off her chest. Kinda give her the courage."

"Penny don't need help wit' that. She knows she can talk to you."

"Apparently it's not that easy. She's been going through a lot, Isis. Shit I had no idea about. Shit you didn't even know."

"Tell me then."

"Penny has been drinking because she couldn't sleep because of nightmares about the rape. She far from being over that. Oh, and get this, she moved out so that she can give me my freedom."

"Freedom for what?" Isis again shrugged her shoulders.

"She feels guilty that I have taken care of her her whole life. She thinks I'm burdened by her. The drinking, of course, cleared her mind from that. And again she swears Jackie didn't have anything to do with her drinking. And you want to know the scary part . . . this time I believe her."

Isis looked stunned. She was not used to me saying I didn't blame Jackie. "So, yep, that's it in a nutshell. I only find out that my sister blames me for her rape, one that she may never get over. She believes she's a burden to me and was willing to sacrifice herself to give me my privacy. So thank you, Isis, for encouraging me to go find all that out. Thank you for sticking your nose where it didn't belong." I was now angry.

"Wait, are you blaming me for this?"

"You goddamn right," I yelled. "I told you I didn't want to go. I told you it was not a good idea. But you had to dig your heels in and force some shit."

"Oh, no, you will not blame me for this. This ain't on me. I had no idea that Penny had anything to say to you. I had no idea the rape was a part of this. There was no way I could have known." Isis threw her hands in the air like she was tossing caution to the wind.

"But if you had left it alone, then just maybe . . ."

"Just maybe what?" Isis put her hands on her hips. "What?" Isis squinted at me. "Maybe Penny's mind would have changed about the way she felt? What exactly do you think would have changed, Secret? Please tell me. Because I need to know, what is it about encouraging you to do something that Penny really wanted you to that caused any of this? I'll wait." She crossed her arms across her shoulders.

I was not feeling the card she was playing. "Don't make this bullshit about Penny; the fact of the matter is, I trusted you, so I went. Now my mind is fucked up."

"Again, it ain't my fault, Secret. You need to stop running and pointing your goddamn finger. What happened to Penny ain't going away, and the fact she turned to alcohol to silence the demon says that she was suffering. And for whatever reason, she didn't come to either of us. Her family, her sisters. But now she has the courage to release some of what she is feeling. It ain't all about you. So stop feeling sorry for yourself."

"You think I don't know that? I never said it was about me. But I'm the reason she was raped. I may as well have poured the liquor down her throat. I'll never forgive myself, Isis."

"Well, you should try."

"Just fuck it. 'Cause you don't get it."

"Know what, I'm done. I ain't gone sit here and argue wit' you. When you get out yo' feelings, give me a call." Isis stomped toward the front door. She suddenly stopped and turned to me. "Oh, and I had an idea for the business. That's why I came by. Or maybe you changed your mind about that, and you can call me up and blame me for that, too." She exited the door and slammed it.

I was just sick over the Penny situation, and I couldn't believe I had just flipped the whole thing on Isis. Deep down, I knew none of it was her fault, but I was angry and confused. I wasn't sure what to do or think. One thing was for sure, all the crying had done nothing to soothe my pain. And I still had no resolution. What I really needed to do was relax, and I could only think of one way that I could do that. I strolled over to my in-house bar and grabbed a brand-new bottle of Jack Daniel's. Removing the top, I thought about Penny and pictured her saying that Jackie was not the cause of her drinking. Her words echoed in my ear. I snatched up a shot glass and headed for my bedroom. If Jack couldn't help me get my thoughts together, I was certain nothing else would.

# Chapter 35

# Isis

I raced down the interstate, upset as I replayed the things Secret said, as she blamed me for the visit to the therapist. I could not understand why she blamed me. All I had been trying to do was fulfill Penny's wishes. She really wanted Secret to come to the session, as the therapist had requested. It would be good for them. And I still believed it has been. Penny was able to release feelings and thoughts, which might be helpful in the future for her recovery. I only wished Secret could see that.

I wasn't sure when I had decided to go to Bobbi's house. I didn't even know if he was home. But at some point my car must have pointed itself in that direction, because the next thing I knew, I was pulling up to the condo that he was renting. I sat in the car and held onto the steering wheel as I stared at his front door. The engine in my car was still running. I contemplated just pulling off, but it felt as if something was pushing me toward the front door. Slowly, I turned off the ignition and climbed out of the car. The walk up to the front door felt more like a stroll as I put one foot in front of the other. I took a deep breath before ringing the doorbell. I prayed Melvin didn't answer the door. Sometimes I felt like he was Bobbi's second shadow.

Bobbi's eyes stretched wide when he opened the door and realized it was me. But I guess I had to be honest: I was probably the last person in the world he expected to show up at his door. Hell, I was shocked that I was there. "Isis, hey." He seemed nervous. "Is everything okay?" he followed up. I almost laughed, even though I was upset. I was the one who was supposed to be nervous, not him.

"Nothing. I just thought I would stop by," I lied. "The invitation is still open, right?" I said. He had given me his address and told me to feel free to stop by whenever I wanted. This just so happened to be the first time I had thought to take him up on that offer, and I didn't know why. Although we were cordial again and I gave him business advice, I didn't consider him a friend like that. I wasn't ready to accept him back into my life like that. I probably never would, and I was more than okay with that. But why was I there?

"Of course. Like I said, whenever you ready . . . Come on in." He ushered me inside. I stepped in but stood by the wall. He smiled at me, then shut the door. "I was sitting down in the den watching a movie and having a drink. Would you like to join me?"

"I guess so, since I'm here." I shrugged my shoulders. I didn't have anything else to do but go home, because I refused to go into the office. I followed Bobbi into what I assumed was his den. It was pretty laid back, as I would have imagined Bobbi would have it. He had a huge black sectional with some tables and a seventy-inch television screen. "Where is Melvin?" I asked.

"At home. He came by the store earlier after you left, said he was going home to chill."

"You mean he don't live here wit' you?" I was truly surprised.

Bobbi laughed. "Nah, we ain't doin' that no more. You know how it is when the Jeffersons move up." He grinned.

"Yeah, I see how you livin'. I remember when you was sleeping on that beat-up couch at Melvin's crib. Oh, and fighting those cockroaches." I laughed.

"Aye, I know. That was fucked up . . . But I can't front; those were good times." He smiled, but it slowly faded. I thought maybe something was on his mind. Or maybe thinking about Melvin's crib revived old memories of what he had done to me. "Would you like me to get you something to drink? I have wine, pop, Hennessy, you take yo' pick."

Usually I would have gone for the wine, but to be honest, I really needed something a bit stronger. Maybe I could shake the argument I had had with Secret.

"Fix me a shot of that Hennessy, matter of fact, make that two shots."

"Damn, you sure?" He glared at me.

"Very." I smiled. I turned my attention to the television. He was watching one of our old favorite movies we used to watch together, *Negotiator* with Samuel L. Jackson. I sat back on the sofa.

"Just thought I'd bring the whole bottle." Bobbi set the Hennessy on the table along with two shot glasses. "And since you goin' hard, I figured I'd go hard wit' you." He filled my shot glass, then his. He looked at me. "Let's do it." At the same time we raised our glasses and took it down.

"Agggh." I grunted out loud as the brown liquid tortured my throat but in a good way. "Hit me again." I pushed my glass over so he could refill it. This time it tingled my toes, rolled through my feet, then forced itself up through rest of my body all the way to my brain. I had to shake my head just to gather my thoughts.

"Yeah, that brown has that effect," Bobbi commented as he observed my reaction to the Hennessy.

"I swear. It's the beast." I cosigned.

"I'm really glad you decided to come by. I wanted to thank you for stopping by the store today. That was dope. You know, having you support me and all."

"Hey, I was glad to do it. Besides, I wanted to witness some of the questions I had answered for you during your process. Even though I know you were all being modest. Be honest: you didn't really need me."

"Aye, of course I needed you. I wouldn't ask if I didn't. Please believe that."

"If you say so." I smiled. He was lying, but whatever, if he wanted to make me feel like he really needed me to put his store together just to talk to me. Cool. I wouldn't rain on his parade.

He was now staring at me. I wondered if I had something on me. "You straight?" he finally asked.

"I'm good." I grinned. That Hennessy was already doing itself justice.

Bobbi poured another shot, drank it down, set down the glass, and turned to me. "Now when you gone tell me what's bothering you?" I looked at him with the intent to protest his persistence, but I had to be honest, Bobbi knew me well. When we were together we had been close, able sometimes to read each other's thoughts. At least we had been until his deceit.

"Ain't nothin' worth dwelling on." I wanted to keep it at that without going into details. That was specifically the reason for the Hennessy shots: to clear my mind so I could think about something other than the argument with Secret.

"Isis, I know we just getting back to where we can have a real conversation. But believe me when I say I'm here for you. If you need to talk about anything, whether it's something that's bothering you or not, I'm here for you." As much as I wanted to deny it, I could see in his eyes that he was being sincere. Or was I seeing what I wanted to see? Secret's words for me not to trust him crept through my mind. But there were all his apologies made since, and his situation had been complicated. Maybe I could soften a little bit and share my small problem.

"Secret and I had an argument before I came over. I was upset and just stormed out."

"Hey, you shouldn't even worry 'bout that. Y'all use to beef all the time about petty stuff." He smiled, but I wasn't smiling. Secret was really mad at me, and I didn't like it.

"This ain't petty. She really pissed at me. I don't know for how long."

"Aye, I wouldn't even worry about it. Y'all friendship too strong. From what I know, y'all sisters. And sisters be back talkin' by tomorrow. Especially you and Secret." I knew he was right, but it didn't make me feel any better. I thought about the things Secret had said about Penny, then the pain that had been on Secret's face. She was really hurt and blamed herself. I started to regret, to wonder if I had done the right thing by insisting that she go to the session. I still believed I had made the best decision. What if she hadn't gone? Then Penny would have felt there was no solution other than turning back to the bottle.

Even though she was upset, I had to stand strong in my decision to encourage her to go. Not to mention that I honestly believed that Penny needed to release her thoughts and emotions. Secret never wanted to address her emotions head-on. But like I had tried to tell her, this was not about her; it was about Penny. And what was best for Penny was Secret coming to the session. Now it was done. There was nothing else left to do but move on and hopefully start some healing. Just the thought of all the heartache and pain on all sides sent tears racing down my cheeks.

"Not the tears. I got you. Everything gone be cool." Bobbi scooted across the sofa over to me. Before I could even protest, I was buried deep in his arms. And I didn't want to be released. Nothing in me said to back away, resist.

Instead I consented to everything that followed from the gentle kiss he planted on the tip of my nose. Holding my face up to his, I looked him in the eyes and, surprisingly, I saw everything that I used to see when we had been together. When we

were happy, when I believed that we would be together forever. And I wanted him just as bad as I
had then. Wrapping both my hands around the
back of his head, I pulled his lips down to mine.
Prying his lips apart, I pushed my hungry tongue
inside and kissed him for dear life.

Bobbi gripped me so tightly yet so gently, I
moaned and kissed him deeper, and he met me
stroke for stroke. I was craving him. I tugged at his
shirt and pulled it over his head. Pushing him backward until he was lying flat on his back, I climbed
onto him. Taking my tongue, I kissed his chest until
I couldn't take any more. With his hands up my
shirt, he found my breast. I sat up and pulled my
shirt over my head. Sitting up, Bobbi found my bra
and undid it. He buried his face in my breast. I
couldn't hold on any longer. I instructed him to
take off his pants. No sooner than they hit the
floor did I all but tackle him back to the couch.
Climbing on top of him, I rode him stallion style
and released pressure I had been holding in for
months. Bobbi smiled as I released all over him. I
fell onto his chest, relieved.

We lay on the couch but decided to take it to
the bed. All night we went round for round. I
quickly remembered the old days when we would
tear each other apart all night. Somewhere in my
reminiscing or exhaustion from our sex play, I had
fallen asleep. I woke up to Bobbi in a deep sleep
and the quiet of his house. Looking around the
room, I was well aware where I was, and I remembered exactly how I had gotten there.

I glared over at Bobbi, and I knew right then
and there that this was not what I wanted. I appreciated that he had been a shoulder when I clearly

needed one. But I regretted that I had allowed my weakness to let my guard down. Hell, but to be honest, my body had needed it. Bobbi had given me exactly what my body screamed for: multiple orgasms. But I could not allow it to go any further. I started to wake Bobbi but decided I wasn't in the mood to discuss it. Slowly and as carefully as I could, I slid from under the covers. He was still deeply asleep. I looked around for my clothes but remembered that we had come to the bed naked. My clothes were in the den. Tiptoeing through the house, I grabbed my clothes, slid them on, and slipped out the front door.

I drove straight home and jumped in the shower. The events of the day that had driven me to Bobbi's house played in my mind. I thought about how mad Secret was at me. I wondered how mad she would be if she knew I had slept with Bobbi. I could hear her cursing him out and calling me stupid.

# Chapter 36

# Secret

I was so tired of lying around the house and feeling sorry for myself. That shit was played, and it damn sure was not solving anything. I had to do something to move on the next thing, whatever the hell that was. So when Kirk called rattling on about a shipment and shit that Isis and I did every day anyway, I decided to head over to his house to hang out with him, since he clearly wasn't doing shit, either.

"What's up? I was surprised as hell that you wanted to come hang out wit' me." Kirk opened the door, jabbering about nothing.

"Listen, that's exactly the reason nobody come visit you. Because they got to hear this shit." I blew past him and headed straight to his playroom, where he spent all his time. Kirk had the room tricked out for lounging. It was a game room and den all put together. It had a pool table, arcade games like Pac-Man, and a movie theater off to one side. And of course a complete bar.

"Here you go." He chuckled.

"Where's that catered food you said you had over here?" I asked.

"It's down there on the bar."

"You expecting company or something?" I was nosy.

"Nah, I just got that food so I could relax and watch a movie or something. Plus, I wanted soul food, no bullshit."

"Well, good, 'cause I'm hungry." I wasted no time grabbing a plate and filling it. He had fried catfish, cabbage, sweet potatoes, mac and cheese, cornbread muffins, and buttered beans. I put some of everything on my plate before finding my seat in front of the theater screen. "Why you watchin' this depressing-ass movie." I referred to *Malcolm X* movie starring Denzel Washington.

"Aye, you trippin'. This ain't boring, it's educational. This is what you need to be focused on."

"No the hell I don't. You trying to make me start a race riot? If not, you should put on something else." I forked some mac and cheese into my mouth.

"You just complicated. How you gone come over here and ruin my movie." He got up and put in another movie.

"Oh, okay. Now this I don't mind." He put on *American Gangster*. I got comfortable in my seat and smashed all of my food. "Damn, that was good. Compliments to your caterer. You always pick the best ones."

"No doubt. I can't be eating no bullshit. You know, since I ain't got no wife to take care of me."

"Yo, that's your fault. Stop messing wit' these hoes and you'll find a wife. Maybe," I joked.

"Aye, I'm good. I'll get a wife 'bout the same time somebody wife you."

"Fuck you, Kirk." I chuckled. "Ain't no nigga out here good enough for me. Besides, I don't play that bullshit. I would fuck one of these lame niggas up out here." I laughed, but I was serious. I did not play games.

"So what's up? What really brings you through? 'Cause you don't ever come check up on ya' boy."

"Don't act like that, Kirk. You know I be checkin' up on you." I decided to beat around the bush a bit longer.

"Nah, a nigga ain't got yo' attention like that. So what's up?" He scratched his forehead.

"Nigga, don't act like that. I always call you. So petty." I sighed. "But you right. I got shit on my mind . . . I'm a little heated with Isis 'bout some shit," I admitted. It didn't sound right, those words coming out of my mouth. Especially talking to someone else.

"Word. Not ya' girl. You got to be on some bull-shit."

"That might be true, but it's how I'm feelin'. At least that's what I think. 'Cause I also feel bad even sayin' that shit."

"What's up, then?"

"Man, it's just some shit going on wit' Penny. You already know we been going through some shit 'bout the therapist and all that . . ." Kirk nod-ded his head in agreement. I had given him a little information on it the last time we spoke. "Well, Isis suggested that I go to the therapist. Just to support Penny, 'cause she really wanted me to come to the session that the therapist suggested I attend. I told you I was against that shit one hundred percent."

"I remember," Kirk said. "Shit, I didn't think you was gone go through wit' it.

"Aye, and I wasn't, but Isis convinced me it was for the best. So I did it. Turns out I should have followed my first mind . . . It was crazy."

"Damn, what happened?"

"What didn't happen is the real question for you to ask." I shook my head. I hated reliving it. I had to check my emotions before saying anything. If not, tears would be all over the place, and I wasn't trying to go back there. "Penny still in pain; she says the drinking was to suppress the nightmares she still suffering from because of the rape . . ."

"Man, that's fucked. I figured she wasn't over that shit. Damn." Kirk balled up his fist. It still hurt him knowing what had happened to Penny, even though he had dead that situation soon as she found out who was responsible.

"Even worse, she moved out because she felt as if she was smothering me. She wanted to give me space. But, Kirk, she didn't say it, but she blames me. I just know it."

"Nah, I don't believe that. I can't even fuck wit' that thought, Secret. Get that shit out ya' head." He looked me in the eyes. I fought back the tears that were threatening to fall. No matter how hard I tried to suppress them, they fought harder to reveal themselves.

"Listen, this shit got me fucked up right now, Kirk." I sniffed back the tears but couldn't shake the knot in my throat.

"Yo, but why you mad at Isis?"

"She the one sent me to find all this shit out.

Had she left it alone, I could have avoided all of this."

"And is that what you really wanted? You don't think you needed to hear all of this eventually? Clearly Penny needed to get this off her chest."

I knew everything he was saying was the truth. "I know." I slowly nodded my head in agreement.

"Isis yo' girl. I ain't never seen shit come between y'all. And you know she only told you the truth. You had to go."

"I know. And deep down I know I'm not mad at her, but I need to point the finger. This way I don't have to come to terms wit' shit. Ya' know." The tears finally escaped my eyelids. There was nothing else I could do to fight them.

Kirk was to his feet too fast for me to protest. He bent down on his knees. Taking his right hand, he brushed at the tears that ran down my cheeks. "Hey, you always trying to be so tough. At least you been that way since I been knowing you. Let somebody be there for you sometimes."

Kirk had never looked so fine to me as in that moment. I saw not only a friend but a confidant. Slowly Kirk brought his face to mine and gently kissed me on my lips. I trembled from the effect. He eased back, but I reached out for him and pulled him back in. This time I took the lead.

I kissed him gently on the lips, something I rarely if ever did with a man. Slowly I allowed my tongue to ease into his mouth. And, damn, it felt good, and to my surprise Kirk was a good kisser. I assumed a gangster like him would kiss only as thugs do: aggressively and full of lust. But it was actually full of passion. Fuck foreplay; I didn't need it. I was instantly dripping wet. I reached for Kirk's belt. I was on fire. Without one word, he lifted me up and carried me through his huge house, up the stairs to his bedroom, and laid me down on his bed.

He pulled off my shirt and bra, and I arched my back from pure pleasure as he sucked both my breasts. His tongue tasted the tips of my nipples like they were diamonds in the rough. Juices flowed down my thighs in anticipation of him. I could never have guessed Kirk had skills like that.

"I need you inside me, Kirk," I all but begged. I couldn't wait much longer. He stood up, and his member sang to me, it was so thick and hard. I lifted my hips in the air ready to force it inside. Kirk smiled. He kissed the center of my stomach, then came back up to my lips. I moaned out loud as he slowly entered me.

"Shit," he mouthed, looking me in the eyes. He took a steady pace and ground me to the best orgasm I ever had, I was sure.

Afterward, we lay in silence in each other's arms. I opened my eyes and it was daylight. I couldn't remember even dreaming. I was still in Kirk's arms. I could not believe what had happened between us. Kirk and I had been friends since we were kids, then business partners. And now here I was in his bed in his arms.

"Good morning," he said as he stirred.

"Hey." I eased out of his arms a bit. "What time is it?" I asked.

"Let me check." He reached for his phone. I used that as an excuse to ease out of his grasp.

"Damn, it's ten-thirty," he announced. "And I got like twenty missed calls." He chuckled.

"Them niggas ain't used to sleepin' in late," I

added. My phone started ringing. I reached for it. The number wasn't familiar, but I still answered. "Hello," I answered, but got quiet as a recording signaled it was a call from the jail. Then I heard Jackie say her name in between pauses. My first instinct was to hang up, but something stopped me.

"Secret," Jackie said my name almost as if she was afraid. I was silent for a second.

"I'm here," I said.

"Thanks for answering." I could tell she was nervous.

"Why you locked up, Jackie?"

"Just some petty old shit they found on me. I been in here for a week."

"Hmmm, how you get my number?"

"Penny gave it to me." I wasn't shocked to hear her say that.

"She know you locked up?"

"Yeah, I told her." I didn't say anything. I was silent again. "So listen, I have visitation today, and I was just wondering if you could . . . if you had time would you come down here and see me. Now I know how you feel but . . . I . . . just thought I'd ask."

"Jackie, I just woke up . . . I gotta go, though." I ended the call. I just didn't know what to say to her.

"That was your mom?" I'm sure he was even surprised I answered the call. Hell, I was, too.

"Yeah, she locked up for something . . . You know how it is wit' her. Could be anything."

"I know . . . Did she say what she want?"

"For me to visit her or something." I blew it off.

"Damn, she asked you that?"

"My thoughts exactly." I snapped my neck.

"Can I get you some breakfast?" He glared at me.
"Nah, I got shit to do. I'ma get up outta here.
I'll hit you, though." I all but jumped out of bed,
grabbed my clothes, and raced to the bathroom.
On my drive home I didn't know what to think
about first: sleeping with Kirk, which was still a
complete shock to me, or the fact that Jackie had
actually called me and asked me to visit her in jail.

I felt so alone. I couldn't call Isis, because I was
sure she was still upset with me. And the last thing
I wanted to do was bother Penny. What I did do
was jump in the shower and let the water soothe
my mind back to life. It was time I did some thinking on my own. I was known to be strong; here was
the time for me to do that in order to pull myself
out of the dumps.

Without any plans, I dressed, jumped in my Escalade, and drove down to the jail. No decision in
my mind was ever made I just did it. Inside, I
checked in, and my name was on the list to visit
Jackie. I guess she was serious when she asked me
to visit. I wasn't sure what this was all about, but with
Jackie there wasn't much that could surprise me.

I was checked in and in my eyes treated like a
criminal, then taken back. I sat down in front of
the glass and waited for them to bring her back. I
wasn't prepared for the emotion that tried to take
me once we were face-to-face. I put on my cold
face, thought it was easy.

Jackie picked up the phone first. Reluctantly, I
followed. I didn't know if I wanted to hear anything stupid she might have to say. Even more, I
wasn't sure why I was even there. It would have
been so easy for me to never come down.

"Hey, I didn't actually think you would come."

"In that case, I guess you wouldn't blame me?" I looked away for a moment. Jackie stirred so much up inside me. But I wasn't there for that.

"I'm just glad that you did . . ." She paused. "Penny was really upset when I called. I didn't want to call, but I knew she might look for me. And I didn't want her to worry." I almost rolled my eyes at her. After all she had done to us, now she cared if Penny worried about her. That shit was comical to me.

"Yo, Jackie, why am I here? You asked me to come here . . . Why?" I was not about to beat around the bush. Like I had told Kirk earlier, I had shit to do.

"That anger that you give me I deserve. I brought you here today because it was time."

"Time for what?" I got loud. I looked around to see who might be watching us. Thankfully, we were the only ones visiting.

"I need to explain some things to you about my life. Maybe then you can see why I'm so fucked up."

"You mean excuse. You want to excuse the things you did. So that you can feel good 'bout ruining our lives."

"Not at all. I just want to share my life wit' you. If you will allow me to."

I was mad. I didn't want to hear from her. I put the phone on the hook. I wanted to get up and walk away, but my legs wouldn't allow me. Reluctantly and with some force other than my own, my hand went back to the phone. I picked it up and put it to my ear.

"Spit it out," I said through my gritted teeth.

"I never told you and Penny 'bout me growing up. I had a twin brother; he was killed, though, when I was a teenager. But our mother married this man named Robert when we were about eight. Now he was nice enough to us. He kept food on the table, and he didn't beat us. But at night he would rape me and my brother in front of each other . . ." Tears ran down Jackie's face as she seemed to stare out into the distance. My heart nearly dropped out of my chest at what she had just said. I couldn't imagine that happening to any child. "One night my mother came in the room, and he was on top of me. And I thought, finally we are saved, she going to kill him. Instead she stood in the door and asked him was he finished. I looked at my brother, confused. Robert said to her, 'No I haven't done him yet.' My brother and I watched in horror as our mother turned and left the room. All that time she knew that she chose him over us; she gave us to our predator so that she could have a husband. This went on until we were fourteen, when my brother was hit by a car and killed. I ran away and never went back home. See, I had been on my own until I had you." Her eyes came from the distance and found mine.

"So when I had you, I knew absolutely nothing about love. See, I had rid myself of that a long time ago. But I tried; then came Penny and I continued to try, but I was so full of my old life. See, it was always there. I never had a good night's sleep because Robert's face was always there when I closed my eyes. That is, until Penny's daddy introduced me to my cure. And that became more important to me than anything. 'Cause, see, I was free of pain. Then there was you and Penny needing to be taken care of, fed, and loved. I resented that. Mainly, because I felt love for you two; as much as I tried not to, I did. So I started to beat you to convince myself I didn't love you. That no one had ever loved me, so you two didn't deserve it. But the truth of the matter is I love you two so much. I fought it, but it just wouldn't go away. Then one day you hated me the way I hated my mom, and I figured, mission accomplished."

Tears ran down Jackie's face, and I had to fight to keep mine in. For the first time in my life I saw her as the damaged adult that she was. Now I knew why we never knew about her mom. I could remember as a kid asking her about her mother. And I remember that she got that same distant look on her face that she had just now as she remembered her mother. I didn't want to feel sorry for her, but I understood. How could a mother allow her own kids to be raped just to keep a husband? I was sick for her.

I rubbed my face from frustration. "Why tell me this now, Jackie?"

"You deserve to know, Secret. You have always been my strength, believe it or not. You stood up to me, no matter what. And I heard you, believe me, I did. But I was just so fucked up back then, I couldn't come back from it. Then, the past few years, I just been ashamed to admit my truths. 'Cause I didn't want to face them. I never in my life told anyone 'bout what happened to me and my brother until now. I'm seeing a therapist while I'm here. Ain't the best, but it feels good to get it out. I had to apologize to you, baby girl. And let you know that I love, truly love you and your sister. I'm just damaged goods." She shrugged her shoulders.

For the first time in my life I saw that she truly did love us, because it was written all over her face. And I admitted to myself that I loved her, too; that's the reason I was so emotional when it came to her. Our history would forever be tainted. Healing may not even be possible. But I cried for the twin girl and boy that were my mother and my uncle.

"Listen, you keep getting your help while you're in here. I got to get going, though. You got my number." I hung up the phone and exited before I broke down in front of her. I wasn't ready to open up to her like that yet. I was my mother's daughter.

# Chapter 37

# Isis

Once again my plate was full: not only did I still have Secret angry with me, now I had slept with Bobbi, making matters worse. I didn't know what the hell was going on with me. Here I was supposed to be focusing on getting money. I had told myself that's where my focus was, but here I was, out here pissing off my best friend and jumping into bed with an old partner who had betrayed me in one of the worst ways. I was just not making good decisions. But I was going to get it together.

I got up early and went into work to tie up some loose ends with some paperwork on a few deliveries that I had promised I would get done. Then I made the drive down to see Felicia. I had to speed all the way there, because I had left the office later than I had planned. I did not want to miss the visiting hours. Thankfully, I made it just in time for the cutoff. I got checked in and was happy when Felicia made her entrance.

"Boy, am I glad you see you," I admitted right away. I was not in the beating-around-the-bush mood. I need to make every second count so I could tell her everything that was going on with me. Except I would conveniently leave out the part about me sleeping with Bobbi. That bit of infor- mation might cause her to smack me for being so dumb. Honestly, I wouldn't be able to blame her.

"What's going on now?" She jumped right in.

"Secret is mad at me. It's been a few days, and I haven't heard anything from her. I even think she's avoiding me at the office."

"Well, have you tried calling her?"

"No, I have not." I crossed my arms like a spoiled kid. "Why do I have to call her first? She al- ways gets her way." I pouted.

"I swear, if you and Secret don't both grow up al- ready . . . Tell me what happened?" Felicia finally asked me.

"Okay, Penny's therapist wanted Secret to come in to see her. Long story short, I convinced her to go, for Penny's sake if anything. Because Penny really stressed to me that's what she wanted."

"So did she go?"

"Yes, and that's where the drama come in. At the session Secret finds out that Penny was drink- ing because she still was having nightmares about the rape. Also Penny admitted she moved out be- cause she wanted to give Secret her space. Even though Secret didn't want her to move out. But Penny feels she was smothering Secret. Anyhow,

Secret now blames me that she went to the meeting to find all this out."

"But these were things that she needed to know," Felicia said. She seemed confused.

"Correct, she did need to know. But she ain't gone admit that to herself, so she blames me. Now I feel bad because she hurt." I thought of Secret and hated when we fought.

"Aww, this gone be okay. Secret just need some time. Trust me, she knows what you convinced her to do was the right thing to do. She had to find out how Penny feels. All that is a part of Penny healing. Don't worry." Just hearing Felicia's take on the entire situation eased my nerves. For one, I knew she wouldn't tell me anything to hurt me, and what she had said was the only rational thought anyone could have after listening to the situation. Now I just had to sit back and wait for Secret to realize the same thing. I had only told her what was in my heart, and that was to be there for Penny. And honestly, if I had to do it all over again, the outcome would be the same.

"See, I knew talking to you about it would help. I feel better all ready." I smiled from within.

"So what else is bothering you?" she asked, as if it was second nature.

"Oh, I'm cool," I lied. The lady was a magnet, and my problems were pulling me toward her. There had to be relief on my face from the conversation we had just had. How could she see anything else?

"Isis, let's not do this. You belong to me. I know when something is going on. Let's talk about it and get it over wit'." I froze with apprehension.

"I've been hangin' out wit' Bobbi," I admitted.

There was no way I would tell her I had slept with him.

"Why, Isis? Why must you hang wit' this dude? He stole from you. One of the ultimate betrayals from the man who you planned to spend your life with." She reminded me of that as if I had forgot. That was one detail I would never forget. I hated to hear it out loud. "The bastard deserves to be in jail, not be your friend." She looked at me as if surely I was crazy. Shit, maybe I was.

"See, the thing is . . . he apologized to me and paid back the money, every cent." I said that as if she would jump up and say she forgave him, too.

"Wait, he paid the money back? But this still does not make it right. Isis, he stole from you. What's to stop him doing it again?" She had made a point there, but I wasn't done yet.

"Okay, the situation is this. Bobbi had a gambling problem. He owed some guys some money. He didn't know how to tell me, so he just took the money. But he had to disappear until they were paid, because they were looking for him to kill him. And he didn't want to bring that heat around me. But he always planned on paying me back. That's why he was trying to talk to me. He wanted to pay me back and apologize to me for what happened."

"And you fell for that? Sounds like bullshit to me. But, hey, I'm just a bystander." I would have laughed, but I knew she was serious. So instead I decided to explain my reasoning.

"Yes, I believe him. Think about it, Felicia. He didn't have to pay me back. He was gone; he could have stayed gone. Instead, he paid me, and frankly, I believe him. See, back before he ran off, I do remember him getting these phone calls and looking as if something was wrong. I just assumed he worried about his business with fixing the cars."

"Hmmm, okay, say this is the truth. Why out of all the people in Miami you have to hang out with him?"

"Because I forgave him." My answer was simple as far as I was concerned. But I knew how that sounded to someone else. At the end of the day, they only see the wrong he had done me.

"You can forgive him and be done with him." Felicia also had a point. And now with the situation I was in with him, I wished I had done just that.

"And you're right. He opened up a clothing store in Miami, and he asked me for my help with some business questions. Other than that, that's it," I once again lied.

"Well, for your sake, I hope you stay away from him. I don't trust him." Her words reminded me of Secret's. I still didn't see the problem with me being on speaking terms with Bobbi, but lovers was definitely out of the picture. I had to make that clear once and for all.

Felicia and I finished up our visit, and I jumped back on the highway in as much of a hurry to get back to the city as I had been to leave it. I had to see Bobbi. I had called to make sure he would be home when I touched down.

"Come on in." Bobbi opened the door halfway. His eyes were not open all the way.

"Were you asleep?" I asked. From where I was standing, his house looked dark, like the drapes were still closed. It was a far cry from the other day, when I had come by the house and it was lit up from natural light. The sun was still in the sky, so there was no need for his house to be dark, unless it was his choice.

"Nah, I'm up. Just not feeling all this sunlight right now. Kinda got a hangover. I'm on this Extra Excedrin, hoping for some relief. I went out wit' Melvin last night."

"You don't have to tell me. I know how he get down." I grinned. Melvin was a hard drinker when he turned up. "You cool to talk?" I asked out of curiosity. But I didn't really care; I was ready to get this conversation over with.

"I'm straight." He led me to his den. His place was quiet, so he must have been asleep. "You good?" he asked. "I called you a couple times yesterday, and you didn't answer." I had ignored his calls. I hadn't been sure what to say to him just yet.

"I was busy." I decided to keep it at that. I didn't feel the need to say any more. Soon he would understand anyway.

"I thought I had ran you off." He gave a nervous laugh.

"I thought about it." I laughed. "No, I'm only kidding. Listen . . . we had a talk a while back, and I told you we could never be together in a relationship again. Talking, even hanging out is different. We are adult enough to handle that."

"I know . . . I was just thinkin'—"

I had to cut him off because there was no buts involved. "Look, Bobbi, we both grown and we smart. We know one plus one equals two. Ain't no way we can be sleeping together and only remain friends. It ain't that simple."

"So you regret what happened?" He had this sad look in his eyes that I had to ignore. This was not a debate or a compromise. It was actually making things better for both of us.

"It's not about whether I regret it or not. You are missing the point."

"No, I just want to understand. I want to be clear."

"And that's what I'm trying to do is make it clear. So, to make it simple, I will just say we can remain cool. You can call me to talk, ask questions, whatever. But what happened the other night cannot happen again. We cannot sleep together," I added. Hopefully, now it was very clear. I thought I had made it clear to him in the past. But I couldn't blame him, because what had happened between us was not just his fault. We both had played a part in it.

"I will respect your wishes. I be sure not to let it happen again. The last thing I want to do is push you away completely."

Disappointment was all over his face, but I refused to feel bad. It was what it was. He had ruined it. Now, regardless of what feelings he had for me, or wished I had for him, he would have to deal with it. I was not changing my mind. Our existence in each other's life was what it was. Two exes now on speaking terms, and in my opinion, good speaking terms.

# Chapter 38

# Secret

After talking to Jackie, I felt a little better about things. It put a lot in perspective for me. And as much as I hated to admit it, she had some right to bitterness at life. But it didn't excuse what she had done to Penny and me. Because of her, we were just another fucked-up generation, possibly to pass that down to the next. There was no way I could let that be me, especially if I ever had kids. Poor Penny, though: I didn't know if she would ever be okay again. It was bad enough she had grown up with Jackie as her mother, then to be violated by rape. She was truly suffering, but she was fighting to win. And the only person I was thinking of was myself, by feeling sorry for myself. Isis didn't deserve my bullshit, either. I was always taking things out on somebody else when I felt cornered. It was my way of staying in control and feeling like I was winning.

But I needed my best friend and couldn't go one more day without talking to her. So this morning her number was the first I dialed. I invited her over for lunch and margaritas. The doorbell rang, and I all but ran to open the door.

"I'm so sorry for being a bitch." I threw my arms around Isis. I was hugging her so tight, I was sure I was cutting off her air supply.

"I accept, but please let me go so I can breathe."

"I swear you so weak. Can't stand no pressure," I teased.

"I knew you would miss me sooner or later. Now my stomach gets to reap the benefits."

"Fo' sho'. And I cooked your favorite. P. F. Chang's."

"Really, you took the easy way out. Ask me if I care?" Isis strolled straight toward the kitchen.

"Do you care?" I teased.

"Hell, no. Now please fix my margarita first."

"I got you. I already had one."

"What I tell yo' selfish self 'bout startin' before me."

"Aye, what you expect comin' from me." I laughed. "But, damn, bitch, what you been doin'? I missed the shit out of you."

"Same ol' going to the shop—and I went to visit Felicia. To tell her about your trifling ass." Isis sipped her margarita. "This good, Secret," she complimented.

"You know this." I tasted my margarita and was equally satisfied. "What Felicia say?"

"She don't take us seriously, basically." Isis grinned. "So what you been up to? You ain't been to the shop."

"I know. I needed to get my thoughts together."

I pulled plates from the cabinet and filled them with stir-fry. I passed Isis her plate.

"Thanks, I'm hungry." She went for the table. "Have you talked to Penny?"

"I called her to check on her. She cool."

"What about you? You good?"

"I'm straight." I sat down at the table. "I talked to Jackie." Isis's chewing slowed.

"And?" she asked, then swallowed her food.

"She in jail on some old bullshit charges. She called me up and asked me to come down and visit her . . . I went."

"Really." I knew Isis would be shocked. "Damn, what'd she want?"

"It was really deep, Isis. I wish you could have been there . . . basically she wanted to explain why she was so fucked as a mother when it came to raising us . . ." I had to slow myself. Just the thought of the things Jackie had told me that had happened to her forced a lump into my throat.

"What'd she say?" Isis asked again. She lifted her glass to her lips and took another sip. I told her what Jackie had said.

"No way." Isis's mouth dropped wide open just as a tear slid down her face. "That's fucked up." Another tear slid down her other cheek. She wiped at the tears as they continued.

"Yep."

"Did she ever say how it ended?"

"Not really, just that her brother had been hit by a car and died. And she ran away. She never went back home. She raised herself the best way she could. Then she had me and Penny. But she was so damaged, until Penny's daddy introduced her to the bottle. It was a rescue from hurt and pain."

"That's crazy. I should have known it was something, though."

"So there it is in a nutshell. Penny and I were products of somebody already fucked up by force." I shrugged my shoulders.

"So did y'all talk?"

"Nah, not really. I mean, I listened and told her she had my number. I had to get out of there. But she did apologize and told me that she loved Penny and me."

"Did you believe her?"

"I think I do. But fuck all this sad shit. What's good? We got to hit the club or something. I need to relax."

"Aye, I'm good wit' that. But guess what?"

"Spit that shit out. You know I don't do guessing games." I sipped my drink.

"I picked me up a new whip. A Panamera Porsche. It's bangin'."

"That's what I'm talkin' 'bout. Time you pull out coins."

"You better know it. I cashed out on that baby."

"Is it outside? 'Cause you know I gotta bend a corner in that."

"It's at the crib. But I got you tomorrow."

"No doubt."

"Sooo . . . I got to tell you something. Promise you won't flip out."

"This must be bad. So hell, naw. I ain't promisin'."

"Come on, Secret. You always makin' me promise some crazy shit." She tried to bring up old stuff. I twisted the corners of my lips.

"Aye, but my stuff be legit. Yo' shit be off the wall. Uhh, uhh, I ain't promisin'. Spit it out."

"I swear you don't play fair. You better not flip, though."

"Come on, Isis. Stop playin' around." I was so anxious, I could barely sit still in my seat.

"I slept with Bobbi," she said quickly.

I placed my hand on my chest. I was scared for a minute that she might say something crazier. "Bitch, why you do that to me? I thought you was about to share some real juice." Her facial expression told me that she had expected a whole other reaction from me. And I didn't blame her: normally I would have gone berserk. But I had my reasons why I could not.

"So you not shocked? And you cool wit' it."

"I didn't say I was cool wit' it. But I'm not shocked. I knew that nigga wasn't hangin' around you for nothin'. You really thought he was interested in your boring-ass friendship?"

"Ha, ha." Isis laughed. "Whatever. I ain't boring; please believe that. But it didn't even go down like that."

"Hmmm, really." I grinned. "Exactly how did it go down? Please do share." I sat back in my chair and playfully crossed my legs. I picked up my margarita and licked the salt off the rim.

"See, you got jokes." Isis smiled. "But if you must know, I went over to his place when you were mad at me. He ended up being a shoulder to lean on, and it kinda happened. But like you even said, I needed it."

"Oh, so it's my fault." I laughed.

"Yes. It's your fault." She placed the blame on me.

"A'ight, I'll take that. You were sexually frustrated. All work and no play. I was starting to believe that you were dating Custom Hot Rides," I joked. Isis spent all of her time at that place. I wished all the time that she would go out and have fun, meet a man or something, but she always had an excuse.

"Whatever. But real talk, I'm good . . . So I was also thinkin' I could get that old bank deposit slip from you that showed Bobbi had cleaned out our bank account." I was surprised that she still remembered I had that.

"What made you think of that old thing?"

"Trust me, I never forgot about it. But now I feel like I can get rid of it. It's a part of a pain that I want demolished forever. You still got it?"

"Yep. In the safe in my room. You know the code; just get it out."

"Thank you for keeping it for me all this time. Tonight I plan to have a burning ritual with it."

"Aye, whatever makes you feel better. But his bitch ass better not make me ride down on him."

"Trust me, he's scared of you." Isis laughed.

It was time I told her what had happened between Kirk and me. She would not believe it. "Well, I guess I might as well tell you that I slept with Kirk."

"Wait, what? You slept wit' who?" Isis's mouth was wide enough to catch flies.

"I slept wit' Kirk." I dropped my head in shame.

"I knew it. You two slick-ass creepers been hidin' that shit forever. I knew it, I knew it," Isis repeated over and over, waving her right hand in the air.

"Nah, it's not like that, though. Kirk really is my boy."

"He ya' boy, a'ight. That much I agree." Isis chuckled. I knew she being sarcastic.

"No, for real, though. It was not like that. Just like you did with Bobbi, I went over because I needed someone to talk to. I was telling him about Jackie and Penny, and one thing led to another, and then it just happened."

"Umm." Isis looked me up and down like she was sizing me up.

"I ain't lyin'," I continued to explain.

"So you sayin' there were no strings attached? That you don't feel nothin' for Kirk."

"Man, listen. Kirk is my friend and I love him. Like a friend. That's it," I added. "This might mess that up." I was worried. Kirk had been my boy forever. I valued our friendship more than anything, even the money we got together. I would be really messed up if I lost his friendship.

"If that's how you feel, you gone have to tell him. 'Cause Kirk got feelings for you. I been told you that long time ago. He might want to take this thing to the next level."

"I know. I can feel it. The way he touches me explains it all. Damn, why did I let that happen, Isis?"

"Trust me, I understand. That's how I felt after I got it in with Bobbi. That was the last thing I wanted to happen between us. I didn't want it to confuse things after I had already told him that we couldn't be together. But when you vulnerable, crazy shit happens."

"I know. I should have never took my lonely ass over there. But he mentioned catered soul food, and I was already depressed. Shit, I bolted my ass up outta here." I laughed.

"I would have, too." Isis chuckled. "Did he have mac and cheese?"

"Yep. And it was bomb." I licked my lips as demonstration.

"Hey, mac and cheese make you do some strange thangs," Isis joked. "Real talk, though, you just got to tell him. Like you said, you and Kirk are friends first. I think he will understand. You just got to be straight up wit' him. I'm sure he wondering what you think, too. Have you talked to him since?"

"He called, but I didn't answer. I figured I'd text him later, once I had time to think."

"When was that?" she questioned.

"Yesterday," I revealed.

"Did you text him back then?"

"Not yet." I dropped my head in shame. "He called again this morning."

"Did you answer?" Isis squinted at me. She knew the answer before I said anything.

"No." I felt bad, but it was the truth.

"Really, Secret." Isis playfully rolled her eyes. "You are full of shit. I guess he knows. So you don't need to tell him nothing."

"Aye, I wanted to answer. I just couldn't bring myself to do it."

"If you don't put on your big woman drawers and stop playin' them damn games . . ."

"I know. I'ma hit him up tomorrow. I might even just drop by his crib."

"Thanks, and be a grownup about it." Isis playfully shook her head like she was disappointed in me.

"I got this."

"I got one question, though. We both know that
Kirk is fine as hell; ain't no questioning that at all.
But can he BONE?!"

I should have known she would ask that. I
picked up my glass and finished off my no longer
cold margarita. "Yes!" I shut my eyes and yelled.

"I knew it. Go, Kirk. My boy hit that." We stood
up, reached over the table, and slapped five. "After
that bit of news, I need a drink."

"I do, too. I'll grab some wine." I wasted no
time getting to my feet.

"Cool. While you do that, I'll grab that receipt
out of the safe." Isis headed toward my room,
where I kept the safe. I raced to the cooler by the
bar, where the wine was kept, and grabbed two
glasses. I couldn't wait to sip and talk more shit
with my girl. Back in the den I popped open the
wine and prepared to pour.

"Secret, what the fuck is this?" I looked up to
see Isis standing over me with the two bricks of cocaine that I had forgotten all about. I had meant
to get rid of them, but it had slipped my mind.

I wasn't sure what to say, but one thing was for
sure: I didn't feel like lying. "That. That ain't shit.
I'ma get rid of it; just put it back." I tried to play it
down and started to fill the glasses with wine.

"So since when is having two bricks of cocaine
'ain't shit'? What's up?"

"Listen, I was given that as a thank-you. I didn't
know what to do wit' it. Long story short, I threw it
in the safe and basically forgot about it."

"Who gives out bricks of cocaine for gifts? At least I
don't know anybody who does that." Isis hunched
her shoulders.

"Come on, Isis, don't make a big deal out of this."

"Don't make a big deal," she mouthed sarcastically, then paused. She had a look in her eyes like a light bulb had just come on. She set the bricks on the table. "So that's it. I should have known. This has got Kirk's name all over it. Just admit it." I wasn't surprised she had figured it out. There wasn't too much you could get past Isis; she always figured it out. I looked at the bricks and remembered the day I had received them. Then suddenly I remembered the incident with Rock.

"Listen, I tried to keep this from you, because you never needed to know . . . I got them bricks as a thank-you from Kirk's connect."

"Wait, you met the connect? The cocaine connect?" Isis's eyeballs looked as if they might jump out of their sockets.

"Yes. Kirk came to me and said he needed me to help him do a job . . . He needed me to distract this dude who was trying to take over some of his territory."

"How could you help wit' that?"

"The guy had a huge shipment coming in that he would use to supply his workers to take over some of Kirk's territory. So he asked me to dance for the guy to distract him while they robbed his shipment."

"So he put you back on the pole to benefit him. Typical Kirk. I ain't surprised." She shook her head with disappointment.

"It was supposed to be simple," I continued on. "But, dude, well, Rock—that was his punk ass name—he decides to put a gun to my head and force me to participate in his freaky shit. I agreed."

A tear slid down my cheek, and not because I regretted what I had done, but the thought of Rock's hand around my throat squeezing tight sent chills down my spine.

"What happened?" Worry was on Isis's face.

"That bastard wrapped his hands around my throat and squeezed . . . I couldn't breathe. I felt myself blacking out; then he suddenly let go. I took that chance and went for his gun . . . I killed him," I released. Now my face was wet with tears. "It was him or me.

"You did what you had to do." Isis reached over and hugged me. "Why didn't you tell me?"

"I wanted to, but I knew I couldn't. I didn't want to worry you."

"You still didn't tell me about the connect, though."

"Well." I sniffed back my anger and pain. "A few weeks after all this, Kirk called me up and gave me a lot of money and rode me out to his connect, who was in town. The guy told me he had heard a lot about the both of us."

"Us." Isis seemed surprised. "As in you and me?" she asked.

"Yep."

"How?"

"Kirk been telling him about us. Dude amped on that shit. He thanked me for having Kirk's back in the incident. Told me I was always welcome wherever he was and gave me those bricks as his appreciation." I shrugged. "I meant to get rid of it, though. Like real talk. I ain't fuckin' wit' no cocaine on my own."

"Good . . ." Isis shook her head, glaring at the bricks. "This madness right here ain't good. I know

Kirk mean well. But it's foolishness like what he got you involved in that is why we got to get our shit together. You should have never been put in that situation with that Rock-ass asshole. And meeting the connect . . . Well . . . I can't front; that's boss shit. But is that what we really tryin' to do?"

"That shit heavy." I kept it real.

"This just confirms what we already know. We got to get our shit together so we can start our shit. 'Cause truth be told, we never know when all this gangster shit gone blow up in our faces."

"Fuck that. We going all the way to the top, like Kirk said. Until then, throw them bricks back in the safe."

"I'll do that. But make this the last time you keep something from me. We in this together, like always."

"No doubt. Boss bitches," I chanted. I had been prepared for what had just happened, but it still felt good getting it off my chest. Now I could continue to focus on the rest of my bullshit.

# *Chapter 39*

## Secret

Two days had gone by, and although I still planned to, I hadn't made my way to Kirk's crib to tell him we couldn't be hooking up. I didn't think that he would trip, but I knew that deep down he was really feeling me. But I knew this was for the best, and I was certain he would agree with that. Now all I had to was work up the nerve to do it. The one thing I knew I would do for sure was roll up a fat blunt to take with me. That fire always calmed and resolved most sticky situations.

"Yo, wait I'm comin'," I yelled as somebody beat my front door down. I wasn't expecting anyone. If it was FedEx with a package, they were for sure about to catch my mouthpiece. "Yo, why the fuck . . ." I boasted as I snatched open the door. I paused at the sight of Penny standing in the doorway. "Girl, why you out here beatin' on my door like the cops? You still got your key. Use it some time." I eyed her

stone face with uncertainty. She was too quiet for
too long. I could swear her face looked swollen, as
if she had been crying. Something was wrong.
"What is it, Penny?" My tone was full of aggrava-
tion. I didn't know what she had to tell me, but I
wasn't up for it if it was bad.

Instead of answering me, she stepped inside and
walked past me. I stood for a second and looked
out the door. I didn't see anyone outside, so I shut
the door and followed her into the den. "Are you
gone tell me today why you up in here looking like
somebody stole your damn bike or something?" I
gave a nervous giggle. My gut wasn't feeling right.

"Secret, you might want to sit down for this."
Penny turned to face me slowly.

"For what? Penny, don't play wit' me. Spit that
shit out . . . Wait, is something wrong wit' Isis?" I
yelled. But I quickly dismissed that. I had just spoken with Isis about twenty minutes before Penny
knocked on my door.

"No . . . It's Jackie." At the mention of Jackie, a
mass of tears escaped Penny's eyes. "She was found
this morning."

"What do you mean 'found'?"

"She overdosed on heroin. She . . . dead, Secret."
Penny sounded as if she was choking on her words.

"Wait . . . you said Jackie, right?" I stood staring at
Penny. Suddenly my chest started to itch. I tried to
scratch away the feeling while I waited for Penny to
answer. Penny just nodded her head for yes. "Nah,
listen, I'm sure this a mistake. I'm gone call down to
the hospital." I lifted my cell phone, which was already in my hand, so that I could see the screen, but
for some reason there was no dial screen there.

"No, Secret, she gone. They already took her

body to the morgue. Karen's mother came and told me. By the time I got down to where they found the body, the morgue was taking her away."

I wasn't sure when, but my legs gave away from under me. I heard screaming and felt Penny tugging at me to get me off the ground. I could see her face and the tears. Her mouth was closed, and I realized the screaming was coming from me. I hurt and ached all over. I felt as if someone had taken a sledgehammer and beaten me. I grabbed at my chest; I felt like someone was sitting on my chest and I couldn't breathe. Penny helped me stand and walked me to the door so that I could get fresh air. The next hour or so was a blur of a bad dream.

"Oh, my God. What happened?" I heard Isis as she burst into the room. Erica had arrived a few minutes before Isis.

"Jackie was found dead this morning. Karen from the old neighborhood, her mother came and told me. By the time I got over to where she was, they were taking her away." I sat in a daze as Penny told Isis what had happened.

Isis just shook her head as tears flowed down her face. "My God, I just can't believe it." Isis looked at me and wiped at my tears. I could see her heart breaking for me and for Penny. Jackie had been in her life for a long time also. Hell, she had dodged a pot or two when Jackie was throwing them at us.

"This shit crazy," I cried. I had a knot in my throat so big, I had to periodically open my mouth wide to get air. My stomach was tied in a thousand knots. I had thrown up six times already. My hands were cold, and I had chills. If I didn't know what was wrong with me, I would have sworn I had a touch of the flu. I felt truly ill. Life just was not open to giving me any breaks; that much was clear to me. Penny leaned in, and we hugged so tightly my body was becoming weak again. I felt as if I might pass out. But Penny held on tight. Then she broke down crying. Erica came over to get her.

"Listen, we here for y'all. We are all family," Isis cried.

"No, fuck this. This just can't be happening." I jumped up. "I need my keys. Penny didn't see the body. The morgue ain't called. It just can't be her," I screamed.

"It is," Penny cried. "I saw her face, Secret."

Isis grabbed me by the waist. "Wait, I called already, and I'm waiting on them to tell me where they took her," Isis reminded me.

"It can't be her, Isis. We just talked and she shared all those things that happened to her with me. I was still mad but I heard her." I continued to cry.

"And it's good you got to talk to her and found some common ground," Isis said.

I shook my head in disgust at myself. "No, there was no common ground. I was still the same mean bitch I always am. And all I did was cheat myself. I could have told her that I felt bad for the bad hand she had been dealt as a kid. That I understood . . . that . . . that even though I hated her, deep down I loved her." I was sick with guilt. Now she would never know. Somehow I always felt that by not showing Jackie my feelings, I was paying her back. But at this very moment I felt as if I had cheated myself, and there was no other hand for me to play.

"I think she knew that you loved her. And she understood the reason you treated her the way you did. That's the reason at last she opened her heart to you. She had to have you see that she was no monster. Just battered, and bruised. Trying to understand the love that she needed to give to you and Penny, but had never received."

"Yeah, Secret, Jackie knew. When she stayed with me for that time, she opened up to me a lot. That's why I wanted you to sit down with her. She wanted so badly to make it up to you . . . to us for the way she treated us. But she struggled with how. I knew her struggle; that's why I forgave her. I had to. I had enough struggles in my life."

Why had I been so selfish and not listened to Penny back then? She had tried to get me to listen. I had refused. And I had not only cheated myself of Jackie, Penny had suffered because of me, too. "I am so sorry, Penny, for what I done to you. Keeping Jackie away from you when you wanted her in your life. Out of meanness in my heart. I cheated you of a chance to have a relationship with her."

"No, you didn't. So don't feel bad. Jackie and I had a relationship. We still talked on the phone. We still met up and took long walks in the park. We stayed connected as best we could. Unfortunately, she wasn't strong enough to keep fighting the struggle of her childhood. She just couldn't outrun it. No matter how hard she tried. And believe me, she tried. She even joined those AA meetings that I attended, but the hawk was also on her back. And that she couldn't kick . . . See, Secret, we are lucky—our lives were bad, in some ways some would say sad. But Jackie's life was a tragedy. And the only time she could outrun it was when she was in another zone."

I was done. I couldn't think any more. There were just too many thoughts running through my head. We sat and waited for Isis's phone to ring so that we could find out where they had taken Jackie. We were up for hours. It started to get late, and I worried we all might go to sleep and miss the call, so Erica ran out to get Starbucks.

Isis stood to answer the knocking at the door. "I hate when people just don't use the doorbell," I mouthed. But I was sitting in a trancelike state. The minutes that ticked by just didn't seem real.

"Aye." Kirk spoke as he came into the room. He walked over and reached down and hugged Penny. She cried on his shoulder for a minute. He then walked over, reached down, and hugged me. "I'm sorry for your loss," he whispered in my ear. I broke down again. I held on to Kirk for dear life. And it felt good in his arms. I was safe; nothing could touch or hurt me. "It's gone be all right." He rubbed my back gently in a soothing motion.

"I know." I tried to suck my cries back in. My voice was shaky. "This is all my fault. I think I'm being punished for not stepping up and forgiving Jackie for all she done to us. The Bible says honor thy father and mother. I should have obeyed. Now I can't." I cried more on Kirk's shoulder. He rubbed my back until I was calm and no longer sniffing. Erica made it back with the coffee, and she also had food.

"Aye, it's good you brought that food. 'Cause we gone need it." Kirk pulled out a plastic bag that had four fat rolled-up blunts.

"Now that's what I'm motherfucking talkin' 'bout. Fire that shit up." I was excited. "Kirk, that's why you my nigga. You know exactly what to do to make a bitch feel good."

"And I should have known you would come prepared." Isis smiled.

"Shi'd, I try not leave home wit'out it. Besides, you know I got you. Kirk to the rescue." He pulled out a lighter, gently sat the blunt between his two lips, and lit it. "Now I ain't selfish; this yo' crib. And yo' crisis. You get to hit it first." He passed the blunt to me, and I gladly reached for it.

"And I want to hit it, too." Penny spoke up. My necked snapped in her direction.

"Oh, hell naw. Yo' ass tried it. I ain't that sad."

"Fuck that, Secret. I need this. Now hit that shit and pass it. Jackie died today, and I need a lift," Penny said matter-of-factly. I looked at Isis for confirmation.

"Puff and give." Isis nodded her head.

"Rotation this bitch." Kirk lit up another blunt.

In five minutes flat the room was filled with smoke I could barely see my hands in front of me. And like always, Kirk had that fire, so all our problems were soon floating above us, where they would remain until that high came down. But Kirk made it clear that wouldn't be soon, because he planned for us to smoke all four rolled ones, and he had spares in the car. So we geared up to pull an all-nighter. By the time the morgue called to tell us where to find Jackie, we were all on cloud nine with hot wing sauce all over our fingers. We had to air, and we chose which one of us was in the better state to drive. We voted on Isis: she was high, but she was the most competent.

One look at Jackie, though, and we all were sober again. This was some shit I would never forget. I regretted my actions, and what I could have done the very last time I saw Jackie.

# Chapter 40

# Isis

Two months had passed since Jackie had died. I guess you could say things were as back to normal as could be expected. Secret and Penny were doing the best they could to move on, and we all had their back. But there is some pain you just can't keep for someone. Being there meant the most, so that's what we did. Business was still booming and getting busier. Kirk was really boasting and pushing that new project he wanted to see come to life in LA. And since shit had gotten kind of crazy around Miami, Secret, Penny, and I were trying to jump on board to go down and help Kirk out.

We figured if anything it would get us out of Miami for a while. We still loved our city mad crazy, but we needed a getaway. Especially Penny and Secret: the death of Jackie was strong in the air. But what I really planned to do in LA was shop. It was

time I had some fun and broke some banks. I was
tired of sitting on all my money. I wanted to spend
carelessly like Secret and be happy about it.

Tonight was huge for us. We had another huge
shipment coming in, and a lot was riding on it.
Kirk had some big boys in town from Korea who
put in a big investment on the shipment. A lot of it
was already spoken for. It wouldn't even make it to
the streets; it was being shipped here and taken
right away. Kirk was proud of Secret and me for
getting the paperwork ready and seeing that the
numbers were spot on so the shipment could go
off without a hitch. It was always a huge risk on the
big shipments; correct weight was key. Secret and I
had worked on this one for a bit over a month;
even through the drama we managed to stay focused on it. I can't lie—I was nervous but also like,
fuck it. Because one thing I was certain of, I was
good at what I did, so my confidence would get me
through, and I would keep stacking my pockets.
There was no way I was about to lose.

But I was wondering who the hell could be
knocking at my door at this hour. It was late, and I
was trying to get out of the house. If I wasn't on
time, Kirk would trip, and I would have to curse
his ass out, and that I didn't need right before a
huge shipment. I needed my nerves intact like the
packages.

I was surprised to see Bobbi standing at my
door unannounced. I guessed he was trying to get
me back. I had stopped by his house the night before unannounced. I still kinda felt bad about the
way things had gone down between us. We hadn't
been talking, so I wanted to be sure we were still

cool. Unfortunately, I had shown up at the wrong time. I had promised myself that the next time I would call first.

"Uh, hey." I was sure my tone gave away that I was surprised.

"Hey. Just thought I might stop by for minute."

"Oh, yeah, listen, I would like to really apologize to you again for just showing up last night unannounced. I really didn't mean to do that. I just . . ."

"No, don't apologize. You good. I have no problem wit' you popping up. We friends." I wasn't sure why he had added that part. But I guessed it was true. "I wanted to apologize for sending you off like that. I just had a date up in the crib. And I didn't want shit to be awkward."

"Oh, it's cool. Dang, I'm sorry I ruined your date." I was surprised to hear he had a date, especially at his house. Not sure why, though, because Bobbi was good looking. I could see any woman lusting after him. I had, too, at one time.

"Well, I thought I'd stop by. I thought I should probably tell you who was in up in the crib last night." I was not sure why he felt the need to tell me that. Him dating was none of my business. I was about to say just that, but he jumped right on it. "It was Courtney." That got my attention. Miami was big—hell, Florida the state was big—but I only knew one Courtney.

"Courtney. You mean our Courtney that works at Hot Rides." I had to be sure we were speaking of the same person.

"Yep, her." He seemed nonchalant.

"Oh, for real." I'm sure the shitty look was on my face. Not that I was jealous or anything. "I didn't know you two were friends," I threw in to be slick sarcastic. He had been to the shop a couple of times, but I didn't even know they knew each other. And I could not believe Courtney was dating my ex. Of course I knew she was no saint; she would date some random woman's husband every now and again. But I never would have thought she would hook up with my ex. He was right: it was awkward.

"Actually, no, we are not," Bobbi announced. "She came into the store a few weeks back. We got to talking, and I kinda invited her over."

"You did. Okay." I guessed coming from Bobbi, I shouldn't have been surprised, I mean look how he had already deceived me. But I wasn't about to even let that bother me. I had bigger fish to fry. This shipment had to be my main focus. No oopses were allowed to be made.

Bobbi stepped on inside the door past me without being invited. I had to get rid of him quickly, though, because I had to get going. "Listen, Bobbi, I'm glad you came by to clear that up, but I really have to get going." I kept it simple. He could never know my business, because low key I still did not trust him. And he had just confirmed I could not.

"A'ight, can I at least use your bathroom before I go? I been holding all the way over here."

"Sure, go ahead." I figured that shouldn't take him long. I was pretty much ready. I was just watching the clock. I made my way to the den to pour myself a glass of wine. I needed to unwind for a bit and shake Courtney and Bobbi off. I was cool; I didn't want to feel no type of way with Courtney. She was cool people, but clearly she didn't live by the code. Not that we were tight friends or anything, but we hung out together a lot these days. I sipped my wine and shrugged my shoulders. Maybe it was a misunderstanding. Either way I was good. Fuck it.

"That sure looks good. Think I can have a quick drink before I get up outta here?"

I started to say no but figured why not. "Make it quick. No small sips." I smiled.

"Hey, I was just thinking when I went to the bathroom how you used to hate Melvin's small bathroom. And it was never clean enough for you." He chuckled.

Images of Bobbi's apartment popped in my head, and I couldn't help but smile as I remembered exactly what he was talking about. "I swear I hated that entire nasty apartment."

"You stayed having me clean that bathroom over and over every time you had to use it."

"I swear, no matter how many times you did it, it still was disgusting. And that bed and that couch. Just ugh." I was squeamish just thinking about it. "Remember when he had those bedbugs?" Bobbi shook his head and laughed.

"Man, them damn things took over. I kept telling him to call the office and report it."

"I remember. He kept talkin' 'bout they gone charge him. If it hadn't been for you, he probably never would have reported it. And them trifling nasty-ass girls he brought up through there. I simply cannot with your cousin, Bobbi, and memory lane." I waved it off.

"Trust me, I know. Now I look at us, you know, his crib and mine. The shit we able to afford now versus the shit we couldn't back then ..." He shook his head. "It's just a lifetime ago. But I feel the blessings, though."

"I know, right." I had to agree with him. I could relate when I thought about my own situation with Secret, Penny, and me. We lived in a small apartment, struggling, just trying to make it, with the hope of doing better. But never did I imagine us having half of the things we did. Granted, the way we got them was not the best. However, I still thanked God, because my heart was in the right place and one day I wanted to be legit. And I would. "We all had it hard." I sipped my wine.

"Yep."

I looked at my cell phone. The time was ticking. I had to get going. "Listen, I got to get going. So you need to chug that wine down."

"A'ight. I'm gone get out ya hair." He lifted the glass to his lips and emptied it of its liquid. "That's that." He smiled, set his glass down, and started for the door. I followed him so I could lock up.

"See you later." I started to shut the door as soon as he stepped out into the night air.

"Aye, don't forget to call me later when you're not busy. I leave for New Jersey, remember?"

Actually, that had slipped my mind. He had told me about it a few weeks back. "That is tomorrow." I stalled but quickly remembered I had no time to waste. The shipment was key. Nothing could stand in the way of that. "I'll hit you up." I smiled, then shut the door. I went back into the den to get the wineglasses. I took them into the kitchen and loaded them into the dishwasher.

Bobbi was really leaving the next day. I couldn't say that I would miss him, but I had actually gotten used to him being around. I knew he was eventually coming back because he still had the business here in Miami. But he had made it clear that his main focus was the store in New Jersey, where he had made a home for himself since he had been gone. Melvin would be in charge of the day-to-day for the store in Miami. So who knew when Bobbi might come back? What was really odd was that I didn't even know why I was having any thoughts about him leaving, but for some odd reason, I wasn't sure how I felt about him being gone again. It was for the best, though, for reasons just like this: I wasn't sure about him not being around. But I was certain that I didn't want a relationship with him.

# Chapter 41

# Secret

Gearing up for this shipment that would be going down tonight was like mad pressure for it to work with no problems. But no pressure at the same time. Isis and I had worked hard to make sure everything went the way it was planned, and I had no doubt that it would. But I needed to stop by to see Kirk before heading into Custom Hot Rides for the night. I had promised Isis that I would stop by Kirk's house to pick up a file that had some numbers on it for this small package was due to come in an hour before our big shipment.

I still had not talked to him about what had happened between us as far as us sleeping together. I knew he hadn't bothered me because of the loss of Jackie. He knew I had taken it hard. So I figured he was giving me time, and I appreciated that. But my mind was made up; I knew us continuing to be friends was the only option. Since I had a little time to kill before being at the shop, I figured I would talk to him about it while I was at his house.

I pulled into his circular driveway. Isis's name lit up on my cell phone. "What's up, Isis?" I answered.

"Hey, don't forget about the package." She referred to the file I was picking up from Kirk.

"Aye, don't worry. I told you I got. I actually just pulled up. I'ma handle this and get in gear."

"I'm wit' it" was her reply. With that I ended the call. When talking on the phone, we tried to keep business conversation at a minimum, never actually saying what we were talking about.

After shutting off the engine to my truck, I made my way up to the door. I rang the doorbell about six times before Kirk finally opened the door. "Damn, nigga, I was about to kick this bitch in. What the hell is you doing up in here?" I stepped past him and looked around.

"You just impatient." He shut the door.

"Whatever." I turned and headed toward his den–lounge area. Just as I expected, he had a bottle of Hennessy out and a freshly rolled blunt.

"Shit, you know exactly what to do when ya' girl comin'." I smiled.

"No doubt." He sat down.

"Wait, I ain't interrupting nothing, am I? You got one of them thirsty bitches up in here?" I always called his chicks thirsty, because in my opinion they all were gold diggers. Not that Kirk gave a fuck. He had plenty of money.

"Why you come in here wit' that shit all the time. Ain't nothin' up in her but the bills." He picked up the blunt.

"Good, I can smoke in peace. Last thing I need is to have to slap one of your stupid bitches." It had been a time or two I had to check his hoes because they thought they were crunkier than they really were. They saw this half-breed skin of mine and took it for weakness until I got in that ass.

"You wild, girl." He lit the blunt.

"Hey, you got that file ready? Isis will kill me if I forget it."

"Right there." He pointed to the table. "So what's up?" He looked at me. I could see from the look in his eyes what he was thinking. He passed me the blunt. I took a puff, let it out, and sighed.

"Listen, I been wanting to talk to you about what happened between us. But, as you know, shit been crazy wit' my life." He reached for the blunt and nodded his head in agreement. "You know we been friends for a long time. Cool as fuck . . ." I added. I needed to really stress where I was coming from. "You were there for me when I didn't have nobody. Made sure I was straight. . . ." Kirk had hit the blunt three times, and it was burning short. I needed to get to the point so that he could pass it back to me. "What I'm tryin' to say is, our friendship means a lot to me. I won't risk messing that up for a relationship. What happened between us was nice. I mean, I really enjoyed it." My middle thumped just thinking about it. I damn near wanted to rip his clothes off for one last go-round. But I chilled.

I was done talking because I didn't know what else to say. I glared at Kirk to get a vibe of what he might be thinking. For some reason, though, I kinda got the feeling he wasn't all the way there. He seemed to be listening but not all the way in tune. "Yo. what's up? Pass the blunt or something." I spoke up.

"Ahh, mad bad. Here." He passed it to me. I almost got the feeling he had just joined me in the room. I hit the blunt, then exhaled. "So you cool wit' what I said?"

"Yeah, I get it. I mean, you know I want you. But I get it." He reached for the blunt.

"Naw, nigga, not so quick. You done hit this bitch five times while I was talkin'. I'm making up." I hit the blunt again. While exhaling, I again saw that distant look of strangeness in Kirk's eyes. Something else was on his mind, or I was tripping. "What' really good, though?" I passed the blunt back to him.

"Everything good. Ready for this shipment."

"Nah, what's up, Kirk? What's really on your mind? I know you, nigga, like you know me. And I can tell when something ain't right. What's up? No bullshittin'."

This time there was no hesitating; there was definitely something up. "Listen, I don't want you to trip out. Be cool when I say this."

"What?" I was impatient. Kirk had never seemed to be worried about shit. His head was always one step ahead in the game. He made the shit look easy. But right now the world seemed to be on his shoulders. And somehow I felt it had not just got there. Maybe this was what Isis had been asking me about. How had I missed the signs until now?

"I think someone is after me. I ain't sure, though." He actually seemed paranoid. This was not the time for this. Especially tonight. Too much was riding on the shipment.

"Who after? And why?" I inquired.

"Shit, if I knew that, I would be straight. But I just don't know. Can't put my finger on it. I think they followin' me. I had my niggas follow me to see if they saw anybody tailing me, but ain't nobody see shit. I don't know, maybe I'm just trippin'."

"Maybe, hopefully so. You in for the night, though? This shit goes down in less than six hours," I reminded him.

"Aye, we good. I ain't worried. Shit just fuckin' wit' me that I ain't sure. It's like cat and mouse. I'm a killer. I don't fuck around wit' it. I just fuck niggas up," he said matter-of-factly. "I done did a lot of shit, and you know that. Hell, I ain't halfway done." He laughed, hit the blunt, and let it out in the ashtray. "Fuck all this, though; forget that shit I said. We gone do this job tonight, then we gettin' ready. We gone get all this fuckin' money. We ain't got no fuckin' problems. You still game?"

"Shit, you know I'm down to get this money wit' you. But right now I need to use the bathroom and get my ass outta here."

"No doubt. You know where the bathroom at?" He pulled out another blunt, ready to roll up.

"Damn, Kirk, stop with them blunts, or I ain't gone never get outta here." I laughed and stood up just as the doorbell rang. I headed for the bathroom.

I had to hurry up and get going before Isis called me tripping. I frowned at the thought that I couldn't smoke the next blunt with Kirk. After flushing the toilet, I thought I heard loud noises, but I dismissed it. After fixing my clothes, I turned on the warm water from the sink to wash my hands once again. I thought I heard loud voices. I turned off the water but didn't hear anything. As I dried my hands, I heard what sounded like bumping or, worse, a scuffle. Then the loud voices again. I realized there was definitely some yelling going on. I cracked the bathroom door.

I made the voices out to be male. Kirk's was one of them. He called someone a "nigga." My heart sank. I needed to see what was really going on. Quietly as I could, I opened the bathroom door wide enough for me to step out. Taking slow, light steps, I made my way down the hallway and to the corner, where I could see into the room where Kirk had been. I paused as I heard a loud *thunk* like a table being slammed. I caught the center of my chest with my right hand. I took in a deep breath and continued. I needed to see what was going on.

Then I heard an unfamiliar voice say, "This is for killin' my brother."

"Who is your brother?" Kirk's voice sounded faint at best.

"Guess you kill so many motherfuckers you can't remember. Well, this one you will wish you could remember if you could remember. My brother was Rupp." Rupp was the guy I had set up to be robbed as revenge for raping Penny. I froze at the mention of his name. And it was the most shocking piece of information I could have imagined hearing. Not that Rupp had a brother, but that he had found Kirk and actually had the nerve to come to his house. I steadied myself up against the wall and straightened my posture before finding the courage to peep around the corner.

My breathing and my heart seemed to stop as I saw Kirk lying on his floor on his back with a man standing over him. And it was no mystery to me that he held a Ruger pointed at Kirk's head.

Kirk said, "You got me, my nigga, so let's do it."
Tears ran down my face as I watched him be the
strong man that I knew him to be. Not afraid of shit.
I could not believe what I was seeing. I watched as
the Ruger pumped not one but two bullets into
Kirk's skull, then one to his chest. I had to cover my
mouth to keep from screaming out loud. Suddenly
I realized I was there with the guy alone. Quietly, I
somehow found the strength to find a place to
hide, which turned out to be in the closet of one
of Kirk's guest rooms.

I was crying silently and shaking real bad as I
slid behind the clothes to get to the back of the
closet. Rupp's brother's face was now clear to me.
He had been the guy who had come into Custom
Hot Rides months back and started fake drama
about his car being messed up by them and refusing to pay. Kirk had had his crew throw him out of
the shop. Now I saw that that must have been a
part of his plan to figure out who exactly Kirk was.
But how did he know anything about Kirk? Did he
know who I was? Was he looking for Penny? After
all, Penny was the reason Kirk had killed Rupp.
And I was the reason Rupp had kidnapped and
raped Penny. Was he the mystery of that cat and
mouse game that Kirk speculated about, that
someone who was following him around? Maybe
Kirk hadn't been paranoid at all. But I would probably never know. I heard footsteps getting closer
and closer to me; in fact, they were right in front
of me.

# Chapter 42

# Isis

Everything at the shop was set up and ready to go for the sit-and-wait, which meant we had plenty of snacks and a blunt for the night while we patiently waited on our shipments. But Secret had not arrived yet. She was supposed to be stopping by Kirk's house to pick up some paperwork that we needed for this small shipment we had coming in. But it had been over an hour since I had spoken to her, and I thought she would have arrived by now. Knowing Secret, though, if Kirk had pulled out a blunt or two, she was not leaving until she hit them both. That was her; but she also knew how important the night was, and Kirk did, too. So I was sure she wouldn't play around with that.

I picked up my cell phone and dialed her number but got no answer. I guessed that if she was running a few minutes behind, she didn't feel like hearing my mouth, because she knew as soon as she answered the phone I was going in. I ended the call and tried again, and it was the repeat of the first call: ringing non-stop until the voice mail came on. I decided leaving her a message was a waste of time, so I canned that option. I was hungry, so I fished a steak taco with cilantro and onions out of the stash I had ordered and picked up. I bit into it and was in taco heaven. Lucky for Secret, it calmed my nerves.

I was almost done with my taco when the banging on the front door got my attention. I knew it was nobody but Secret; she was famous for forgetting her keys to the shop. Stuffing the rest of my taco into my mouth, I rushed off toward the front door. As I got close to the front entry door, I slowed my pace as I realized that it was not Secret at the door but Bobbi. I had just left him less than two hours ago and told him I had to work. So I was clueless as to why he was standing outside of Custom Hot Rides banging on the door.

"Ahh, what's up, Bobbi?" I asked with my eyebrows raised.

"Aye, I know you busy, but I really would like to take you out to late-night dinner when you done here."

I couldn't believe he was in fact talking about dinner. What part of work was he confused about? "Bobbi, I told you I have work. I ain't talkin' late night. I'm talkin' early morning."

"Hey, beggars can't be choosers. But I really want to take you out. Like I said, I'm leaving tomorrow, and this means a lot to me." I just glared at him. At the moment I was agitated that Secret had not shown up. Instead, I was for the second time in the same night staring down Bobbi and his persistence. I looked over his shoulder; still there was no Secret. And here he was standing in my face like eating with me was in his last will and testament.

"A'ight, Bobbi. I'll eat wit' you, but it will be hours from now if you can stay up."

"Can I stay up? Girl, I'm a night owl. I know you remember," he joked.

"Yeah, I remember you sleeping well through the night," I reminded him. I gave a light chuckle.

"I got this. Trust me. I'm in."

"Cool. I'll call you when I'm done here."

"Well, I was hoping I could drive you. You know, like a date . . . Wait, hold up. I know how you feel about us and dates. But I just wanted to take you out, me the driver, you the passenger." I really wasn't in the mood to protest. I really just needed to get rid of him and fast.

"Whatever, I'll call you when I'm ready. Now you gotta go." I all but pushed him out the door.

"And I promise I will, but can I please use your bathroom?"

Annoyed, I sighed. "Bobbi, no, you have got to go." I was tired of being nice.

"Please. I promise to hurry," he begged.

"Hurry your ass." I rolled my eyes, annoyed. He rushed off toward the back. I walked back to the office to grab my phone to see if Secret had called, and if not, to call her again. Checking my phone, I discovered there were no missed calls from Secret. I dialed her number again, and there was no answer. A funny feeling was suddenly in the pit of my stomach. There was no doubt in my mind that Secret was running late. She would not be this late.

Not when it came to business. I started to call Kirk to find out what time she had left his place.

I heard footsteps. I turned around. "Bobbi, you finis—" Instead of finishing my sentence, I was stunned that I was staring down the barrel of gun. And to my complete horror, it was Bobbi's hand holding the gun in my face.

For a minute, we just stared at each other. I thought about the first day I ever saw him standing the parking lot of the apartments that Secret, Penny, and I lived in at the time. I could see the sweat that dripped off him as he stood up straight from under the hood of his cousin's car, which he was working on. Suddenly, I could remember the scent of the Polo I had bought for him on the first Christmas we had spent together. I could see us rolling around in my bed playing. Then I remembered the heartbreak I felt when I realized he had stolen from me and run off. How sick I felt at his betrayal. Somehow I had been a fool and allowed him back into my life. And for the second time, he was here to hurt me again, maybe this time permanently.

"Are you surprised?" he had the nerve to ask me. He had this look of satisfaction on his face. I was dumbfounded and clueless, all rolled up into one.

"Actually, I am. Seeing that I truly wanted to believe you were not the scum of the earth that I thought you were. So what is it you want from me this time, Bobbi?"

"Good you asked."

"You are such punk-ass bitch. Constantly stalking a female to come up. So tasteless," I spat at him.

"Who the fuck are you to judge me? Ain't shit you got legit. You think I don't know?" He laughed. "Well, I do. Now here is what you can do for me. I know all about that shipment coming in tonight," he revealed, I was at a loss for words. "Yeah, thought that might get a reaction out of you. I want it—all of it."

"You must be out of your fuckin' mind. Do you know who that shit belongs to?"

"Frankly, my dear, I don't give a fuck. I'm here to collect, and I will tonight."

"Such a fucking snake," I hissed at him. "How do you know about this?"

"Easy, I eavesdropped on a call you had wit' Secret. Remember that bullshit you told me about you were just Customer Service? Like I was stupid enough to believe that. Why do you think I came back to Miami? I knew all about your whole operation before I even touched down. See, I had a cousin who worked for Kirk's scheming ass, and he told me all about you and Secret's position. You might know my kinfolk. He's missing now. I'm sure your boy Kirk had something to do wit' that also. But fuck all, I'm trying to get this money. I just been waiting on you and that cock-blocking, hating-ass bitch Secret to make a way for me to make my move. So thank you."

"Fuck you. Don't be calling me names," I spat. "She tried to warn me about your snake ass, but I refused to listen . . . I should have known better, but here I was stupid, trying to forgive your black ass."

"Just like a female. Y'all always lettin' your guard down too early. But I knew bringing you back into my life was gone be a piece of cake. You been fighting hard to resist me. I see it in your eyes. You still want me. Gone admit it?" I couldn't believe he was using this time to be conceited.

"I just need to know why, Bobbi. After all I ever done for you, I never would have hurt you. I trusted you. And the whole time, I was being taken. Just tell me why." I genuinely wanted to know. What drove him to betray someone who cared so deeply for him and supported him in every way? "I even supported your pipe dream about that drive-up car service shit. When everybody else just laughed at you, it was me who encouraged you to follow through with it."

"I admit the car thing was cool. But it was not enough, it would never take off fast enough for me to get where I was trying to go. See, buss it. I was tired of living in the hood scraping just to get by. But I met you, and I thought you were cute, but I ain't never had it in my head to be in no committed relationship. That changed when I found out about the money. I wanted it. All of it. Then I thought, why not stick around and add to that. So I did . . ." He looked away briefly. His eyes were cold as they fell back on me. He was silent as if I might respond. "I wanted that money and a future. You had it, so you became the prey.

"So just like that, you used me."

"Aye, don't take it so personal. I said I thought you were cute. Money just meant more than you. And the fact of the matter is I never loved you." He laughed. "I'm a funny guy, right?"

"Nope, you a fuckin' idiot. Do you honestly believe you gone take this shipment and ride outta of here on a white horse?"

"Damn right, you just sit back and watch." He was sure of himself.

"Boy, please believe me when I say America ain't big enough for you to hide. 'Cause when Kirk figure out you got this shit, you might as well put the gun to your own head. 'Cause, bitch, you through." I was sure he was unfazed by everything that I had said. But that was because he didn't know who he was messing around with. Kirk knew niggas all over the globe. Bobbi was done. And that much was official.

"See, that's the problem: y'all so busy worshipping the nigga. You don't even see that he distracted." That statement hit me like a ton of bricks. I instantly thought about the odd behavior and vibe that Kirk had been giving off lately. As much as I wanted to deny it, I had noticed it weeks ago. Something was amiss with Kirk; his mind just seemed to be busy all the time. And if I and others could see it . . . That was problem. Kirk always kept a stone face in public. He probably wouldn't even blink if someone was shooting a machine gun right over his head. But lately he had been a little quieter. In thinking about Kirk, Secret flashed before my eyes again. She was still not there.

"First off, all businessmen are distracted at one time or another. But at least he trying. Kirk has his hands full wit' the business, and he still working . . . Stop worrying 'bout over here. We got this." I gave him attitude. I was annoyed with his entire conversation.

"You act like this shit legit or something. Isis, this is a drug operation run by a wanna-be kingpin. The shit gone fall eventually anyway. I'm just giving it a head start."

"Whatever, Bobbi, keep stealing for your come-up. You just jealous that Kirk's business took off."

"Fuck that nigga. After tonight that nigga can work on startin' from scratch. Now what time your hoe-ass friend coming back?"

"She'll be here." I kept it short. He still sounded like we were friends. I kicked myself a thousand times just thinking about the fact that I had actually backtracked and dated the asshole. I would never forgive myself.

"And there is something else I think you should know. That little bitch Courtney, she's dead."

"What do you mean dead?" I was confused.

"I mean it's lights out for the nosy-ass, money-hungry slut. The bitch would do whatever to get some money. Even try to con me, and that's where she fucked up."

"What are you talking about, Bobbi?"

"I killed her ass. Last night when she came over to my crib, I pumped two slugs into her chest. She gone."

Tears stung at my eyes. "Why? Why you kill that girl?"

"See, you not listening, I just told you she was nosy. Turns out the girl I hired at my store was Courtney's cousin. Melvin had been banging the hoe, and she overheard our plans about this takeover. She called up Courtney, and her greedy ass tried to extort me for money. And I was not having that shit. So last night I took care of her and her big-mouth-ass cousin. Actually, you came over when Melvin and I were dismembering the bodies. You showing up really was an inconvenience. I had to hurry up and take off the plastic jumpsuit I had on

to keep the blood from staining my clothes." The
look in his eyes sent tingles up my spine.

"You are a fuckin' monster. She did not deserve
that," I screamed. Suddenly I felt bad. I should
have never believed that Courtney would betray me
by dating Bobbi. I was no longer angry with Bobbi;
I was horrified, dismayed, and pissed. I could see
bloody red. I could not believe he had murdered
Courtney in cold blood.

"Oh, and last. I think it's time you know that
Melvin is not my cousin."

"Who gives a fuck?" I yelled in his direction.
"Your whole pathetic life is built on lies."

"If that's the way you feel, you'll hate this one.
I'm bisexual. Not only is Melvin not my cousin, we
been sleepin' together for years." I felt as if I would
faint as I stood still feeling light-headed.

"You a fag?" I screamed and went to rush him.
But he pointed the gun directly between my eyes.

"Uh-uh. Stay back. This will be painful." I could
not believe what I was hearing. The room seemed to
blur. "Yeah, all the condoms you used to fine around
the house and thought they were some random girl
Melvin was messing wit'. Nope, they were ours." I
bent over and placed my hands on my knees. The vi-
olations from Bobbi's mouth seemed to be never-
ending. I didn't know what was due to come of his
mouth next. One thing was for sure: I felt rage.

"I'm gone kill you, motherfucker." My tone was
calm, but my anger was a raging bull. "You sleep
wit' me and put me in danger. I could have some
sexually transmitted disease or, worse, AIDS." My
eyes blinked, and they were bloodshot red.

"Bitch, don't be dramatic. We used condoms,
remember?" He had the nerve to remind me. He

wore a stupid grin on his face. I was shaken inside and out. I could not believe I had been sleeping with Satan.

"Nigga, ain't shit wrong wit' being dramatic. And I should have known by the sneaky way that you moved that you were somebody's bitch. Taking it straight up the ass, huh?"

Secret stepped out of nowhere and put a gun to Bobbi's head. I was surprised, stunned, and grateful, all at the same time.

"Bitch, fuck you." Bobbi's words were tough but the look on his face was cold, as if he had seen a ghost. "I should have known you would fuck this up. Damn, I forgot to look out for you." He bit his bottom lip.

"Well, I guess the first lesson you should learn is stop talking so fuckin' much and hit the target." Secret pushed his head with the gun. "You a'ight, Isis?" She looked at me.

"Courtney dead." Secret's eyes were full of questions. "He killed her."

"Hoe-ass nigga. Don't worry, this nigga 'bout to meet her in a few seconds." Secret pulled back the trigger.

"No!" I screamed.

"Isis, don't start this shit. I told you before, don't trust this nigga. But naw, you said fuck that and went off playin' hopscotch wit' his ass. Now look at what he done. Up in this bitch tryin' to take what's ours." Secret pushed Bobbi's head again with the gun.

"And you were right about every lowdown, piece-of-shit name that you called him. But make no mistake about it, this asshole's death belongs to me."

"Ha ha." Bobbi laughed. "Bitch, please, tell you

what. You shoot your hoe-ass friend over here, and I'll go ahead and marry you and give you the life you want. 'Cause ain't no other nigga gone put up wit' you. Shi'd, it ain't like you light-skinned."

Rushing across the room, I snatched the gun out of Secret's waiting hand and smashed it across his face. Blood flew everywhere, all over my clothes. His two front teeth landed right next to my feet.

"I might be dark-skinned, but you a toothless bitch. Now you stand there and bleed. And remember the last thing you seen was my dark-skinned face."

"Fuuc . . ." He tried to mumble something, but I was done listening to him.

"No, fuck you. This for Courtney, bitch." I pumped two bullets between his eyes. At first his body stood erect, his eyes half open. Then he fell backward. We could hear his skull crack when it hit the floor.

"Damn, that nigga got a hard-ass head," Secret mouthed.

"What took you so long to get here? I was worried about you." Tears rushed down Secret's face, and she started to sob. "Aye, what?" I asked.

"Man, Isis, Kirk is dead."

"Naw, Secret. Naw." My hands became weak; the gun in my hand almost dropped. I had to grip it. Secret reached for me, and we hugged for a minute, both crying. "What the hell happened?" Secret stepped back.

"I went over there to get the documents, and he was acting strange, something like how you said he was. We smoked a blunt. I asked him about it, and he admitted that he thought somebody was following him but then said it was all good.

"The doorbell rang. I went to use the bathroom. Next thing I hear is loud voices and a scuffle. I sneak out into the hallway to hear the guy say he was Rupp's brother and he shot Kirk. . . . And, Isis, it was that same game that was here a few months back, and Kirk's crew beat up and threw him out."

"Are you sure?" I was stunned.

"Yes, it was him."

"So then what?"

"He shot Kirk. He dead. I had to hide because he searched the house. I hid under some clothes in one of Kirk's closets. He almost found me. But his phone rang and he left."

"This can't be happenin'." I was in utter shock.

"What if he knows about me and Penny? What if he lookin' for us?"

"If he was, he would have found y'all by now. More than likely it was Kirk he wanted."

Secret gnawed on her fist. "You probably right."

"What do we do now?"

"Ain't shit to do but get ready for this shipment."

"How? What about him?" I pointed to Bobbi's lifeless body.

"We need to clean this shit up. It's just like his ass to make a mess. All this fuckin' blood for nothin'," Secret complained. "We got to make this shit happen and quick. We'll clean this up, wrap him up in a sheet, and dump the body. He a bitch, so nobody but his faggot friend Melvin will care.

Her idea seemed okay with me. I looked at the

clock. "We have three hours before the small ship-ment. You got the file from Kirk's house?"

"Hell, yeah. Let's do this."

We worked fast as we could to clean up the bloody mess. There was plenty of bleach in the back that the cleaner used to get the building clean. Secret found a sheet in Kirk's office; who knew why he had a sheet in his office, but we couldn't care less. We wrapped Bobbi up and dragged him to the back door, where Secret had driven the truck around to, then with all of our might lifted his heavy body up and dumped him in the closest gutter we could find.

By the time we made it back to Custom Hot Rides, we both were tired. Lifting Bobbi had been no joke; my arms were sore. And Secret claimed the same about her back. But business was on, as usual, and we fixed ourselves up and prepared. The final shipment was delivered, and it went off as planned. Afterward, Secret made the call to the big man and told him what was up with Kirk and that she and I would make the drops. And like true Kirk girls, we did it. He had taught us well; there was nothing about the business we didn't know. There was no doubt in our minds that he would want us to rise to the occasion and boss up. And with heavy hearts, we did.

# Chapter 43

# Isis

What can I say? With Kirk being dead, we were at a crossroads. Nothing was certain, the streets were on check. And nobody was safe. You had to watch your back from all angles, because anybody could possibly sneak up on you, but Secret and I were on it. Custom Hot Rides was still in business for the moment; we hadn't decided what to do with it just yet. But money was still coming in, and we had gone ahead with the orchestration of a few shipments. I mean somebody had to, or the streets would wild out. Fiends needed their fix, and the workers needed their cash. So it was simple. But this was not our job, and we knew that.

In the meantime, we were trying to get our personal lives back on track. I was focusing more on me—like having some free time—but it came at a bad time, when Secret and I were dang near at the top and becoming fill-in kingpins. Secret and

Penny were still mourning Jackie and trying to move forward. Secret had started seeing Dr. Cesaley Wright for a few sessions, trying to come to grips with her emotions, her love-slash-hate for Jackie. Penny seemed to be healing fast, physically and mentally. Things were crazy but getting better.

"Aye, so what's up? Did you book the tickets for Jamaica last night or what?" Secret was really bugging me about the trip. We had made up our minds that the trip was happening. Regardless of what was going on, we refused to put it off any longer. Life was much too short and the way things were set up around us, we had better not take it for granted. So all of us, Penny, Secret, Erica, and I, were catching a flight and would be lying on the beach in Jamaica in less than twenty-four hours, for an entire week.

"No, I . . ."

"What the hell you mean, no?" Secret cut me off before I could finish. "Did you not tell me you would take care of this? I got my Louis bags out; this ain't no game." She snapped her neck. I laughed. "Ain't shit funny." She rolled her neck in my direction.

"If you would let me talk, I could have said, no, I didn't book it. I called a travel agent this morning, one of the best. She is getting everything set up. And she will call me when she is done."

"Oh, my bad, girl. You know I got bad nerves."

"Whatever. You need to just pipe down. I told you I got this. Just go home, pack your bags, and wait on my call."

"Shi'd, not a problem I can do that. Penny and Erica already packed; they did it last night. After they called me and got ten stacks and hit up the mall."

"I hope you told them they can't take all that with them." I grinned.

"At least I tried. But for real, me and you need to hit up Macy's real quick for some beach wear."

"Aye, now I can get wit' that," I agreed. "So are we good while we gone?"

"Yep, ain't no shipments coming in. And everybody stacked, all corners are covered."

"Good. I need peace of mind while we're away. I set up the appointments for us to look at a few spots for the store when we get back." We were in the process of opening up the shoe store. We just needed to find a spot. We had a few good options; all we had to do was choose.

"Good. I been talking to some good vendors for shoes. We 'bout to fit some feet up in Miami."

"I can't wait." My cell phone rang. "Hello. Yes, I'll be by in a couple of hours. Thank you." I ended the call. I couldn't hide the grin on my face.

"Who was that? Got you showing all your gums," Secret teased.

"That was the travel agent. Our flight leaves in less than twelve hours."

"Yeah, baby. Jamaica, here we come." Secret stood up and danced. "Lock this bitch up and let's go." She referred to the store.

"I'm wit' it. But first let's hit Macy's."

We started to walk out of the office. Secret's cell rang. She had a strange look on her face as she surveyed the number. "Who is it?" I mouthed quietly, only moving my lips.

"Kirk's connect." Her eyes were apprehensive.

"Answer," I mouthed. We had been dealing with his people for the past few weeks since Kirk's death. I wondered if we had made the wrong move on something. All the shipments had been good. Nothing was tampered with or pulled over. So what else could it be? Secret had only called his direct number when Kirk had first died so she didn't have it saved. Other than that, his people got in touch with us here. Something had to be up. I was nervous. The last thing I needed was a bullet between the eyes because something wasn't right.

"Secret here," she answered her phone. I literally held my breath waiting to see what she would say next. "Yep, she right here." My heart really sank when she said that. Why was he asking about me? What had I done? Or who had put my name in their mouth? "Yeah, let me put my phone on speaker."

"What?" I mouthed, stepping backward as if I would take off running.

"He wants to talk to both of us," she answered, moving her lips only. She moved the phone away from her mouth.

"He yo' friend, remember. You met him and kicked, not me," I reminded her.

"We didn't kick. Now come on," she begged.

"I don't want to," I mouthed in a whisper.

"Come on here." Secret yanked my arm, pulling me close to her. "A'ight, we here."

"Isis, right?" I was surprised at how well he said my name. The man ran Miami and many more states. I was almost honored that he knew of me.

"Yes," I said in a clear, steady tone. The last thing I wanted to do was sound weak. Why I cared what he thought, I had no idea. But I did.

"I just wanted to let you two know that I ain't been sleepin' on the work y'all down there puttin' in. But I ain't surprised. Kirk told me that y'all could fill his shoes if anything ever went down." Secret and I both looked at each other. Kirk really had made us sound good. I was stunned he thought that much of us. I mean, all we did was the paperwork. "And he was right. Shit been tight with no hiccups since y'all been in charge. That goes a long way in this industry. There are niggas that's been in the game for years that can step up and do the shit y'all been doing."

Secret and I again looked at each other; we didn't know what to say. All we had been trying to do was keep the streets calm and continue that bread until we figured out the next step. And follow our main rule.

"This is our city. We got to be sure shit legit around here. And no matter what, we hustle hard," Secret added.

"Well, take a bow. With that I got to be straight up. The area need some permanent bosses. Basically Kirk's job needs to be filled. And I think you two are perfect for the job."

I nearly choked on my spit. Had we just been asked to become female kingpins? Again Secret and I stared at each other.

"Well, we kinda—" I started to say something, but he cut me off.

"Tell you what. I got a meeting with a few of the bosses tomorrow. It'll be in Miami. I'll have my people hit you up with the address."

"But . . ." I started again, but he ended the call. "What about our flights?"

"Good question." Secret looked clueless. "Fuck that, we leaving here headed for Jamaica tonight." Secret sounded confident. "Besides, what the hell would we do being female kingpins?"

                        *   *   *

Secret and I both looked up as we heard a plane
fly over our head, and we climbed into an unknown
Cadillac Escalade. We were being whisked off to the
spot for the meeting. I wondered if it would go well
when I turned him down. I was prepared.

"Welcome, first female kingpins." Secret and I
stopped in our tracks as we were greeted with what
I guessed were our new titles. Problem was we had
not even confirmed that we were taking them.
Hell, we had our fights rebooked for today, and we
were scheduled to leave in six hours. So we had to
make this fast. Shit was probably about to get ugly.

*No one betrays better than family . . .*
*No Loyalty*
Enjoy the following excerpt of "Dangerous
Liasons" from *No Loyalty*
By De'nesha Diamond and A'zayler

# Chapter 1

After weeks of a record rainfall, the sun returned to southern California in time for the funeral for Javid Ramsey. It was good turnout of family and friends. Even Javid's estranged parents made an appearance. Of course, they sobbed on one another's shoulders and occasionally cornered the widow for details of their son's tragic end and why there was such a hurry to cremate the body.

Stone-faced and dry-eyed, Klaudya Ramsey gave no fucks about their fat tears and had no interest in assuaging their guilt for having financially cut their son off years ago—and for never welcoming her into the family when she married Javid.

Truth be told, Klaudya didn't even give a fuck about the man lying in the casket. In life, and especially in love, Klaudya had only asked for one thing: loyalty. Muthafuckas act like it's the hardest thing to give to their loved ones when it should be the easiest.

Lieutenant Erik Armstrong and his partner Lieutenant Joe Schneider, late to the service, blended in with the attending guests.

Armstrong kept his gaze centered on the dry-eyed widow while her eight-year-old twins Mya and Mykell looked like their beautiful mother's opposites, especially the boy. His small body trembled and shook with racking, silent sobs before the bronze urn.

Across from the grieving Ramseys stood another stone-faced observer, Nichelle Mathis—Klaudya's young mother. For over a year, the mother and daughter kept the Calabasas' grapevine buzzing. To Armstrong's chagrin, he'd played a part in it all. Only he believed he was helping an estranged mother and daughter heal their relationship, not setting up a death match between the two of them. If only he could have put two and two together much sooner—like the night of the first murder . . .

*The house looked like a war zone.*

*Veteran first responders mumbled to each other that they had never seen this level of carnage in their entire careers. In the center of the living room, a black male, wearing only a pair of silk boxers, lay sprawled across the floor with half of his skull splattered on the ceiling and walls. A bloody bat was clenched in his left hand.*

*"My God," Detective Erik Armstrong whispered, shaking his head. "The whole damn world has gone crazy."*

*"No shit, Sherlock," his partner, Detective Hugh Schneider, grumbled back, taking it all in.*

*The police and emergency responders held a brief debate*

*on whether they need to take the lone survivor, eight-year-old Klaudya Ramsey, to the hospital or straight to the police station. Soon after an ambulance arrived, she was told she needed to see a doctor.*

*Detective Armstrong cocked his head and smiled at the wide-eyed child. "Did you hear me, sweetheart?"*

*Klaudya couldn't unglue her lips to respond or stop the tears from streaming down her blood-splattered face.*

*The cop's concern dissolved into pity. "Poor thing. You're still in shock." He comforted the child. "Is there anyone we can call? A family member?"*

*Klaudya bunched her shoulders and sidestepped the cop's touch.*

*Armstrong took the hint and backed off.*

*It took forever for an extra ambulance to arrive. More people drifted in and out of the girl's face, asking questions. She stared, her bottom lip trembling, while the bodies of her family were carried out on stretchers.*

*At long last, her mother, Nichelle Mathis, was escorted out of the house. She held her head down. Her hands were cuffed behind her back.*

*Detective Armstrong pulled the child closer as they both watched her blood-covered mother marched toward a patrol car. At its back door, Nichelle locked gazes with her daughter.*

*Klaudya shivered. The ride to the hospital passed by in a blur. When a doctor and nurse came to see her behind a curtain, they wore matching plastic smiles and launched the same questions. Frustration wrung more water out of her near-empty tear ducts.*

*The questions slowed to a trickle.*

*"Nod or shake your head if you feel any pain," the doctor instructed before checking out her bruises. It was*

*stupid because she was already in pain. Everywhere. But she refused to nod or shake her head.*

*By the time the doctor and nurse left her alone behind the curtain, their smiles were thin and flat. Later, she was taken to a strange place and led into a kid's room filled with toys. She was told to wait and that someone would be in in a minute to talk to her.*

*"Feel free to play with anything you want," a woman, whose name she'd already forgotten, said. Once the door closed, Klaudya sat trembling in the small room, covered in her father's blood. The bright toys clashed with slate gray walls, giving her conflicting vibes on how she was supposed to feel. She wished she could stop crying. How many times had her mother said that she wasn't a baby anymore? But it was hard, and she was scared.*

*Each tick on the clock matched the rhythm of her pounding eardrums. After two solid hours of it, Klaudya's head ached, and her eyelids were impossible to keep open. She'd nod off and jerk herself awake every other minute. Her next wave of tears was of frustration instead of anger. She wanted to go home and crawl into her bed.*

*Outside the door, she heard the police officers shuffle back and forth in the hallway. Maybe they forgot she was in there. It was possible, she reasoned. Adults always got busy and ignored her all the time. Klaudya wrestled with the decision whether she should leave on her own. She knew where she lived. She'd taken the city bus home plenty of times. Only . . . she didn't have any money. You can't do anything without money.*

*Her eyelids were like bricks again. She caved and laid her head on the table. Tonight's horror sped behind her closed lids. She could still see her father lunging.*

*Bang!*

*Klaudya woke with a jump.*

*A strange woman smiled at her. "I'm sorry. Did I startle you?" She closed the metal door behind her.*

*Lips zipped, Klaudya eyed the woman crossing over to the table.*

*When the woman settled into the chair across from her, she made her introduction. "I'm Mrs. Durham. You're Klaudya, right?"*

*Silence.*

*"Do you mind if I talk to you for a minute?"*

*Silence.*

*"Oookay." The woman held onto her smile. "You're in shock and a bit confused about all the things going on right now—that's understandable. You're probably even scared and that's okay too." She stretched a hand out, but Klaudya jerked away from her icy touch.*

*"Can I ask whether you remember what happened tonight?"*

*Silence.*

*"Do you remember anything at all?"*

*The image of her father's gun firing flashed in her head, but she said instead, "Can I go home?"*

*Mrs. Durham's ridiculous smile vanished, and her thin lips flat-lined. "I'm sorry, sweetheart. It may be a while before you can do that. But we're working on getting you placed somewhere safe. Everything is going to be all right."*

*Tears pooled in Klaudya's eyes. "But . . . but . . ." She swallowed hard, but it was still hard to slow her breathing. "What about momma? She's coming with me, right?"*

*"Aww, sweetie. I'm afraid not." Durham reached for the girl's hand again, and again, Klaudya pulled farther away.*

"I want my momma. Now!" Klaudya's bottom lip trembled.

Mrs. Durham shook her head. "I'm afraid it may be a long time before that happens."


"When can I see my daughter?" Nichelle asked the first officer entering the interrogation room.

"We'll get to that in due time." Armstrong settled wide-legged into the chair across from her while his partner stayed back and leaned against the door.

"She's scared and was in shock when I left her. I have to talk to her and make her understand that everything is going to be all right. I'm going to take care of everything."

Armstrong's eyes narrowed as he watched her fret. She hadn't been processed and was still covered in her husband's blood. Her eyes were unusually wide.

"Calm down, Mrs. Mathis. Your daughter is in good hands. She is being well taken care of."

"But I will get to see her again, right? I can get one of the girls down at the club to bring her in for a visit, right? They do let you do that, right?"

"Mrs. Mathis, we need to go over what happened tonight. We need to know what happened to your husband and your son."

Tears streaked Nichelle's face as she opened and closed her mouth without a single word falling from her lips. Until that moment, she hadn't formulated what she was going to tell the police. Reality hadn't set in. Her daughter may have been in shock, but she was in denial. Nichelle needed a story and quick.

Armstrong cleared his throat and wrangled her thoughts back to the present. "You and your husband have quite the record of domestic violence. He'd called the police on you, *and you'd called the police on him. He'd beat you up and you'd beat him up. Which was it tonight, Mrs. Mathis? And who hurt little Kaedon?"*

*"That was an accident."*

*"But your husband wasn't an accident? Is that what you're saying?"*

*"What? No. He was . . . I was . . ."* Her mouth kept moving even after the words stopped flowing.

Armstrong turned and glanced back at Schneider, who looked down on the woman and shook his head. Sighing, Armstrong turned back to their suspect and pushed her for an answer. *"Tell us what happened to your husband, Mrs. Mathis?"*

Another tear streaked down her face. *"What happened? Shadiq . . . got exactly what he deserved."*

At the end of the eulogy, Armstrong made a sign of the cross while the crowd's gazes crept toward him and his partner.

It was time.

They had a job to do. Together, the two lieutenants marched through the crowd.

"Nichelle Mathis?"

The flawless older beauty turned with her brows already arched inquisitively. "Yes?"

"We have a warrant for your arrest." Schneider flashed the warrant while Armstrong produced the handcuffs to the astonished woman.

"What?" Her beautiful caramel skin flushed.

"You have the right to remain silent . . ."

Nichelle stuttered indignantly as the funeral crowd halted in their tracks to stare.

Armstrong wasn't without sympathy as they led

her back through the crowd. He did, however, make a sidelong glimpse at Klaudya. Her ice-cold expression had yet to change. No. That wasn't right. It had changed. A small smile tugged at the corners of her lips.

Not for the first time, Armstrong wondered whether they were arresting the right woman.

Don't miss A'zayler's

*In Love with My Enemy*

Available wherever books are sold!

# Prologue

"Hey, Free, make sure you be checking your phone," Echo warned.

"Come on, now. You know me. I don't fuck around when it comes to business."

Echo chuckled. "A'ight, bet. I'm set. I'll meet you at the drop in a few."

"Cool. This it, my nigga. Let's eat."

Echo's laughter filled the phone. "Already," he told him before ending the call.

Jalil Donquez Free—Free to the streets and Don to himself—was a hidden loner with a constant intent to kill and no time for the pleasures of a simple life. With his hood covering his head, he took a deep breath and made his way into the club. It was game time. Since he'd gone through the side exit, he was in his seat and chilling within minutes.

Flashing red and white lights flickered across the room as smoke and music filled the dark atmosphere. Heat radiated from one wall to the other as the floor shook from the bass of the music. Men were everywhere, with a barely dressed woman strewed here and there.

Liquor bottles, red cups, and marijuana-filled blunts that were louder than the music rotated from the mouth of one person to the next as the partygoers interacted vibrantly with one another. Pool tables decorated one corner of the room, while sofas, bar speakers, and a homemade bar occupied the rest.

A parade of nudity filled the gleeful eyes of the many men that enjoyed that type of thing, but not Don. That wasn't something that moved him. The naked women were such an irritant for him that they might as well have been flies circling his food at a barbeque. Unwanted, and just in the fucking way. He liked his women a little more respectable and a lot less social. Hood girls that knew their status without hanging out at every party to let the streets verify it.

Being that he hadn't wanted to be there from the beginning, Don sat in a large chair in the corner of the room minding his business. Simply observing his surroundings and chilling. Too many people in one room with too much going on wasn't his scene, but for money he'd do what he had to do.

"Why you always looking so mean? You're too handsome for that," an around-the-way girl known as Mocha whispered into his ear as she leaned over the back of the chair he was seated in.

Don looked over his shoulder with an annoyed look on his face. His brows were furrowed while his mouth held a small frown. He was in no mood to be bothered, and he'd made that very clear from the moment he'd walked through the door. One thing he couldn't stand was a woman that didn't know how to listen. He wasn't the most social person to begin with, but he most definitely hated women with no morals. Specifically, the ones like Mocha. She'd do anything for money, no matter how backstabbing or disrespectful it was.

"Carry your ass on," Don shooed her away with his fingers.

"Why are you being so mean? You ain't been acting like this."

Don blew out a frustrated breath and ignored her while looking at the screen of his phone. He checked his text messages for the thousandth time, waiting on the message from his friend Echo that would get his night going. His thumb was tapping on his screen when he felt Mocha's hands sliding down the front of his chest. She wasn't given the chance to get much further than his collarbone before Don had a death grip on one of her wrists.

"Bitch, you must want to die."

Mocha sucked her teeth and tried to pull her hand free of his grasp, but it wasn't happening. Don squeezed it a little tighter, even twisting it until she whined in pain.

"When you see me, do your fucking job and keep it moving."

"Let my arm go. I got it."

Don applied a little more pressure, this time twisting it harder to one side. When she yelped and dropped a set of keys into his lap, he finally let her go. With no more words spoken, she walked away nursing her wrist. Don watched her rush to

the back corner, where a few niggas he knew from
around the hood were sitting.

He pushed the keys into the front pocket of his
hoodie as he observed her switch back to where
she belonged. Mocha was one woman that did too
damn much. It had been a tedious task to be cordial to her during their brief alliance, but he'd
done it and he was more than happy that it was finally about to be over.

He wasn't surprised when she sat in the lap of
the biggest man in the section, and held her wrist
up to his face as if he was going to do something
about it. Her thick lips were moving rapidly as she
relayed what had just happened. Don watched and
waited. Bishop, a well-known pimp held her wrist
and placed a kiss on it as his pudgy fingers rubbed
her back.

Like Don knew he would, Bishop looked his
way with a grimace. His eyes searched the people
around Don until Mocha whispered something in
his ear. Finally, Bishop's glare found Don's. Un-
moving and unbothered by anything that Bishop
could possibly be attempting, Don peered back.

The frown that had been there earlier disappeared and a simple head nod was rendered. Don
nodded back before looking away. He hadn't expected anything different. He wasn't to be played
with, and even Bishop knew that. He might run
them hoes, but he didn't run Don, and that was
known.

Back in his element, Don leaned back and
checked his phone once more. Still nothing. His
irritation grew by the second. It was a little after
one in the morning and his job was scheduled to
have been completed by midnight. Don huffed

out another ragged breath and stretched his legs out in front of him.

His hands were resting across his stomach with intertwined fingers when he heard a loud commotion at the door. Accustomed to staying alert, he sat up with the speed of lightning. His hand went to his back releasing the large glock nine that had been secured in the waistband of his jeans. He made sure the silencer was intact before allowing his eyes to scan the crowd where all the noise was coming from.

On his feet and sliding further into the darkness he'd just been occupying, Don waited to see what was happening before making any further moves. The bright red exit sign above his head, leading to the unchained door behind him, was the perfect avenue out, if things blew out of hand. His seat for the night hadn't been by chance; Don was a thinker, and so was Echo, so anything they planned was bound to run smooth.

In a room full of niggas he knew nothing about, the exit had been the safest and smartest place to be. For reasons like the one unfolding in front of him. Still unsure of what was going on, or who it was causing the disturbance, Don squinted his eyes trying to see the faces of the yelling men. With the loud music still playing, and the staggering drunk patrons, it wasn't easy to make out the issue, but Don wouldn't relax until it was revealed.

He was squeezing the handle of his gun when he felt his phone vibrating. In a hurry, he pulled it from his pocket and checked the screen. **GO**, was the one word message he'd been waiting on all night. With the skill and expertise of a trained shooter, Don raised his nine and aimed it until the red beam attached to it landed on his first target. Phew . . . body number one. Phew . . . body number two . . . Phew . . . Three. He was done.

An uproar of screams and frantic cries sounded throughout the room as Don hit the exit without looking back. There was no need to—his job was done. He'd killed all three people before the first one's body hit the ground. Positive no one had seen or heard him do it, Don trekked down the sidewalk coolly, but with a little more urgency in his step.

The hood to his black hoodie shielded his head as the cool breeze from the night air brushed against his face. His hands were tucked securely in his front pockets as he bent the corner heading for the big black pickup truck parked on the side of the hole-in-the-wall club he'd just been in.

Don looked over his shoulder once to make sure no one was coming, before snatching the keys out and hitting the locks. Once the door was open, he slid in and backed out of the parking space. The block was empty and dark as he cruised down the street. That too, being a part of strategic planning. From the fifth-floor window of the abandoned apartment building to his left, he'd shot out every street light along that block hours prior. The lick he'd just hit had been in the works for weeks and he had one last step to complete before giving himself a pat on the back.

With no outside help, Don and Echo had hopefully set themselves up to become a part of something much larger than themselves. Something that would potentially alleviate his loneliness and repetitive struggling. Echo had his family, so he was good, but Don was alone. Just trying to make it. He'd been living from one dump to the next since turning eighteen four years ago, and had been putting in work ever since.

Nights had been long, with days that were even longer but he'd made it happen. With nothing or nobody outside of Echo, Don was self-made and planned to keep it that way until the day the city covered his corpse with the dark dirt that would eliminate his light forever.

Echo had been the only family he'd had in years. They'd met in the county jail three years prior and had been hanging since. If it wasn't him, it wasn't anyone. Echo was truly a stand-up guy and the only person that Don halfway trusted. He trusted him with business, nothing personal.

Which was why they'd been friends for years and Echo still knew nothing about his living situation. Anytime they made plays, he'd either meet up at the spot or they hung out at Echo's crib. Nothing more, and Don planned to keep it that way until he could do better. He'd learned long ago to never let another man see him down bad. Hopefully, their current plan would be the open door to all of that.

With his heart beating a mile a minute, Don looked in his rearview mirrors to assure he wasn't being followed before taking the highway en route to the meeting place no one but he and Echo knew about. Well almost no one. Thanks to one lonely night in the basement of a run-down basement he'd been sleeping in, he'd stumbled upon a life changing opportunity.

*It had been freezing outside and way too cold to sleep under his normal bridge, so Don had gone on a hunt to find somewhere warm to sleep. When the raggedy old* building with the boards and plastic up to the window caught his eye, he'd wasted no time kicking the back door in. It had been empty, minus the rats and stray cats that were seemingly unbothered by the other's presence.

Using plastic, and the blanket he carried around in his tattered old backpack, Don made his bed on the bottom floor of the building. It was in the wee hours of the morning when he'd heard voices. Unsure who the men were, and afraid to move, Don lay deadly still beneath the dirty old blanket.

"It's the one they call Bishop."

"The pussy pusher?" The second voice questioned with a tainted accent.

"The one and only."

One of the men cleared their throats before the conversation continued.

"So, he sells dope and pussy? You Americans are a fucking joke."

Don strained to hear the conversation better. It was pretty easy up until the one with the deep accent spoke. He was clearly a DeKalb county outsider. Nobody in Ellenwood sounded like that. Which only sparked Don's interest even more.

"Who gave you the information?"

"One of his hoes. I think her name is Mocha or some shit like that."

"Do you see why I say it's stupid? His own women are selling him out. Disloyalty is something my family doesn't tolerate."

The man that owned the first voice made some sort of noise with his mouth before talking again. "What do you think should be done?"

"You tell me. This is your area, right?"

Although he didn't know him, Don liked the second guy. His tone and wording sounded like a man that *could be respected. In his opinion, the first one seemed to be a tad bit shifty. It was just something about him that didn't sit right with Don. Little did he know; his gut feelings would soon prove to be accurate.*

*"The only way to get rid of him is to kill him, is that something you want done?"*

*"You tell me."*

*"I mean, I could, but everybody would know. He's the man in this city."*

*"So, you mean to tell me I flew out here for this bullshit? Not one muthafucka that I've met since being here has shown me anything to respect." Second voice cleared his throat. "Stop wasting my gotdamn time. Off that man, get me his shit, and call me when it's done. Got it?"*

*By this time Don's heart was booming while his mind did numbers. If that nigga was scared to put in work, he had no problem picking up his slack. He just needed a way to get himself involved without seeming too eager. He lay beneath the blanket thinking over everything he was hearing and the best way in without getting killed for eavesdropping. The foreign man didn't sound like somebody he wanted to rub the wrong way.*

*"Yes sir. I got it."*

*"Good. Call me when you've figured this shit out."*

*The sound of footsteps could be heard clicking across the floor which let Don know the man was probably well dressed. Only nice shoes made that type of noise when being used. With his mind in overdrive, Don lay still for a few moments longer after hearing the door of the building slam closed, and got the break of his life.*

*"Hey, who the fuck is this nigga, man? Trying to call shots when he can barely speak fucking English."*

*Don slid the covers from his head, slowly trying to grab a glance at the man as he spoke loudly on the phone.*

*"The only way he's willing to give me a spot in his*

ring is if I take Bishop out, and I ain't with that shit. I don't give a fuck how much money that nigga talking, Bishop is fucking royalty in the streets, killing him would be a sack move and I ain't going out like that. Fuck nah, nigga. I'm Ellenwood to the death of me."

Don was on pins and needles to sit up as he listened to the man he recognized as Jeff, talk on the phone. Jeff was one of Bishop's right-hand men; no wonder he wasn't feeling the proposition. Don had been hanging around the block doing odds and ends for Bishop and anybody else that paid him the right amount of money since he'd gotten out of his last group home, so he knew a few people. Jeff being one of them.

Though, he had no real idea what this job entailed, something inside of him wanted a part of it.

"I say we set that nigga up and give his shit to Bishop. We don't know his ass, at least we know if Bishop comes up, we all gone eat. This stupid-talking muthafucka might let us do all the work, then feed our asses to the fucking fishes."

What? Don was completely baffled as he listened to Jeff. Bishop was one of the greediest niggas in the hood, and that was a fact. Everybody knew Bishop was out for self, which was why Don had only done business with him once in the past. He promised one thing and had given another, something Don didn't forget. He was a man that took people at their word, so when Bishop burned him that once, their business relationship was over.

Don might not have had much, but he had his respect and he'd die about it. After pulling his heat on Bishop, and killing the two men he'd sent to kill him, Bishop accepted defeat and laid off. Don let him live off street credibility alone, and because of that Bishop kept his distance and allowed Don to do him with no interruption.

*"I'm supposed to meet up with him again at the end of the month. He said I can either have it done, or we can find us somebody else to do business with." Jeff paced the floor with the phone to his ear. "We met at the old barbershop on thirteenth. You know ain't shit in here no more but animals and bums." Jeff laughed. "I just ain't with the shit. I say we dust his old ass and take it for ourselves." There was a pause. "Bet. Go ahead and tell Bishop what's up. I'm on the way."*

*Don's body stilled when Jeff walked past. He held his breath, unsure if Jeff would spot him or not, but when he heard the door slam again he figured the coast was clear. Don waited to move until he'd heard the sound of a car cranking up and peeling out of the parking lot.*

*He wasted no time getting out of the building. With his blanket stuffed into his backpack and a better life on his mind, Don set off into the darkness to find Echo and get them a plan going.*

From that day to his current one, they'd been doing everything they could to get ready for the night at hand. It was the thirtieth and the man would be arriving at the abandoned barbershop within the next ten minutes. Don had just parked Bishop's truck when he saw a pair of headlights shining behind him. He hurried to check his face in the mirror before getting out. He already knew they could only belong to one person. Echo wasn't set to arrive until Don called. Being in the streets, they both knew how first impressions could determine the outcome of life and death. The last thing they wanted to do was bombard the man and ended up dying because of it.

With his hood still on his head, Don stood next to the truck with his hands still in his pocket. His heartbeat thumped rapidly as his hands opened and closed steadily in his pocket. He nodded his head to the beat in his mind as the headlights shined on him. He waited patiently on them to analyze the situation and make their move.

Nearly ten minutes passed with nothing happening, so Don made his first. With his head down and hands still hidden, he walked to the back of the truck and opened the back door. He pulled out the six large bags weighed down with Bishop's re-up money and new product. As a gesture of good faith, he unzipped two of the bags, pulling money out of one, and neatly wrapped drugs from the other.

He held them up, and for another few minutes the air around him was filled with uncertainty and regret, but he'd come too far to turn back now, so he maintained his cool and waited. It felt like forever for the front door to the dark colored SUV to open. Out stepped a big burly man with a long ponytail and a neat black suit. His eyes were shielded by a pair of sunglasses, but Don could tell he was watching him.

The man's large stature seemed to grow another few sizes when he was in front of Don snatching him from the ground. The money and drugs fell to the ground as the man patted him down roughly, snatching on his clothes before snatching his gun from his waistband. He tossed it to the side before continuing his search. When he was satisfied, he stood massively in front of Don.

"Who are you? Where's Jeff?"

Don fixed his clothes while making the best eye contact he could make through the man's shades in the dark night.

"There is no more Jeff, and I'm . . . " Don pondered over his words. "Somebody your boss wants to know." Even with his body shaking in anticipation, Don was confident in his ability and decision making.

The man sized him up as the seconds passed before slapping him hard on the shoulder. "I will kill you."

"There will be no need for that," Don assured him.

With weighted footsteps, the man walked to the opposite side of the truck and opened the back door. A fancy white shoe that lit up the night emerged from the car. A pants leg the same color topped the ankle of the shoe as the other leg followed. When the man was upright, the two men spoke in hushed tones before the person Don was hoping would change his life rounded the door.

He was decked out in all white, from his head down to his feet. Even his hair and facial hair was white. Nothing like what Don had been expecting, but either way, he was there to do business and nothing more. Everything about the man looked expensive. Not that Don was privy to high-end brands or anything like that, but anybody with eyes could see this man was draped in nothing but the best. The iced-out watch and pinky ring further proved Don right.

The closer he got, the more profound his skin color became. The brownish-red hue to it made Don think of the beach. He looked like someone who lived and breathed under the sun and next to the ocean, but the dark lines in his forehead and heavy bags beneath his eyes told a different story.

"So, I've been told you're someone I would want to know? Is that correct?"

Don strained his ears to understand the man's heavy accent and nodded.

"What would make you think I would want to know someone like you?" The older man's eyes trekked up and down Don's clothing. He did nothing to hide his disapproval of Don's appearance. "You look like trash."

Don could feel himself getting hotter, but he took a deep breath and suppressed it. He needed this. On top of that, he couldn't argue with the truth.

"Whenever entertaining money, look the part. You got that?" He questioned with authority.

Don nodded.

"Appearance is everything. People see you before they hear you, and judging by what I see, nothing you have to say may be worth my time." He gave Don the once over again. "Speak, and hurry up."

Don glared at the man with fury burning behind his eyes. The confidence he'd had before had been washed away by the man's insults. In a world where Don had nothing but his respect, he'd fold before he let another man strip it away from him. Especially off the strength of him feeling like he could.

"Humility is also everything. If you present yourself like a self-absorbed jackass, people will treat you as such. Your personality can take you places that your money can't and judging by what I just heard, I'd rather not do business with you." Don kicked the two bags in front of him toward the man before snatching the other four from the truck.

Once they were all on the ground in front of the man, he stood back to his full height. "In these bags are Bishop's most recent re-up and the money he was paid to cap your ass. He got the work from your competition as well as the cash. Him, Jeff, and that nigga Ditto, from up north was planning on taking your old ass out tonight and pushing on without you, but I heard them and stopped the shit. But, I'm sure your head was too high in the clouds to know that shit." Don scoffed.

"How do you know this?"

"Because I heard them say it right after you left here the last time. They weren't feeling your approach, so they were going to push you out altogether."

The man's eyebrows rose. "What were you doing here that night? You work for them?"

Don shook his head once. "Nah, I'm more of an independent contractor."

"Don't fuck with me."

"I'm not. I work for myself and that's it. I do little shit here and there that nobody else wants to do for the cash that nobody else wants to make. I'm homeless and I do what needs to be done to stay fed. That's it."

"Do you know who I am?"

"Nope."

"So, why do something of this magnitude?" He motioned towards the bags sitting between them.

"The night you met with them, I was here on the floor sleeping. I overheard the way you spoke about loyalty and actually kind of respected it, so when I heard that nigga Jeff talking on the phone about all of this, I took matters into my own hands.

I used that hoe Mocha to help me set it all up, and here I am." Don wrapped up his entire month of hard work in a couple of need-to-know sentences.

"And you did all of this with just the help of some prostitute?"

Don shook his head. "I had a friend, but he can come around later. Right now, It's just you and I."

With his hand to his chin, the older gentleman pulled at the white beard as he stared at Don in deep thought. Don waited on his next words, because they would decide his next move. It would take him absolutely nothing to grab his gun from the ground and kill them both before they had time to react. He was just that good, however he hoped it would go a different way. His lifestyle needed a change.

"Where are the traitors now?"

"No longer a problem."

His eyes widened in alarm, but he masked it just as quick as it had come. "I assume that was your doing?"

"You would assume right. Bishop, Mocha, and Jeff. Ditto wasn't here or he would be out of the picture as well." Don shrugged. "I figured you had ways to handle that though."

The air between the men was filled with unasked questions, but neither of them said anything to address them. Don had shot his ball directly into the stranger's court, it was up to him what he was going to do with it.

"Tell me your name."

"Don't have one. Yours?"

A steady hand went back to the long white beard. "Sergio Ortega."

"Never heard of you."

"And you never will." He looked over his shoulder to his bodyguard and nodded his head toward Don.

Before the man or Sergio could move another muscle, Don had fallen onto the ground next to his gun and aimed it at them. The guard had his hand on his waist in what appeared to be his attempt to retrieve his gun, but Don was faster.

"It ain't going down like this. Y'all can take that shit and count it as a favor, but I'm leaving with my life and that's on me." He stood to his feet slowly. "It's up to y'all if y'all do the same." Now in full combat mode, Don's eyes bounced between the two men, but stayed on the bodyguard.

Sergio hadn't moved to do anything, and didn't look like he was about to either.

"What's it going to be?"

"Quick reflexes, I like that."

Don said nothing.

"What is it that you said you do again?"

"I didn't say."

"Who taught you to move like that?"

"The hood."

Sergio chuckled a little before pointing a finger at Don. "You're something special, I can tell. You need a little help in the grooming department, but I can handle that." For the first time that night, he rendered a smile. "How much are your services? Since you're an independent contractor and all." His accent was heavier due to his laughter.

Don found nothing funny, so he didn't laugh. Instead he looked from the bodyguard to Sergio and back again before squeezing his hand around the handle of his gun. He wouldn't move until he was sure they weren't about to kill him first.

The silence grew as they all stood facing one another. Nothing in the air changed until Sergio stepped forward and pushed the top of Don's gun down. Don allowed him to do it, only because he stepped closer and began saying things he wanted to hear.

"I want you to come work for me. Tell me what you're good at." Sergio stood face to face with Don, invaded every ounce of his personal space. "I can use you."

"Use me to do what?"

Sergio laughed heartily. "Grow my empire, son . . . to grow my empire." More laughter flowed from Sergio as he grabbed Don around the neck and pulled him into a small hug. "You ready for this shit?"

Don looked into Sergio's smiling face and said nothing. He was still too busy trying to thank God that his plan had worked out. The only thing he hoped now, was that it was all that he'd been praying for.

"You have any family here, son?"

Don wasn't big on the "son" verbiage, but he'd let it slide for now. Maybe that was just the way he spoke.

"Just the friend I spoke of earlier."

Sergio stopped walking and turned Don to face him. With both of his hands resting on Don's shoulders he stared him in the face. Don's body shook lightly when Sergio gave his shoulders a firm shake. No more movement came from Don's body until Sergio slapped his face lightly. Don pulled his head away to free it from Sergio's range of motion.

Sergio dropped his hand from Don's face before a grin crossed his face. "Don't worry, son, we'll get to know each other soon enough. For now, on to more important things."

"Such as?"

"Take me to the bodies. I need to make sure all of this is true."

Don nodded his head backward toward Bishop's truck. "Your car or Bishop's?"

Sergio raised his eyebrows. "Bishop's?"

"Yeah, I drove it from the spot."

Sergio looked back at his bodyguard as he walked toward the truck. "Anybody saw you do this?"

"No. But if they did, it doesn't matter."

Before getting into the car, he faced Don and observed him quietly. "Where are you living right now, kid?"

"Anywhere and nowhere at the same time."

Another smile. "I fucking love you. Get in."

"In your car?"

"Yes, son, with me. We have somewhere to be."

Don looked around at nothing in particular, just trying to process what was happening and how fast it was happening. He'd been hoping the meeting went well, but he hadn't known it would be of this magnitude. The feeling of it being too good to be true was heavy on him, but he pushed it away. He'd been on his knees before the creator for years begging for a break, maybe it had finally come. Sergio seemed like a cool dude, and was embracing him rather quickly, but that alone made Don a little eerie.

"How do you know you can trust me?" Don asked him.

Sergio clasped his hands together loudly and held them there before raising them to his mouth. He held them still for a few seconds before shaking them toward Don while walking toward him.

"Because I live off loyalty, and you were loyal to me before you even knew who I was." Sergio motioned for Don to come to him. "Come, we have work to do."

This time, Don went with no problem. Sergio was definitely a man he could work with. Not too many people shared his values in life, and anyone who did had to be trustworthy. It took a few minutes for everybody to settle down in the car, but once they did Sergio turned to Don.

"To establish trust, we must be honest with one another no matter what, you hear me?"

Don nodded. "Understood."

"Once we're family, there's no going back. You good with that?"

Don was quiet for a while contemplating how much that statement weighed before nodding.

"Give me your name."

"Free."

"Free." Don glanced at Sergio before sitting back in the seat and looking out of the window. He didn't know what lie ahead, but he did know he was ready for whatever it was.

"Here's to a new beginning, kid." Sergio's outstretched fist hung between them.

Don pressed his against it. "A new beginning."

Don ran his open palms over the front of his jeans while trying to calm his nerves. It was really happening. The moment he'd been waiting for, or so he thought.

"You know, son, it's funny you picked the name Free."

Don looked his way. "What's funny about it?"

Sergio looked his way while digging in his pocket. "Because that's the opposite of what you'll be for the next few years of your life."

Don's eyebrows scrunched up at the sight of the shiny badge hanging from the wallet in Sergio's hand. Though he couldn't read the small words, the big FBI abbreviation hadn't lost his attention yet.

"Man, what the fuck!" Don slid down in the seat at the same time as two more large trucks pulled in behind him with flashing blue lights in their window.

Everything after that happened at the speed of lightning. All he knew was that Sergio's words definitely held some truth. Free was indeed the last thing he would be for years to come. But . . . who the fuck told? Don closed his eyes trying to think of any loose ends, and they popped back open immediately. *Where the fuck was that nigga Echo?*

# Connect with
## Us

Visit us online at
**KensingtonBooks.com**
to read more from your favorite authors, see books
by series, view reading group guides, and more.

for sneak peeks, chances to win books and prize packs,
and to share your thoughts with other readers.

facebook.com/kensingtonpublishing
twitter.com/kensingtonbooks

*Tell us what you think!*

To share your thoughts, submit a review,
or sign up for our eNewsletters, please visit:
**KensingtonBooks.com/TellUs.**